It Looks Like This

It Looks Like This

Rafi Mittlefehldt

CANDLEWICK PRESS

Copyright © 2016 by Rafi Mittlefehldt

First edition 2016

Library of Congress Catalog Card Number pending
ISBN 978-0-7636-8719-9

16 17 18 19 20 21 BVG 10 9 8 7 6 5 4 3 2 1

Printed in Berryville, VA, U.S.A.

This book was typeset in Granjon.

Candlewick Press
99 Dover Street
Somerville, Massachusetts 02144

visit us at www.candlewick.com

For Mom and Dad
and for Kathryn and Bill

Do you know we brag about you, too?

FIRST

It looks like this:

Pink, mostly.

Puffs of orange just below.

The fiercest yellow way ahead, far, far ahead.

Red slashed all across.

All of it fading to blue, getting deeper and deeper as you go out.

Underneath all that is the ocean, reflecting it back. All I can hear are the waves and the seagulls, all this calmness surrounded by an eruption of colors, deep strong colors.

I only saw this once in real life. We stayed up late and walked to Mill Point Beach in the middle of the night. There was no light anywhere and we sat, blind, and we said nothing. We didn't speak for the longest time, just listened to the ocean.

Then the blackness started melting.

This is what it looked like when the sun finally came up. I was so tired, we both were, but we did it anyway.

We only saw it once because there wasn't much after that, and now we can't ever go again.

This is what I see when I want to remember the good parts. This is what I see when I think of him, when I let myself think of him.

TWO

We moved to Somerdale a little before the start of the school year.

"We" means me and Mom and Dad, and my little sister, Toby, and our dog, Charlie.

Dad has a job with a textbook publisher as a sales rep. The publisher is in New York City, but Dad sells to small bookstores and colleges in our part of the country. His region used to be the Midwest but now it's the Middle Atlantic.

Dad says they got rid of one of the sales reps to cut costs so they had to change everyone's regions around to make up for it.

We came to Somerdale from Sheboygan Falls. I miss Wisconsin. But Dad says if we have to live in Virginia, we might as well live near the ocean, and Somerdale's right on the edge of the beach.

We used to live near Lake Michigan, which is kind of like a small ocean. I used to stare across the lake when we went to the shore to see if I could see Michigan across the water.

I never could because the lake is so wide. It was easy to pretend it was the ocean and we were right on the edge of the country.

And now I guess we are.

Mom and Dad were happy we got to move in the summer because then me and Toby didn't have to worry about switching schools in the middle of the year.

They told us that when they first said we were moving.

Mom and Dad sat us down in the living room. They said it was a Family Meeting. Sometimes we have Family Meetings but not really that much. Toby and I sat on the small red couch that always feels kind of rough but not too bad, and Mom and Dad were standing and then Dad says, We have something to tell you.

And then they told us we were moving.

Toby said, What about Marla?

Her voice was real flat and low, which is how it sounds when she's her maddest.

Dad said, I'm sorry, Toby, but we don't have a choice. You'll make a new best friend in Virginia.

Toby raised her eyebrows.

She said, Marla's not my best friend, she's my

BFF. We're supposed to be best friends forever, not best friends till middle school.

Dad sighed.

Toby said, That's why it's called a BFF, not a BFTMS.

Dad said we might not like it much at first but it would be an adventure and we'd like it after a while. That's when Mom said we got lucky that we were moving in a good season.

I didn't say anything.

Toby said, I don't want to move in any season.

I don't remember a lot before Sheboygan Falls because we had lived there since I was three and Toby was just a baby. We moved there from Milwaukee right after Toby was born.

There's only one memory from Milwaukee:

Walking in between Mom and Dad in the park near the lake, holding both their hands so that my arms are raised over my head because I'm so small and they're so big. We are walking along the edge and it's around dusk.

The sun is really deep orange and it's coming through some of the buildings and getting in my eyes but it doesn't bother me. Next to us the water is getting blacker and blacker, but there's still a sliver of orange that is reflecting the sunset.

I look up at Dad and he's looking back at me and he's grinning so wide.

Then he and Mom lift me up together by my arms. My

feet leave the ground and it's like I'm floating, and I laugh and laugh.

That's all, though.

Everything else is just fuzzy and barely there.

Somerdale wasn't bad at first.

At first things were just new and everything felt different, and it was a bit weird.

But there was a lot that was the same. The same kind of house and the same kind of town. Just different people. Like when they used to get a new actor to play the same character on a TV show after the old actor quit or something. Different people but basically the same.

No one seemed to notice me at school on the first day, which was fine with me.

I mean we were the new kids, but it was the start of the year and there were a lot of new kids. Also it was the start of freshman year for me so a lot of the kids didn't know each other anyway if they came from different middle schools. And plus Toby was eleven and just starting middle school, so I bet it was the same with her.

So there wasn't much to notice. That was fine with me.

At first it was just like that.

I walk Toby to school every day that the weather is good. It usually is, especially at the beginning of the school year. I mean it can be hot sometimes, but there's also a lot of cool breeze coming in from the ocean.

Dad likes to talk about the cool breeze coming in from the ocean. He says it's another good reason that we moved, so we can be near the water.

Even though we were living near the water in Wisconsin.

The school is a mile from home and it takes about twenty minutes to walk there.

Toby and I leave at seven o'clock in the morning. We walk a bunch of blocks past other houses that look a lot like ours with dark red bricks and two trees each in their front lawns.

Then we turn onto this one street where the houses are bigger and different colors, with yards and gardens and horseshoe-shaped driveways.

This is where some of the richer people live, but I mean most everyone in Somerdale has money.

After that we turn onto a bridge that goes over this wide creek. The rich people's backyards face the creek.

Once we get over the bridge we are basically on school property. The school has a lot of land, though, and has a small woods on the side near the creek so we have to walk by that first.

The high school and the middle school are right next to each other on adjacent lots. Dad says this was to Save Taxpayers' Money.

He says it with this kind of approving smile, thin and short. He always has that same expression when he's talking about Saving Taxpayers' Money.

We will get to the schools with a few minutes to spare, and sometimes I give Toby a dollar for a muffin or a cookie or something. Even though we always eat breakfast at home.

Just 'cause she's kind of cool.

Then I'll squeeze her shoulder and she'll go off to the middle school and I'll go off to the high school.

That's just about every day the weather is good.

Toby and I are just turning onto that one street where the rich people live when I see Victor.

Victor's a kid in a couple of my classes, Biology and Art. I don't really know him or anything. In Biology he sits with another kid, Fuller, and they talk a lot. Mrs. Ferguson gets annoyed at them.

I don't think they've known each other long. On the first day of school, Mrs. Ferguson had us all sit in assigned seats at eight different tables. Each table has four stools around it and a sink off to the side and gas hookups for Bunsen burners. It's kind of like my seventh-grade Science class.

Victor and Fuller were put together at one of the tables. I'm at the table behind them. I watch them sometimes because I have to face them when Mrs. Ferguson is at the front of the class. They didn't talk to each other much for the first week.

I mean they would say small-talk things like Can I borrow a pen? or What page are we on?

I watched them. After a week or maybe a bit longer, Victor said, Hey.

Just like that.

When Fuller came in, I mean.

Fuller looked at him for a bit and then said, Hey.

That was it, though.

But the next day they started talking a bit more.

After a couple weeks they seemed to be friends.

This morning Victor's standing at the edge of one of the driveways and smoking a cigarette and looking at his phone. He has on black jeans and a green T-shirt too big for him. He brings the cigarette up to his mouth, holding it between his first two fingers, and then he takes a drag. And then he pulls the cigarette back down with his thumb and index finger.

He keeps doing that, switching his fingers, and then he looks up from his phone at us. His hair gets in his eyes and he brushes it away. Straight and parted and really, really dark.

I can't tell if it's his house or not, but I sort of doubt it 'cause he's smoking, and he'd probably get in trouble if his parents saw him. It's a mostly gray house with weird spires that remind me of Disneyland and a long, winding gravel driveway. There are three really wide willow trees.

I love willow trees.

I've never smoked before, except one time to try it when my friend Kris back in Sheboygan Falls got one of his stepsister's packs of Virginia Slims. That's supposed to be a girl's cigarette but it was all he could get.

We both tried it. Kris could do it pretty easily because I think he'd done it before. He said he got a buzz going.

I tried to inhale it like he showed me, but it just made me cough a lot. Kris said that happens to everyone the first time but then it gets better.

I didn't really want to try again, though.

Anyway, Victor seems to know what he's doing, like he smokes a lot. I bet he does.

He just keeps smoking and staring at us as we turn onto the rich people's street and walk toward the bridge over Blushing Creek.

After we get past a few houses, Toby says, Who was that?

I say, Nobody, Toby.

She says, Is he in your grade?

I say, Yeah.

She doesn't say anything for a minute.

Then she says, He smokes like a damn pro.

She's always saying stuff like that. I mean stuff that normal eleven-year-old girls don't say.

I say, Don't say damn. Mom'll get mad.

She giggles a bit and says, Whatever you say, Mike.

I'm leaving the bathroom right after Biology and I hear:

You're Mike, right?

just as I open the door.

I sort of stop in my tracks because it takes me by surprise. The door starts closing and it hits the back of my heel. It hurts a bit, but not that much because I have thick sneakers on.

I look around and it's Victor. He's standing off to the side near the water fountain.

I say, Yeah.

He says, Mike Mike Mike.

Just like that. Three times really fast, kind of under his breath. He isn't smiling or anything but he isn't frowning either.

He says, What are you always looking at in class?

I say, Huh?

He says, In Ferguson's. You're always staring at me and Fuller.

I don't say anything.

He says, Why are you always staring at us?

I say, I'm not.

He still doesn't look mad or upset. He doesn't look anything, just blank.

He says, I see you staring all the time.

I say, You sit in front of me and I'm just looking that way because Mrs. Ferguson is talking.

He doesn't say anything.

For a couple moments we just look at each other. I don't know what to do because he isn't doing anything and he doesn't really have any expression on his face. He's looking at me like I'm a rock or something.

11

After a while he blinks and says, Don't stare at me in class.

And he walks off.

I have some friends.

I'm not like a popular kid at my school or anything but I have some friends.

These are my main friends:
• Ronald
• Jared
• Terry

Also there are some kids in my classes that I talk to sometimes, but we don't really hang out after school or anything.

Terry is a friend from church, but he goes to a different school, so I only see him every now and then. We don't have a lot in common, really. He's in my youth group and seems to like talking to me for some reason, so we became friends. But we aren't like best friends.

Jared and Ronald and I hang out after school and on weekends and stuff. Plus we eat lunch together.

I met them at freshman orientation just before the school year started. They were nice to me and I didn't know anybody.

Victor walks away, and I watch him leave, not sure what to do.

Then I go to lunch. I usually get to the cafeteria late

because Biology is kind of far away from that part of the building.

The tables are either square or circle and seat four or five kids. Sometimes kids put them together when they have big groups. They aren't supposed to, but usually the teachers don't do anything because they don't care and everyone knows it's a stupid rule anyway.

Jared and Ronald and I always sit at the same table, a square one in the far corner, near the band hall and the side entrance. We like it there because it's more open and we can watch people walk in and out of the school and around the elective classes.

Jared is already there when I show up.

I sit down and say, Hey.

He says, Hi, dude.

Sometimes Jared says dude even though it sounds weird coming from him. He's taller than me, taller than most kids, and really skinny and kind of awkward. He has a kind of nasal voice, but not like ridiculous or anything. His hair is straight and really dark brown, and it hangs down over his ears and covers his face a bit. He has a big nose, which I think he's self-conscious about. He's kind of pale and has red lips.

I asked him once why he says dude like he was a football player or something, and he rolled his eyes and said, I'm being ironic, dude.

I don't mind that he's awkward, because I know I am too.

I say, Where's Ronald?

A voice really close by says, Right behind you, dumbass.

Ronald comes around and sits down. He doesn't look anything like Jared at all. He's a bit shorter than me but not as skinny, and his hair is kind of curly and strawberry blond, and really messy. He said once it was because he was part Welsh, and that's also why he has light skin and all those freckles too. He likes to wear loose button shirts and jeans that cover the backs of his shoes.

I say, Hey, Ronald.

He says, What's going on, Mike?

Ronald frowns at his spaghetti. He looks a bit disgusted but also kind of resigned. They have spaghetti every Wednesday, and Ronald always gets it even though he complains about it and even though he could get something else if he wanted.

He picks up one of the strands of spaghetti and holds it in front of his face, pinching it between two fingers. He looks at it for a few seconds, not saying anything. Jared and I watch him.

Then Ronald leans his head back, lifts the spaghetti high over his face, and lowers it into his open mouth.

Then we hear someone approaching our table. Jared looks up. Ronald doesn't notice until he hears the girl's voice.

She says, Hey, are you using this chair?

She's older, maybe a junior or senior, dressed in shorts

14

that are probably too short for the dress code and a bold turquoise shirt with short sleeves. She has really bright glittery lipstick and auburn hair and she's very pretty.

Ronald brings his head level again and just looks at her. There's a tip of spaghetti hanging out of his mouth. His eyes are wide. Very slowly, he sucks the spaghetti tip into his mouth and starts chewing.

He says, Hey there.

The girl looks back at Ronald. She still has her hand on the fourth chair at our table. I can tell she doesn't know what to say.

Jared says, No, you can have it.

His voice cracks just a bit.

The girl smiles wide and says, Thank you!

And then she takes the chair and leaves.

We all watch her go for a while, and then Ronald turns to Jared and punches him in the arm.

He says, You idiot, I was talking to her.

Jared snorts and rubs his arm. He says, She didn't want you, she just wanted the chair.

Ronald turns back in the direction she went and shakes his head, slowly. He says, Man, she was smoking.

I look over. In the distance I can see her sit down at one of the big groups of two tables pushed together.

I say, She had a lot of makeup on.

Ronald says, Yeah, that's what smoking is.

* * *

We are in the middle of doing depth exercises in Art.

Mr. Kilgore has us draw two of the same objects, one near and one far away, and explains how to draw one of them smaller than the other to give the illusion of depth.

It is kind of pointless because I already know how to do all that, but Mr. Kilgore gets mad sometimes if you don't do things his way. He tells us exactly how to draw lines between the two objects to make a convergence and tells us about shading and how that can help with the illusion.

Mr. Kilgore likes to make us follow a bunch of rules when we draw. It's pretty stupid. I told Mom that once, but she said that it might look that way but maybe he knows more than he seems to.

I didn't say anything to that. Maybe she was right. But I sort of doubt it, to be honest.

I'm doing everything Mr. Kilgore says:

I draw two paddleboats, like they used to have on the Mississippi River.

I make one big and one small.

Then I draw lines for the sides of the river, going away from the viewer.

I draw some more lines to make the current and the wake from the paddles, and make all the lines look like they are converging.

It is everything Mr. Kilgore says to do.

If he didn't have us always follow his rules exactly all

the time, I probably would draw something else, but it would still have depth. It would look good.

Plus paddleboats are harder to draw than converging lines anyway.

Mr. Kilgore comes by. He bends down to look at my drawing and I can smell his aftershave. It smells like my dad's.

He pulls down his glasses to get a better look, letting them rest just on the tip of his nose.

I can see his big bushy brown mustache through the lenses. The hairs are magnified and look tangled and dense, with gray ones twisted in here and there. I try not to, but I look anyway. He has four lines going across his forehead, which make him look like he's deep in thought. Above that he's mostly bald, except for some brown hair along the sides.

One or two strands stand up on the top of his head, because of static.

He studies my drawing for a while and says, That's not bad, Mikey.

Then he sort of smiles, but not really, and walks off.

I hate it when anyone calls me Mikey and he knows it, but he still sometimes does it anyway. I keep drawing for a bit, but then I hear this sort of snickering sound.

I look up and I see Victor and Tristan and Fuller laughing about something.

Victor and Tristan have been friends for a long time,

not like Fuller. I could tell because they were talking like they were friends even on the first day of school. By this time Fuller is sitting with them in Art, so I guess now he's friends with Tristan too.

I don't like Tristan.

I see them laughing quietly to themselves, and then Victor kind of points in my direction and Tristan looks.

My ears get hot.

Then they start laughing again, and they keep glancing at me while they laugh.

I go back to my drawing and try really hard not to look up. For a while I barely move.

Then Mr. Kilgore says, Cut it out, Tristan.

Then they stop laughing. I glance up really quick and see that they still have these smiles on their faces.

I know Victor and Fuller are telling Tristan about me staring in Biology.

I look back at my drawing and realize I'd accidentally made this big black spot where I pressed the pencil too hard. I wasn't paying attention because I was concentrating on not looking at Victor.

I just look at it for a while wondering if I could erase it, and then I hear, really soft:

Hey, Mikey.

It's Tristan. I bend over my paper and pretend to keep drawing. Then he does it again:

Heeey, Mikey. You gonna stare at me too?

I just keep working on my drawing like I don't hear.

Then, super quiet this time, so that I almost don't hear
it for real,
    Come on, queer.
    Then Mr. Kilgore says, louder this time,
    Tristan, cut it out. There's no need to talk.
    Then all three get quiet for good.
    I just keep drawing.

THREE

These are the classes I like: Biology, English, French.

These are the classes I hate: PE, Art, Geography.

I don't care that much about Algebra.

That's mostly going by who the teacher is and what other kids are in the class, though. It would be different if I was just talking about the subjects themselves. If it's just the subjects, I would switch Art and Biology.

Either way I don't care that much about Algebra.

It sucks because I like art a lot, I just don't like Art class. Sometimes it makes me mad that I have a teacher I don't like in a class I should like. I don't think I would mind so much if Mr. Kilgore taught Biology.

In Art class I just sit quiet and keep my head down and draw what I want to draw. Usually Mr. Kilgore doesn't care. Usually he leaves me alone, but sometimes he's in a bad mood.

Mrs. Ferguson is all right. She's sarcastic a lot and she acts tired and annoyed about stuff, but you can tell she doesn't mean it.

When Mr. Kilgore acts annoyed, he means it.

A couple weeks after Victor told me to stop staring at him, there's a new kid in my French class.

Our French teacher is Madame Girard. She makes us call her Madame instead of Mrs. because that's how they do it in France.

When I told my dad that, he sort of chuckled a bit and said, I hope she's not that kind of madam.

I didn't really know what he meant but Mom gave him a look.

Madame Girard is teaching us about verbs, about the structures of past tense and present tense and future tense. She's writing it all on the chalkboard, the same kind of sentence three times but with different tenses for the verb on each line.

Adrien ate the cake.

Adrien eats the cake.

Adrien will eat the cake.

She says it in English and then in French and then repeats it a couple more times: English then French, English then French.

She makes us say the three verbs in a row so we can hear the difference:

a mangé — mange — mangera

She makes us say it again:

a mangé — mange — mangera

In the middle of the third time, she stops and lowers her piece of chalk. She is looking at the back of the classroom. Everyone else turns around to see what she's looking at.

I stare for a second at the little white dot where her chalk had just been, right below *mangera,* and then I turn around too.

There's a kid standing just inside the classroom. I think he's been there for a little bit because the door is always open and Madame Girard wouldn't have heard him. This is what I remember:

Dark jeans, stress marks on the right pocket in an outline of his phone.

Navy blue T-shirt, kind of tight.

Black Converse shoes, white laces. Dirt smudges on the tips.

Short dark hair, tight curls.

Light brown skin. Strong jaw around thick lips.

Green eyes.

He's holding a spiral notebook in one hand and a crumpled yellow slip of paper in his other.

For a second no one says anything, and then I hear Madame Girard's voice from behind me:

Oui?

He raises the hand with the slip in it. I look at Madame

22

Girard. She isn't really frowning or anything, she just looks expectant. I can see the clear outline of her lipstick, where it ends and the rest of her mouth begins; I can see the plump curls in her hair, mostly bright auburn but gray just at the roots; I can see a tiny, tiny clump of mascara over one set of lashes.

Her eyes are on the slip. I can tell. I watch her watching it.

Then she walks over to him in six great strides. The end of the silk shawl that she always wears around her shoulders flutters as she walks by. I feel it tickle my cheek as I turn to watch her go.

Madame Girard says something to the kid. He nods and then she points to an empty desk a row over from mine and one seat back. He walks over to it.

Madame Girard turns back to the class and gestures airily at the kid and says,

Je vous présente Sean.

After the last bell I walk over to the big circle where the buses are.

They park there in the horseshoe waiting for all the kids to get on them, mostly freshmen and sophomores who can't drive. They sit and wait with their big engines turned on, twenty buses idling and growling at each other.

I walk through them and I can taste the exhaust, invisible but heavy and bitter, carried by warm gusts

23

blowing in between and under the buses and into my face and through my hair.

Diesel exhaust tastes different from regular car exhaust. It's heavier and more powerful and it stings.

I walk in between the buses and through the horseshoe and onto the lawn on the other side and across a big track field, and then I'm in front of the middle school.

Toby is waiting for me. She sees me coming and picks up her backpack, swinging it onto her shoulders. It is pink and worn at the edges, and looks huge against her small frame.

She smiles when I get near, squinting against the sun behind me, and says,

Let's go.

That's what she always says when I pick her up, every time.

The middle school lets out half an hour before the high school, but Mom doesn't want Toby to walk home alone.

I think it's dumb because it isn't ever dangerous. I mean there isn't any crime or anything. But Mom says there is lots of traffic with all the older kids driving all at once.

Toby is supposed to wait outside for me, but sometimes she just hangs out in the choir room until just before my school lets out.

She loves choir. Her teacher is supposed to be really nice. I don't know, I met her once, and she was really cheerful and everything but kind of too cheerful.

That day I walked into the choir room because Toby wasn't outside. I knew where it was because Toby had told me once. I opened the door and poked my head in and looked around. Then I saw Mrs. Deringer by the projector thingy. She had a tissue and was wiping it across a plastic sheet covered in a bunch of color-coded musical notes she had drawn. I watched on the opposite wall as a giant hand appeared and ran across the square of projected light, leaving a clean path through all the color notes and staff lines and clef marks on the sheet.

I coughed a little and she looked up.

She said, Hi there! Can I help you?

I said, Um. Is Toby in here?

She smiled even bigger and said, You must be Mike!

I nodded.

She said, I've heard a lot about you.

I didn't say anything.

She said, Toby's really fond of you!

I didn't say anything.

She said, So, you're picking her up?

I nodded.

She said, Toby just left. She wasn't outside?

I said, No. I'll just wait for her out there.

She said, Okay, sweetie! Have a good night!

I thought that was kind of weird since it was only three o'clock.

I said, Okay,

and then I closed the door and turned around, and Toby was walking toward me from the hallway. I guess she'd just gone to the bathroom.

She looked at me for a second, and then giggled and said, Let's go.

This time Toby is waiting for me outside.

We turn back toward the high school, and I walk her across the big track field, around the horseshoe of buses this time because they're already leaving.

We walk past the entrance to the high school and then alongside the student parking lot.

There's a really long line of cars trying to get out of only two exits. We're walking along the line toward the road that would take us to the bridge, and then I see Sean.

He is sitting alone in a faded blue jeep that looks pretty old. There are a couple rusted spots along the side and the back chrome bumper is sort of crooked.

I look at the insignia on the back and it says Ford Bronco. I never heard of that kind of car.

Sean glances over and sees me. He kind of stares for a second and I can't tell if he recognizes me from class since it's his first day, but then he turns back.

A minute later he gets out of the parking lot and turns left in the direction Toby and I are going, and drives off, picking up speed.

I watch the Ford Bronco go over the bridge and toward our neighborhood and then disappear as the road curves, the sound of his engine accelerating and chasing him and then disappearing too.

Toby and I walk on.

That night it rains.

There is a little bit of it that starts coming down when Toby and I get home, but it's just small splatters here and there.

But overhead it's deep, deep gray and the sky looks so angry, and I can already smell the dust that gets disturbed and blown around when it rains.

I stop at the door when we get home and Toby walks in, but I turn back and look at everything outside. The trees are kind of waving already in no real pattern and the light is dim but raw.

I like how it looks and feels right before a rain.

Dad is in a bad mood.

He's kind of quiet through dinner and scowls most of the time. It isn't only because of the rain but the rain doesn't help.

The first real crack of thunder comes right before dinner.

Another couple come a few minutes later.

Charlie runs into the bathroom after the second crack. He always does that during a thunderstorm. He goes into the bathroom, sort of slinking in with his tail down, and crawls into the bathtub and sits there, shivering.

He's a beagle. Dad says beagles are really expressive dogs, like they get excited really easily but also get scared pretty easily too. It's true.

Plus Charlie's still young, just under two years old, so he hasn't grown out of being scared of the thunder yet.

Before Toby and I get up to clear the plates, we can hear the rain coming down in what seems like one big endless wave, beating against the roof and the door and the windows and just pouring.

It is almost completely dark even though there should have still been about an hour of sunlight left.

I always know how much sunlight is left in the day because I check the weather every morning, and then again when I get home.

Part of the reason is because I'm interested in weather and part is because I'm interested in astronomy. Mom got me a star chart a year ago for my birthday, and it shows me what stars I'll be able to see each night and when.

It's a bit different each night because of the tilt of the earth and how close the earth is to the sun on any given day.

So that's how I know there's still supposed to be an hour left of sunlight.

Dad is in a bad mood because of work.

When he got home today, he said that he would have to go to New York in a couple months, to the main office.

He said, They're having another goddamn sales conference.

He wasn't saying it to anyone, really, just saying it out loud.

Mom said, Please don't say that word, Walton.

She sounded kind of cross and I think that put Dad in an even worse mood.

Dad really hates sales conferences. They only happen a couple times a year, but he complains about them every time.

He says he has to sit around in boring meetings all day listening to editors talk about all the new books they're going to publish a year from now. Except Dad's company only publishes textbooks, so the presentations are really dull and repetitive.

But mostly it's because he hates going to New York City.

He says the hotels his company finds for him are always damp and musty and the streets are always crowded and the people are always pushy and they smell like fish.

I don't really get how an entire city of people can all smell like fish, but he says it's just a bunch of different bad smells that are always in the air and the people who live there absorb it and in the end it smells like fish.

I've never been to New York City.

So Dad is already in a bad mood because of the

conference and the rain and Mom, so then after dinner he sits down and starts watching a baseball game.

It's the Milwaukee Brewers against the St. Louis Cardinals.

He kept saying after we moved that he was going to have to learn to be a Nationals fan. He started watching their games at first, but then after a couple weeks he went back to the Brewers.

In the middle of the game, the TV makes a loud popping noise and then everything goes dark.

For a second all I can see is the streetlight coming in through the windows and all I can hear is the rain beating against the house.

Then Dad says, God —

He cuts himself off, though, either because of Mom or because the lights come back on right then.

He looks at us, at Mom and me and Toby, and then turns to the TV.

It's just a blue screen now.

He picks up the remote and flips through a few channels, but all the channels are like that, just solid blue.

Dad sighs and leans back on the couch. He looks at me.

He says, Mike, you thinking of taking up anything at school?

I don't say anything for a second.

Then I say, Like what?

Dad says, Like a sport. I dunno, you used to play basketball.

Toby says, That was in like elementary school.

I used to play basketball in fourth grade, but I never really liked it. It was just something Dad suggested I do and I thought it would be cool and gave it a try, but I didn't like it. I wasn't that good.

Dad gives Toby a look and then turns back to me.

He says, Well, do you think you'd want to give it a try again?

I say, I dunno.

He says, What about something else? Like swimming or football?

I say, I dunno. I'm already in Art.

He says, Yeah, but you need a sport.

I don't say anything.

He says, Mike, I asked you a question.

I say, I don't want to do swimming or football.

He looks at me for a while and then turns back to the TV. He picks up the remote, presses the power button, stands up, and goes to the kitchen.

I can hear the fridge door opening and then, a second later, the hiss of a bottle cap.

I get up and walk down the hallway to the back door. I open it and walk out into the garage and sit on a crate.

I just sit there and watch the rain, watch it come down in sheets, watch it cover everything and blot the sky. It drums against the houses and the mailboxes, bangs against cars parked at the curb. It pours down driveways and into the streets, building into rivers that carry leaves and twigs

31

and bits of trash away, swirling them down the block and into the drains. I watch the rain come down harder and harder, watch it wash the asphalt and the grass, and wonder if it will wash me away too.

Everything is still wet the next morning.

It stormed for a long time, into the night. I woke up twice from the thunder, the last time at four thirteen in the morning. I could even hear the thunder in my dreams.

When I have to get up for school, it's over, but the whole world is soggy.

Toby and I walk up the road toward school, past houses and houses that all look like mine.

Whenever we pass a block, I slow down and kind of look left and right down the side streets.

After a while Toby says, What are you looking for?

I say, Nothing, Toby.

But my face flushes a bit and I think she notices because she says, Then why do you keep looking down every block?

She always notices things.

I say, I'm just looking to see how much water's backed up. Or if any trees fell down in the storm.

Toby doesn't say anything, just keeps staring at me as we walk. I try not to look at her but I can tell she's staring, so finally I turn my head a bit and say, What?

She looks away and shrugs.

She says, Your face is all red, that's all.

I don't say anything. But I keep looking down the streets.

Toby stops bothering me about it, though.

A couple blocks before the one with all the rich people, I look down one of the streets and see an old, faded blue Ford Bronco parked in the driveway of a house.

The house is a two-story, like ours. White trim, red bricks, two trees turning orange with the fall. Like ours.

I stare at it for a bit, actually stopping this time. Right above me is the street sign: Hyacinth Court. I read over the white letters of the sign a couple times.

Then Toby and I go on.

I don't look down any more streets after that.

FOUR

Mom drives me to the mall.

I don't want to go but it's getting late and I know I have to at some point, and I figure I might as well just do it.

Toby comes along and she and Mom go off to look at new school clothes even though school started last month. But a week ago Toby tore her pink pants and got mud on her good shirt while she was at school.

She says it was because she slipped on the wet ground when she went outside during lunch and landed right on the curb and tore her overalls and smeared her shirt.

But she looked a bit funny when she told Mom about it and I wondered.

They go off to look at clothes and leave me alone, and I walk over to the Grand Slam store.

On the way I pass by a lot of teenagers, kids a couple years older than me, boys and girls holding hands or friends in groups just wandering around.

I don't know why anyone would go to the mall for fun.

I walk into the Grand Slam store and stop at the entrance. It is big and packed with stuff, sports things like jerseys and baseballs and running shoes and tennis rackets. Stuff all over the place, on tables and displays and on shelves that go all the way up to the ceilings. It's ugly and it kind of overwhelms me, and I just stand there.

Someone says, Can I help you?

I look at him. It's a kid a few years older, a senior or maybe just out of high school. He has on khakis and a purple polo shirt with a small yellow logo in the corner. The ends of the shirt hang untucked over his belt. His hair is a bit greasy and he's thin, thinner than me.

I say, Yeah.

He says, Well, come on in, then.

I walk in.

I make sure to watch Dad's face when he opens my present.

I hand it to him in the morning, before work. I have to get up earlier than usual to catch him before he leaves.

He takes it in his hands and looks at it, a box Mom helped me wrap in colorful blue and yellow paper. Here and there it says GETTING OLD in cartoony letters.

Dad smiles just a bit and says, What's this?

I say, Happy birthday.

And smile back a little.

He opens it and I look up from the box and watch his face. The creases around his eyes and forehead look heavier than normal because it's so early. Some steam from his coffee drifts up and brushes against his cheek, puffing out when he breathes through his nose.

The corners of his mouth turn up just a hair when he sees what it is. I watch the creases near his eyes shift and grow. It looks like his eyes are smiling.

Dad says, Super Bowl Thirty-One.

He is reading the side of the ball, reading it through the box.

Dad says, The Packers won that one.

I say, Yeah.

I knew he'd know. Dad opens the box and very carefully takes the ball out, holding it with two hands like it is made of glass.

He turns it over in his hands. Very slowly, he brushes his fingers over the label.

He says, This is great, Mike.

I just sort of smile a little more.

He looks at it for a long time with that small smile, not saying anything. Then he looks up.

He says, Do you want to throw it around a bit with me sometime?

I look down. I can feel my smile getting wider but

thinner, lips pressed together like I do in photos sometimes, and hope he doesn't notice.

I say, Yeah.

Sometimes I get to French class early.

It's because I have Algebra right before. Algebra's supposed to be in the Math Wing, which is really just a bunch
of classrooms all in the same corner of the building. That's
where most of the math classes are.

They do the same thing with other subjects. There's a
Science Wing and a History Wing and an Elective Wing.

But then when the school got too big a while back,
they had to build a whole new section that they still call the
New Wing even though it's about twenty years old. And
some of the classes are in there.

Both Algebra and French are in the New Wing.

So sometimes I go to my locker in between, but usually
I just bring my stuff for both classes and go straight from
Algebra to French.

I do this two days after my dad's birthday.

It's cool because normally no one's there yet so I have
the whole place to myself, except Madame Girard. But
she's always at her desk not paying attention anyway so it's
like I'm there alone.

Sometimes I get there before the last person in the class
before mine leaves. So I watch them go, and then a minute later the next person in my class shows up and it's like

I saw the transition between periods that usually only teachers see, and it's a little weird.

This day Sean is already there.

Madame Girard isn't even in the room. She's talking to Mr. Pietre, who is a senior English teacher. I pass her in the hall.

Sean looks up when I walk in, and I sort of stop for a second because I'm not expecting to see anyone and it's just a bit off-putting.

We look at each other. There is a moment where we just look at each other and it's like everything else pauses.

And then I walk in and take my seat, one in front and to the right of his.

He says, Hey.

He says it right as I'm sitting down, so I'm just barely hovering over the seat, staring at my hand flat on my desk supporting my weight.

There's another pause and for just a second I know I can make this pause go on forever if I want.

And then I sit down and turn and say,

Hey.

My voice is hoarse from not speaking in a while so it comes out rough.

He says, I'm not really new.

I look at him.

I say, Huh?

He says, To the school. I'm not a new kid or anything.

I say, Okay.

Neither of us says anything for a while.

Then I say, Why'd you start this class so late?

I watch his face relax a bit, like he's waiting for me to ask this.

He says, I was supposed to be in this period, but they put me in another one and it conflicted with Basketball. So it took them a long time to sort it out.

I say, Oh.

He says, I'm supposed to be in Basketball fourth period, but they put me in English in fourth period. So I had to get the counselor to change it around. It kind of messed up my whole schedule.

While he is talking he looks less and less relaxed, like he doesn't like what he is saying but he can't help it. I don't understand why. He is drumming his fingers on his desk, a steady *brrrum brrrum brrrum*.

I say, Oh.

He doesn't say anything, just looks down.

His fingers go *brrrum brrrum brrrum*.

I say, That must've been annoying.

Brrrum.

He looks up. His eyes fix straight on me like he's trying to look through me, and the longer he does the more I start to feel like he can, like he is seeing the dusty chalkboard and the poster of conjugations and Madame Girard's desk, all of it right through me.

I stare back because I don't know what else to do, and all I can think about is how green those eyes are.

Then the corner of his mouth turns up, just barely.

He says, I'm Sean.

I say, Yeah. Mike.

And then people start coming inside the classroom.

Me and Ronald and Jared go to Ronald's house after school. I don't have to walk Toby home because Mom's picking her up today.

We meet up just outside the main entrance after seventh period and get on Ronald's bus with him.

The school has a rule that you can only take your own bus. You have to fill out an ID form at the beginning of the year and give it to the driver, so he knows all the kids on his bus. He's not supposed to let other kids on.

But Ronald's driver is this old guy who doesn't care.

So we get on and ride over to Ronald's neighborhood, which is right next to mine. It's an older neighborhood, though, and Ronald's house is only one floor. But it's pretty cool.

We go in and Ronald dumps his backpack right near the door and walks straight to the kitchen. He grabs three Coke cans and puts two of them on the kitchen table.

He cracks open the third can and starts guzzling, his Adam's apple moving up and down with each gulp, staring at Jared and me the whole time.

Then he tilts his head back dramatically and lifts the

can a couple inches above his mouth, letting the last drops fall in.

He crushes the can in his hand and lets out a long, roaring belch.

Then he says, Halo?

Jared grabs his can from the table and says, Sure, dude.

I'm not great at Halo.

I mean I'm not that bad, but definitely not as good as Ronald. Mom doesn't like violent video games, so we don't have it at home, so I don't get to practice as much.

But I'm all right, I guess.

We're all on the blue team, playing against other kids online. Ronald and Jared are out killing the other team and trying to get their flag. I have the sniper rifle, so I'm perched on top of some high building or something, looking out for red team people to shoot.

Ronald says, So I found out that chick's name.

I blink and say, What chick?

Ronald says, That hot girl who took our chair from lunch.

The game erupts in a bunch of explosions. Jared's character jumps in a little ship and starts flying around in random directions.

Jared says, That was like three weeks ago.

Ronald says, Yeah, and she didn't get any less hot in three weeks.

Jared holds down the fire button, and his ship starts shooting at whatever he's facing.

Ronald says, Dude, watch out, you almost got another blue guy.

Jared tries to turn the ship around, but it careens out of control. He crashes into a cliff wall and blows up.

He leans back and says, So what's her name?

Ronald says, Leah.

I see a little movement of red through my rifle scope. I hold still for a second, and then it comes back and I shoot.

The game says, Head shot!

Ronald says, Nice, Mike.

I say, She's older. Like a junior at least.

Ronald shrugs.

He says, What can I say, I like older women.

The front door opens. None of us turn to look at it. It's just Ronald's mom.

She walks into the living room a minute later and says, Hey, boys.

I say, Hey, Mrs. Pilsner.

She says, Mike, come on, it's Jeri.

I don't say anything. It's kind of weird to call adults by their first names.

She says, Ronald, you need to move your backpack.

Ronald groans but doesn't take his eyes off the game.

His mom says, Ronald.

Ronald says, Mom, I'm like a second away from getting the flag.

His mom says, I don't even know what that means.

Ronald says, Mom, okay, I'll move it in just a second. I gotta kill these kids.

More explosions come from the TV, and Ronald's character suddenly does a flip into the air and lands hard, dead.

Ronald grabs the headset and shouts into the microphone:

Fag fag fag fag fag fag fag—

Ronald's mom says, Ronald! Jesus!

Some laughter comes from the other team through the TV speakers.

Ronald says, Mom, they're totally ganging up on me.

His mom says, I don't care, I don't want to hear that from you! Besides, they're like twelve years old.

Jared says, Some of them are probably thirty.

Ronald's mom rolls her eyes and walks over and picks up the headset from the carpet. She says,

Sorry, friends! My Ronnie needs his din-din.

Then she leans over and hits the power button on the Xbox. The screen blips twice and then goes blank except for the words

HDMI 2 NO SIGNAL

in blue.

We all stare at the screen.

Ronald's mom turns to walk out of the room and says, I'm ordering some pizza if you two want to stay. Ronald, move your backpack.

* * *

We're eating pizza and drinking ice water. Ronald wanted Coke, but his mom saw that we'd already taken some and said we probably should cool it on the soda.

That's how she said it, that we should probably cool it. She doesn't really talk like a mom sometimes. I bet she and Toby would get along.

She's wearing jeans and a large sweatshirt. It's not really cold but Ronald says she gets cold easily.

His parents are separated. His dad lives in Arlington and doesn't really come by ever. Ronald says it's better that way, that his dad is kind of a jerk.

I like his mom. She's nice and laid-back and jokes around a lot. She wears casual clothes and always seems pretty relaxed. There are creases around her gray eyes from smiling so much. That's my favorite part.

She takes a big bite of pepperoni and looks over at me. She chews a moment, then with her mouth still full, says,

So you getting used to Virginia yet?

I have a sip of water.

I say, Yeah, I guess so. I mean it's not much different from our old town. Except the weather.

She says, Oh man, I bet. I have a friend in Chicago I used to visit every now and then. Damn that city gets cold in the winter. And you guys were farther north, up past Milwaukee, right?

I nod.

She says, Yeah. You're in for a much milder winter than you're used to. Which is nice if you're the outdoorsy kind.

I say, I'm not really.

It kinda comes out before I really think about it.

But Mrs. Pilsner just takes another bite of pizza and says, Not much for sports?

I just shake my head.

She says, What elective are you taking this year?

I say, Art.

She raises her eyebrows.

She says, No kidding? You draw?

Ronald says, Yeah, he's pretty good, but he has Mr. Kilgore, who's an enormous douche.

Mrs. Pilsner says, Ronald, shut up.

But she's smiling just a bit.

She says, Well, that's pretty cool. I wish I had some kind of artistic talent.

I say, My parents would rather I did sports.

She looks at me again and takes another bite and chews for a minute, her eyebrows scrunched. Then she says, Really?

I say, Yeah. Well, my dad, anyway.

She chews, considering me. I start to feel a bit embarrassed. I can't tell if she's expecting me to say something. I look away and have another sip of water.

Then she says, Well, that's dumb.

She smiles a bit after that and says, But don't tell him I said that, since I haven't met him yet.

* * *

Sean is a few people ahead of me in the pizza line a day later. I don't see him at first because I'm looking for the pepperoni slices.

Sometimes they run out of pepperoni early.

They only have one left that day so I get it and then a slice of cheese. And then I look up and I see Sean leave the pizza line and go check out. I didn't even know he had the same lunch as me.

And then I remember that it makes sense because a lot of the athletes at school have that lunch period, and Sean said he's in Basketball fourth period.

I get my food after him and start walking toward my usual table. I can see him walking a bit ahead of me, going sort of in the same direction.

Then suddenly he stops and sits down at a square table where three other kids are sitting.

It's Victor and Tristan and Fuller's table. I look away immediately.

I kind of turn to give their table a wide berth.

I hear Victor: Hey, man, how's it going?

And then Sean: What's up, man?

They don't see me. I walk past and get to my table.

Ronald says, What do you keep looking at?

I say, Nothing.

I've been glancing over at Victor's table without realizing it.

Jared says, You are definitely looking at something.

Ronald looks over in the direction I've been looking, moving his head around to try to get a better view.

He says, Is it that Leah girl?

I shake my head and have another bite of pizza. Then I look back at Victor's table.

I say, Do you know Victor Price?

Ronald nods.

Jared says, He's a dick.

Kind of loud.

I say, Did you guys know him in middle school?

Jared says, Yeah. He used to be mostly quiet and not that cool or anything, but then in seventh grade he made friends with some eighth-graders.

I say, How did he get older kids to be his friends?

Jared says, They were his brother's friends or something. But after that the other kids started thinking he was cool. It totally pushed up his stock.

I think Jared's being ironic again, but I don't say anything.

Ronald says, I knew him in elementary school.

Ronald has lived in Somerdale all his life. Sometimes, especially when he gets mad or excited, a little bit of an accent comes out, same as me, only southern and not midwestern. He always hates it when that happens and tries to cover it.

He says, In third grade. He was in my class for part of the year before he moved to another neighborhood and went to another school.

Ronald takes a bite of his pizza and chews for a bit, glancing at Victor's table. He has a bit of sauce on his chin, which he wipes on his sleeve.

He says, Some of the other kids used to make fun of him. Only a couple times, though.

I say, That's weird, to think of other kids making fun of him.

Ronald looks back at me, then takes another bite.

Jared says, Why are you asking about Victor?

I shrug and say, He stopped me in the hall a few weeks ago and told me to stop staring at him in Biology.

Ronald says, Why were you staring at him in Biology?

I say, I wasn't. I was looking at the teacher and he sits in front of me. It was weird.

I kind of wish I hadn't said anything.

But Ronald shrugs and looks back over at the table.

Jared says, Who's that other guy they're sitting with?

I say, Sean,

kind of blurting it out.

Then I say, He's in my French class. He's okay.

Jared says, He looks older.

I look at my pizza and nod.

Miss Rayner told me once I had to use more descriptive words in a story, especially when talking about characters. She said I needed to learn to Paint a Picture.

Miss Rayner is my English teacher. I like her all right.

Here's me Painting a Picture:

Victor is about my height, almost exactly my age. I know because I heard him talking about what he got for his birthday last year and he said his birthday was December 16. Mine is December 31.

He has slick black hair, parted on one side. Some of his bangs cover his left eye. His eyes are dark, dark brown, just short of black. He has darker skin, like a permanent tan. He wears oversize shirts because he thinks he's too skinny, but you can tell he's athletic.

He walks with sort of a swagger, the kind that people have when they think other people are watching them. Every day he wears the same dark red Nikes.

Tristan is taller and definitely athletic. He has red lips and pale skin, light brown hair, gray eyes. His cheekbones are really high, and his mouth is always a bit parted. Kelly Ramirez says he looks like a model. Maybe he is.

Tristan always looks annoyed to me, or maybe bored. Except when he's laughing at me. He wears a lot of polo shirts and fitted jeans, not those baggy clothes. Probably to show off his muscles or whatever.

He's always getting in trouble at school for having his phone. He's pretty dumb about it. The school won't let you take your cell out during the day except for emergencies, and if a teacher sees it, they confiscate it and you have to pay like twenty bucks to get it back at the end of the day. He uses it in the hallways all the time, probably texting girls or something, right in front of teachers. He's even done it in class. He has to pay to get it back like once a week and he doesn't seem to care.

His parents probably have a lot of money.

Fuller has a shaved head. He has kind of a pointy nose and sloped forehead. Girls still go after him. He always has a girl around, though not as many as Tristan.

I don't remember what kind of stuff he wears. Fuller is the least memorable person at our school. For me. I don't know why.

Miss Rayner is in her mid-forties, so not young like Mrs. Ferguson but not as old as Mr. Gardings, who teaches Algebra and is like ninety. He has a hearing aid and shuffles around in class all day in checkered suspenders and a bow tie, like he doesn't know it isn't 1940 anymore.

Miss Rayner is pretty tall, almost as tall as Jared, and keeps her hair in a ponytail and wears jeans with a T-shirt tucked in every day. She speaks in a loud voice with a thick southern accent and smiles a lot.

She had a husband who taught at another school, but he left her for one of his former students. That's what all the kids say, anyway.

That's why she is Miss and not Mrs.

The weather report says clear skies all day when I check Saturday morning, so I take Charlie on a walk.

Sometimes I like to go for a walk, either by myself or

with Toby or with Charlie or all three of us, just walking around.

I don't feel like being around another person on Saturday so I take Charlie. We walk up to the park, him sniffing the ground most of the way and pulling right and left on the leash when he thinks he smells something, tail always up and wagging slowly, back and forth, back and forth.

I like watching him when we walk, because he's always so excited to be anywhere and it makes me laugh sometimes thinking about how easily he gets to be happy.

We pass along the creek for a few blocks and then get to the park, making a big circle around the neighborhood swimming pool and the tennis courts and the jungle gym for the little kids, and then around to the basketball court.

There is a kid playing basketball by himself. I watch him as we approach. He dribbles the ball to a certain spot, plants his feet, then looks up at the basket. He stays that way for a couple seconds, aiming, and then shoots.

And then he gets the ball and goes to another spot.

He makes every shot.

I watch him do this a few times as Charlie and I get nearer and nearer. And then when we are about to pass by, he turns our way and it's Sean.

I stop for just a second, almost tripping. It's only a second and then I recover. But Sean sees it and he looks up.

He says, Hey!

And he walks toward me.

Charlie looks up from where he's sniffing, one paw in the air. He sees Sean and then starts howling, like he always does with strangers. But he's wagging his tail.

Sean smiles at him. When he gets near, he swoops down with the ball under one arm and pets Charlie.

Charlie's tail wags even harder, and he licks Sean and whines and tries to climb all over him.

Sean stands back up.

He says, Mike, right?

I say, Yeah.

He holds the ball in both hands in front of him, kind of spinning it between his palms. He looks around at the park and the houses.

He says, You live around here?

I say, Yeah. On Whittaker.

He says, Oh cool. I live just a few blocks away.

I don't say anything. I know where he lives.

Sean spins the ball some more and then says, You wanna play?

I say, What?

He says, Basketball. You wanna play a bit?

I say, Um.

He looks at me.

I say, I'm not very good.

He says, Don't worry about it. Come on.

And then he turns and starts walking back toward the court.

I stand there for a second and then follow him. Nearby is a sign pole, where I tie Charlie's leash. He whines when I walk away, wanting to join me.

I stand on the court, feeling really dumb and not sure what to do. I'm bad at sports and I haven't played basketball since fourth grade, and even then I was pretty bad.

Sean says, We'll play Around the World. You know that?

I nod.

He says, Okay, first shot is from the side.

He walks over to the edge of the court where he can shoot from the side of the basket.

I hate side shots because you can't bounce the ball off the backboard, so it's a lot harder to get it in.

Sean bounces the ball twice, looking down and planting his feet. Then he looks up, aims for a few seconds, and throws the ball.

It rises and pauses and then falls again, all in a wide arc that looks like it's guided by wind.

There is the quietest *whoosh* as the ball passes perfectly through the net.

I get the ball and walk over to where Sean took his shot, and I turn around and look at the basket.

Charlie whines.

I hold the ball in front of my face, looking just over the top of it. In my head I imagine the arc that my ball should make, the parabola that Mr. Gardings would make us draw in Algebra to describe it. I imagine the ball as a tip of lead on paper, going up in one smooth stroke, passing all the points allowed by its equation, ending with the net. I imagine a perfect shot.

I bend my knees and throw the ball, and it goes up and comes down a couple feet short of the net.

It bounces hard against the concrete, a loud smacking sound that echoes against the houses across the street from the park.

The bounce takes it almost as high as the basket, and then it comes down with a muffled thud in the grass.

It rolls a bit and stops.

I don't make eye contact with Sean.

I say, I'm not very good.

He smiles wide, coming just short of a laugh.

I tense for a second before I realize it's a friendly smile and he isn't laughing at me.

He says, Well, you just gotta put more into it and you'll do fine. Trust me, I've seen a lot worse.

I don't know what he means by putting more into it. More what? But Sean gets the ball and throws it back to me. I catch it and realize he wants me to try again to see how I do.

So I plant my feet and hold the ball in front of my face and think about how Sean looked when he threw the ball.

I will myself to put as much into it as I can, and then I aim and take my shot.

The ball hits the side edge of the backboard and ricochets off at an angle.

I hear a yell:

At least you hit something this time, faggot!

My ears get hot right away. I know whose voice it is before I turn around.

Victor is across the street, behind me, smoking a cigarette.

He's watching us with a big grin on his face, a grin that looks nothing like Sean's.

Then he notices Sean, and that smile falters. Just a bit, but I can see it from where I am.

He says, Hey, Sean!

I turn back. Sean is staring across the street at Victor. He doesn't respond, just looks at Victor in this strange way.

I watch Sean and Sean watches Victor.

Then I say, I gotta go home.

And I walk past Sean on the court and untie Charlie and walk away.

When I get home, Dad and Mom and Toby are watching a movie. I recognize it right away: *Marley and Me.* It just started, I can tell. I've seen this movie a thousand times.

Dad looks over as I walk in.

He says, Just in time, buddy. Pull up a couch.

He pats the space next to him.

I let Charlie off the leash, and he bounds over to the living room and jumps up right where Dad patted. Dad tells him to get down and Charlie jumps off without stopping, his tail still going crazy.

I go over and sit down next to Dad.

We all really like this movie even though it's kind of stupid. But part of why is because we make fun of it as it goes on.

It's not a bad way to spend a Saturday.

The next Monday Sean isn't sitting with Victor.

I leave the lunch line with my tray and make my way to Ronald and Jared at our table, and glance over and see Sean sitting with the other basketball kids on the other side of the cafeteria.

I look at Victor's table. He and Tristan and Fuller aren't really talking. Victor's eyes keep darting over in Sean's direction. He's scowling.

I sit down with Ronald and Jared, smiling just a little.

FIVE

This is my dad:

Stern, sensible, serious.

He has rough hands that look especially big and wrinkled next to Mom's tiny smooth soft hands. He has hair growing out of his knuckles, and his nails are irregular from sloppy clippings and calcium deposits. They are a man's hands.

They are attached to a man's arms, to a man's shoulders, to a man's body.

His dark brown hair thins out on top. He combs it down neatly, but sometimes it sticks up when there's wind.

He doesn't smile or laugh much, and his dark eyes usually make him look businesslike.

He shaves every day, even weekends, but there's always a bit of stubble by afternoon.

He wears a tie on a button-down every day, even weekends, but loosens it at home.

Toby asked him once why he wears good clothes all the time.

This was back in Wisconsin. We were all sitting at the dinner table.

She said, Dad, why do you keep your tie on when you get home? And why do you always wear it on the weekends?

I think she was asking because she'd been hanging out with Marla a lot and noticed how different her family was from ours. How they just wore casual clothes and how Marla and her younger brothers didn't have to call them ma'am and sir and how they even let Marla have her own iPhone.

Dad stopped with his fork and a piece of chicken an inch from his open mouth. He put the fork down and looked at Toby like he was about to say something serious, which is how he always looks.

Then he said, It's important always to look your best, every chance you get, Toby.

Like that.

Toby just shrugged. Everyone kept eating.

Mom seems to agree.

She wears khakis and cardigans all the time. Like Martha Stewart, sort of. Not anything fancy, but still.

I don't think that kind of stuff is as popular as it used

to be, since a lot of other kids' moms wear regular pants or shorts or whatever they want around the house.

Jared's mom always has sweatpants on when I go over, but that's because she likes to jog and work out a lot.

Ronald's mom wears jeans and a sweatshirt with a hood, like she did the other day when we were playing Halo. She looks pretty good for a mom.

But my mom wears khakis and cardigans.

Once I saw old pictures of her from college, before she met Dad. She wasn't wearing khakis in them, but this weird outfit with denim and neon all over it.

I asked her why she was wearing that, and she said back then she didn't dress as nice. Plus neon was really in fashion at the time for some reason.

Mom goes to a nail place every Saturday to keep her hands looking soft and smooth and nice. Her fingernails are always polished. She wears light makeup, even on weekends, and wears her hair down every day.

When she walks around the house, she does it without making a sound, with a grace that makes it look like she's floating more than walking.

Sometimes it seems like she could float away with the wind if she wanted to.

I know we're kind of an old-fashioned family. I think I realized it for the first time in fifth grade, when I met my friend Kris. His family is a lot more like Ronald's than like mine.

Sometimes though I see other people that are like my parents. Well-dressed, conservative, kind of formal. Kids who also aren't allowed to have their own cell phones.

Usually I know them from church.

Sunday we go to Grace Fellowship.

Mom and Dad go every Sunday. They used to make Toby and me go to church every week too when we were younger, but they gave up a couple years ago when Toby started complaining about it a lot.

But they still make us every now and then. Usually it's Dad's idea. Mom doesn't care so much, but Dad is always pushing to get us to go.

So Sunday we go.

The parking lot is already full, because we left later than normal. Toby dragged her feet getting ready until Dad shouted at her to put on a dress or he'd leave her behind. That was kind of stupid because Toby wanted to be left behind. Dad realized his mistake right afterward and told her to hurry up or she'd have to go to church every week for two months.

Toby was especially slow getting ready today because the church choir wasn't going to sing this week. I heard her mumbling under her breath after one of the times Dad yelled at her.

She said, What's the point of going if I'm not going to sing anyway?

I asked her once why she joined the choir, since she hates church.

She said, Yeah, but I like choir.

She was lacing up her church shoes when we talked about it. It was a few weeks before, but I remember that because she seemed really aggressive when she pulled at the laces.

She said, Plus it makes the service go by faster.

She tied another knot, even harder than before.

She said, Plus it keeps Dad happy.

We're still five minutes before the service starts, but Dad likes to get there really early. Extra time for self-reflection, he says.

We circle the lot, looking for a space. Dad is annoyed. I can tell because he's tapping both thumbs on the steering wheel and muttering under his breath.

He finally finds a spot and parks, and we hurry inside.

It's a big church, like the one in Sheboygan Falls. Dad likes big churches.

We walk down the center aisle, passing hundreds of people, looking for the closest possible seat in just the right pew. People are talking and laughing, greeting each other before the service starts.

I'm looking up as I walk, staring at the high, painted ceiling. I pull at my collar, stiff and tight from lack of use, bright white from the bleached wash Mom gives it regularly. Dark red tie hanging down, anchored by a navy sweater vest. This over creased black slacks and shiny black shoes.

I don't like this look but Mom does, has always loved it, so I pretend to as well.

I love the ceiling. It bows out from me in a wide dome, every inch of it covered in images of people from the Bible frozen in place, acting out pieces of famous Scripture.

I don't think Dad likes it. He said once it's the sort of thing that belongs in a Catholic church, not an Evangelical church.

The paintings are the only thing I like about the church.

I'm sitting next to my friend Terry. I don't like going to church, but I do like getting to see Terry. It's like a trade-off.

Terry is absorbed with the sermon. He goes to church every week because his dad is an elder, but I think he'd go anyway. He's never seemed super-religious, but he's definitely more religious than me.

Toby's on my other side. She looks bored and is obviously not paying attention. She slouches against the pew and her dress bunches up. She hates this dress.

Mom sits next to Toby, listening to the sermon with her hands clasped in her lap. Every now and then her lips move with the pastor's as he quotes a passage from the Bible.

Dad sits at the end of the row, eyes closed, but I

know he's not sleeping. He sits straight up, back not touching the pew, chin up, small smile. I know he's listening to every word. He likes to keep his eyes closed during the sermon, to only hear it and concentrate on the words.

I stare past the preacher, watching the light shine through the stained-glass window behind him, making it glow. Pastor Clark is a young man in his late twenties or early thirties. He always smiles in person but looks kind of strained on the pulpit. His voice comes in waves, loud and then soft, a shout and then a whisper. He moves his arms as he talks, and I watch them weave through the air.

Pastor Clark talks about a story in Matthew, about a Roman centurion who comes to Jesus to have his son healed. He talks about Jesus curing the boy, about the centurion's faith, how Jesus praised the man afterward.

Pastor Clark talks about John next, about the centurion's faith being the key to salvation and how to stop sin.

He talks about Massachusetts, and his voice picks up. He talks about a wave of other states after and it picks up more.

I can't look away.

Then he talks about the Supreme Court, and now he's shouting, and I can almost hear the congregation hold its breath when he slams the pulpit with a white-knuckled fist, and now, finally, I look down.

My head feels heavy. I'm staring at the back of the pew in front of me, at the frayed corner of the New Testament sitting in the slot at my knees, burgundy cloth cover, gold text.

I listen to the congregation. Everyone holds their breath, everyone lets out their breath at the same time. I listen for that sigh.

I look over at Terry and he's as engrossed as everyone around him.

Dad and I are in the backyard. Terry's here too. He came over after the service, like he does sometimes.

Dad's still wearing his church clothes, a nicer version of what he wears every day. I'm wearing mine, too, but now my starched shirt is untucked and my tie hangs loose outside the vest.

He has the Green Bay football in his hands and wants me to back up a bit more. To go long.

It's not a huge backyard but I step out a bit farther. He throws, a sidearm toss aimed high, and I squint as it travels up toward the sun. Terry watches with me, from his spot in the triangle we've made.

I catch it, barely. It hits the crook of my elbow and almost bounces out of my arms but I catch it.

From across the yard Dad yells, Use your chest!

He clamps his arms to himself in a bear hug, demonstrating.

He says, Let it hit your chest and wrap your arms around where it lands.

The ball smells new. The Green Bay decal is bright in the daylight.

I hold it in my right hand, putting my fingers over the laces like Dad's told me a thousand times before.

He nods at me, and I throw.

It wobbles, like it's caught in crosswinds. Terry watches it go back the way it came, with this look on his face like nothing could bother him, mouth set. He watches it go end over end, somehow staying in the air.

But it makes it to Dad, at least. He catches it in one hand, easily, and looks upward for a moment as if taking in the sky.

It's blue. Flawless.

After a while he says, Needs more follow-through.

Almost to himself.

He says, Keep your arms moving after the throw.

I nod, and suddenly he smiles. A real smile.

He says, Don't worry, kiddo. Takes practice, like anything.

I blink, and then nod again, but slowly. Then Mom comes out.

She says, Mike! Get out of those clothes if you're going to throw the ball around.

She sounds exasperated but looks at Dad when she speaks.

She says, I didn't get him those shoes so he can scuff them up.

Dad chuckles.

He says, That's enough for now, anyway. Let's get washed up for dinner.

I nod, trying not to let the relief show on my face. But I know he sees it anyway.

Terry is on my left on one of the long sides of the table. Toby is across from us.

Mom and Dad are at either end.

It's a bit cramped on my side because we're forcing an odd number onto our rectangular dinner table. But it's good to have Terry here.

Every Sunday we have a big dinner in the afternoon, like two o'clock. We have it whether Toby and I go to church or not.

Lately we've been inviting Terry. Mom and Dad know I don't see him much besides church so they don't mind. Plus they think he's a good influence on me.

I guess he is.

He comes home with us from church and eats dinner with us and maybe we hang out a bit, and then Dad drives him home.

Dinner today is roast chicken, lemon sauce, garlic mashed potatoes, steamed cauliflower.

The cauliflower is for me, I know. I used to hate it but then it kind of grew on me a year ago. Mom started making it for me once she noticed that I was eating it more often.

She's good about stuff like that.

It's quiet for a while. There's just the clinking of forks.

Then Dad says, You playing any sports, Terry?

We usually don't talk that much at the table, but Dad likes to keep conversation going when we have company. I guess that's sort of his sales rep instinct.

Terry goes to a different high school, up in Laurel Pointe. He's on the freshman baseball team there. Dad already knows this but is asking anyway.

Terry says, Yessir.

He always addresses Dad like this, and Dad lets him because I think part of him likes it.

He says, I'm in baseball at school. We've only had a few practice sessions so far, but I think I'm getting along all right.

Mom says, Oh, that's great!

Dad smiles.

He says, You think he'll take you on varsity next year?

Terry smiles and looks at his plate and says, Oh, I don't know.

But then he looks back up and there's this sort of light in his eyes.

He says, But there are always a couple sophomores that skip JV. Like the really good ones. Maybe even three this year . . .

Terry looks over at the wallpaper, trailing off, thinking about his chances at baseball.

He looks back down after a while.

He says, But yeah, I dunno.

Dad watches him the whole time, that strange smile still on his face, his own fork dangling just above his plate. A drop of lemon sauce falls from the tip and lands on his mashed potatoes.

He says, Well, don't count yourself out yet. I bet you could be one of those two or three next year.

Mom says, I'm sure if you keep up your practices, you'll do just fine.

Terry smiles at his plate.

There's another of the pauses between conversations, more clinking of forks. I wait for Dad to say something. He always will.

After a while, he does:

That was an interesting sermon.

Terry nods to himself a bit while he chews, as if thinking, and says, You think so?

Dad says, Yes, about that passage, and then about the courts and all those states. Very thought-provoking.

Toby says, I thought it was kind of weird.

Dad looks at her and Mom frowns.

She says, Toby.

Toby looks at her with an expression that's supposed to look innocent but doesn't. She says, What?

Mom's eyes dart to Toby just for a second and she says, There's no need for that.

Toby shrugs and says, Well, it's true.

I can tell Mom is wondering if Toby is saying this to

annoy Dad or to annoy Terry. Terry's dad doesn't help write the sermons or anything, but his family is very close to the pastor's. It's a church family, even more connected than we are.

It's the kind of family Dad probably wishes we were.

Toby and Terry don't get along very well. They're not like enemies or anything, but they get under each other's skin. It's weird because Toby likes all my other friends, and her friends are usually pretty cool even if they're too girlie and excitable sometimes.

Terry keeps poking at his food, and it looks like he's trying to decide whether to say something. He knows Toby likes to push his buttons, but sometimes he can't help himself.

But Dad cuts in before Terry gets a chance.

He says, Toby, eat your dinner.

Toby rolls her eyes. She picks at her food with her fork, moving a piece of chicken from one side of the plate to the other.

Dad watches her a bit to see if she'll say anything else. And for a while it looks like she might too.

Instead she gives him a look that only she can, one that I don't think Dad would let anyone else give him. Then she goes back to her chicken.

The rest of dinner is silent.

Terry and I walk Charlie after dinner.

I let Terry hold the leash because he likes to. He

always says he wishes he had a dog at home but his mom is allergic, so he likes hanging out with Charlie when he comes over.

Charlie pulls at the leash left and right, going from tree to tree, but Terry's used to him now.

He says, Your sister didn't like the sermon much.

His voice is reserved and I decide he's not annoyed about it anymore. Terry is good at keeping control of his feelings and not letting things bother him. He might at first, especially with Toby, but after a while he treats any argument with her like a casual debate.

He's pretty mature for his age.

I say, Yeah, she usually doesn't like the sermons.

He says, Is it just the church in general?

I say, Yeah, I think so.

Charlie lifts his leg in front of a signpost, then bounds across the sidewalk to sniff at a clump of weeds. Terry's arm and the leash follow like a divining rod.

Terry says, What did you think of the sermon?

I don't know how to answer at first, so I'm just quiet.

Terry doesn't pester me, he just waits. He knows that I don't talk that much and that when I don't answer right away, it doesn't mean I'm ignoring him.

Dad usually gets impatient when I do that, though.

Finally I say, I dunno. I mean I kind of didn't get it either, but it's Pastor Clark's job to say what the Bible says, right?

Terry nods.

Then he says, What do you think about the whole faith-getting-rid-of-sin thing?

I shrug.

I say, I guess that's what I've always been taught.

Terry says, But do you believe it?

I think about it for a bit.

Then I say, Yeah.

Terry nods again. Neither of us says anything for a few seconds, maybe a minute.

Charlie pulls side to side, side to side.

Then Terry says, I hope so.

I look at him, then back at Charlie.

I say, What do you mean?

Terry's forehead is scrunched together. He looks uncomfortable but determined to say what's on his mind.

He says, There are just a couple things that I have trouble with.

He pauses.

He says, Like, sin things.

He pauses again, then opens his mouth as if he's going to say something more, but stops.

I wait a second before I prod him.

I say, What kind of sin?

It's like he's been waiting for me to ask. He says, Porn.

I don't say anything, I just nod. I get the sense right away this is a bigger deal to him than to me.

For some reason I'm a little disappointed.

SIX

It's November.

We're learning about light in Art class.

Mr. Kilgore has put an old-fashioned teapot on his desk. It's pale blue, squat, with yellow flower designs running in a circle along the top.

He has us draw it, and then after twenty minutes he shines a light right on the front and has us draw it again.

I'm halfway through this second drawing when I glance over at Victor.

I don't know why, I just do.

I notice Victor look away right when I glance over, but our eyes meet for a split second before he turns. He was looking at me.

He's at his table with Tristan and Fuller, but they're not talking to each other. Everyone's concentrating on the teapot.

Except Victor.

I mean he's drawing it now, but he does it like someone going through the motions, as if he knows he's being watched.

I look at the side of his face, his small ear, his short sideburn, his dark skin, black hair. I know he knows I'm looking at him.

I think about how he's been ignoring me lately, and I wonder if he and Tristan and Fuller just got bored making fun of me.

Then Mr. Kilgore speaks.

He says, Mikey, do you want to pay attention to your work?

I start in my chair. His voice is loud and unexpected in the stillness of the room. I look up, and he's peering at me over his glasses, mustache quivering. He looks annoyed.

I say, Yeah, sorry.

A couple kids snicker. But not Victor.

Mr. Kilgore says, Let's get back to drawing, then.

On my paper, one teapot sits next to part of another, which seems to glow in certain places.

I look over at Victor again, just for a second.

He's still drawing.

Then I turn back to the teapot.

* * *

I get to French class early, like usual, and Sean is there, like usual.

He smiles just a little and nods when I walk in. It's just him and me and Madame Girard in the room.

Madame Girard is at her desk, going through a bunch of papers.

She doesn't look up when I walk in but says, *Bonjour, Monsieur Matthis.*

That's me.

I mumble back, *Salut.*

I'm looking at Sean, though, and he's looking at me. For a minute we look at each other that way and it's like we're alone, Madame Girard too busy with her papers to notice, lost in thought at her desk while Sean and I share some secret something. I think about how we're staring too long, how it's past the point where it'd get uncomfortable with anyone else, and for a panicky second I wonder if I'm being weird, if I'm the one staring and Sean is wondering why, but then I see the slightest upturn in the corner of his mouth and I know it's not true.

I break the contact and sit down, one ahead and one to the right of him. And then the world goes back to its normal speed. Kids walk into the class, and it gets louder and louder.

The bell rings, and Madame Girard gives her papers one last examination and then stands up beside her desk and looks at her class for the first time.

It's quieter now but not totally quiet.

Madame Girard tells us we're going to start our semester-end projects.

Everyone groans.

She talks about the timing. The semester ends in six weeks, which is a pretty long time. This is going to be a big project.

Everyone groans a bit more.

Madame Girard smiles at this. I think she's enjoying it.

Then she tells us what she calls the good news: While we're welcome to work on the projects alone, we can team up with a partner in the class.

There's some murmurs at this.

Slowly, casually, I turn my head over my left shoulder.

Sean is already looking at me, his eyes locking on mine.

He smiles.

Ronald and Jared are talking about Kelly Ramirez when Sean walks up.

Ronald's had like a huge crush on Kelly the last few weeks and likes to talk about her whenever he gets a chance.

He says, Her lips are plump as shit. Like berries.

Jared says, Berries?

Ronald pokes at his meat loaf. He shakes his head.

He says, And her boobs are just, like . . .

He trails off, distracted by thoughts of Kelly Ramirez's boobs.

He says, Amazing. Just amazing.

Ronald looks up at Jared, who is watching him.

Jared takes a bite of his cookie and chews for a little.

Then with his mouth full, he says, What happened to Leah?

Ronald shrugs. He says, Leah's old news. Kelly's where it's at.

Jared says, You don't have a chance.

Ronald takes a forkful of meat loaf, unfazed. He's heard this before.

He says, I got a chance.

Jared says, Kelly likes really muscular guys. She dated like every athletic kid in middle school, and she's doing it again in high school.

Ronald says, Dude, I got a chance.

Jared says, I don't think I've ever seen her with a skinny kid.

Ronald says, I'm not as skinny as you. Plus I'm gonna start working out.

Jared says, She's dating Tim Gruetske right now. His arms are gigantic.

I say, You're gonna work out?

Ronald burps.

He says, Yeah. I got a membership to the Y.

I say, The one on Terbocker Street? How?

Ronald says, My mom has a membership. They let you add a family member for half price. I think Mom kinda liked that I wanted to do it, 'cause she's always trying to get me to eat healthy anyway.

Jared says, You're gonna work out with your mom?

Ronald says, I dunno. Yeah. Maybe. Or actually, she takes weird classes there and doesn't really lift weights or anything. So while she does that, I could do my thing, you know?

Jared says, Does she know you're only doing it to get Kelly Ramirez, which by the way will never happen?

Ronald says, Or I could just bike there whenever I want anyway. It's pretty close.

I say, What kind of workouts are you going to do?

Ronald says, I dunno, stuff to get my muscles bigger. Bench presses, dumbbells, that kind of thing.

I think about this for a while.

I say, Have you ever worked out before?

Ronald says, I went with my uncle once, just—

But then his eyes flick upward, over my head, and he stops.

I turn around.

Sean's standing behind me, looking down at me. He's holding a tray of food, just standing there.

He says, Hey.

I say, Hey.

He says, Hey, so I was thinking, that project?

I say, Madame Girard.

He says, Yeah. Yeah, you want a partner for that?

I say, Sure.

My mouth is dry.

He says, Cool. Okay, well, you wanna come over maybe tomorrow and work on it?

I say, Yeah, sure.

He smiles.

He says, All right, cool. Talk to you later.

And walks away.

I watch him go a second before turning back around.

Ronald's watching him too.

He says, What's his name again?

Jared says, Sean.

Jared has a good memory.

Ronald says, Didn't he use to sit with Victor Price?

I say, Yeah.

Ronald watches a bit more, following with his eyes as Sean finds his table, then blinks and looks at me.

He says, He's not anymore.

I say, Yeah.

Ronald shrugs and says, You got a big project in French?

I nod.

He says, That sucks.

He thinks for a bit, then adds, And me, I got girl problems. You and me, we got a lot on our backs, bro.

Then he holds out his fist to bump mine. Ronald does stuff like that sometimes. It's one of the reasons I like him, because he never cares what anyone thinks of him, except Kelly Ramirez.

I fist-bump him back.

It's raining, but only a little.

We're close to the ocean so we get a decent amount of rain, but sometimes the rain that comes is just constant drizzle, barely above a mist but never-ending.

One of the first days after we moved here, Dad came with me to walk Charlie. It had been humid and overcast all day, gray and dull, and we were both wondering if it was going to rain. And then just a couple minutes into the walk, we felt the first tiny drops. It stayed that way, just kind of sprinkling, never turning into the downpour we were waiting for. When we were almost back home, Dad suddenly said,

This rain has no ambition.

He looked up a bit after he said that, letting the spray hit his face, walking slowly even though Charlie was pulling at the leash. Then he looked over at me and winked.

Today is one of those days.

I have a raincoat, and I'm walking up Plum Hollow Drive. School let out an hour and a half ago, and it feels weird to walk in this direction at this time of day and without Toby.

I pass block after block. No one's outside and I have the road to myself. The whole neighborhood.

Finally I take a left onto Hyacinth Court. It's a street I've never been on, and I walk slowly, taking in the block, looking at everything.

All these houses look alike but there are still small differences. There's a house with a big American flag on a pole; there's a yard with a tiny landscaped cactus garden; a lawn with four giant oak trees lined up like soldiers, one two three four.

I count the houses on my left side as I walk. At five, I stop.

It's a red-brick house with white trim like everyone else's, but I look for those tiny differences. There's a small mound in the yard covered in shrubs, with a tall tree on either side. Two piney bushes flank the garage door. The address is hand-painted in charcoal gray along the curb.

In front of the garage, a faded blue Ford Bronco, old and weary-looking. Next to it, a shiny gray Lincoln.

I walk up to the front door, thick wood with panels of murky colored glass. I don't hear anything, so I listen harder.

Once in fourth grade, our teacher made us write down what we hear when it's quiet. No one understood what she meant at first, but she just told us all to stop and listen, and we'd start hearing small things that we hadn't noticed before. After a little while, it worked. I wrote about the sound of the building's heater turning on and off, the wind against the windows, the scratches of pencil and paper. She said sometimes people get so used to background noises that they don't even realize they're there anymore.

I try it now, and then I start hearing. There's a small computer keyboard sound of rain against the hood of my coat, a steady wind, and a dog barking miles away.

I ring the doorbell.

It only takes him a second; through the glass I can see movement but can't make out his figure. He opens the door and he's wearing jeans, different from the ones he had on at school, jeans with holes. A plain white T-shirt, no shoes, no socks. His feet are mostly covered by the bottoms of his jeans.

Sean says, Hey, come in.

I step inside.

The entrance is tiled, like our house but a little nicer. Rooms open up on either side, and straight ahead I see the living room, past a bent staircase that leads to a second-floor balcony.

He says, You gotta take your shoes off or my dad will flip.

I take off my raincoat first. They have a little coat stand near the door and I hang it there, and then I take off my shoes and put them as neatly as I can near the door. I hear movement from another room behind me while I'm doing this and turn.

Sean's parents walk into the entrance hall. His dad is pale with sandy hair, but they still look a lot alike. Same lips and jaw, same eyes.

Sean's dad holds out his hand.

He says, Mr. Rossini.

I shake his hand, which seems weird to me but I do it anyway.

I say, I'm Mike.

He says, Good to meet you, Mike. We're about to head out to a movie, so you boys will have the house to yourselves.

His expression is really hard to read. There's just a bit of a smile but not really. His eyes stay on mine and don't waver, like he's trying to read me. It makes me a bit uneasy.

Finally I turn to Sean's mom, really just to avoid Mr. Rossini's gaze. She's wearing a simple gray dress and a handful of necklaces. She has dark brown skin, darker than Sean, and straightened black hair that hangs down to her shoulders. Every strand stays perfectly in place when she moves. It looks like she spent a lot of time on it.

She looks very sure of herself. Confident. Nothing really like my mom.

I say, Good to meet you, Mrs. Rossini.

She takes my hand but only nods once, slowly, in response. Then her eyes flick over to Sean.

She says, He's here to work on a project, so make sure you actually get some work done.

Her eyes dart back to me right after she says the last bit, and for a second my heart skips. But then she winks at me. Her expression doesn't change.

Sean says, I know, Mom.

Mr. Rossini says, Sean.

His voice is suddenly stern.

Sean says, I mean, yes, ma'am.

Mr. Rossini says, Really, though, I want to see some progress on this.

Sean says, Yessir.

Mr. Rossini says, See if you can get through a quarter of it, at least.

Sean says, Yessir.

His voice is a bit clipped now.

Mr. Rossini says, It's a big part of your grade, remember.

Sean says, Yessir.

Mrs. Rossini pulls at her husband's hand and says, All right, we're going to be late.

Mr. Rossini looks at me and says, Okay, boys. Be good, and don't tear the house down.

They walk out the front door. Sean closes it behind him.

He looks tense for a minute. He's facing the closed door but I can see him blink a few times, from the side.

Then he lets out a deep breath through his nose, slow, and his body relaxes.

He turns suddenly to me.

He says, You want anything to drink?

I'm not really thirsty but I say, Uh yeah, I'll have a water.

He spins on the tiled floor and leads me into a dark sitting room through the doorway on the left, and through that into a huge kitchen filled with light. Coming from the small den with the drawn curtains, I have to blink a bit as the daylight still streaming from the windows mixes with the overheads and stings my eyes.

He grabs a glass from a cabinet, reaching up high to get it, and puts it under the spigot in the fridge door.

There's a loud humming sound, and then I hear a controlled stream of water. Sean looks at me.

He says, Any trouble finding the house? I always give shitty directions.

I shake my head. I already knew the street from before and it wasn't hard to find the car.

He hands me the glass of water, condensation already forming on the side, and pulls a Pepsi from the fridge and cracks it open.

There's a moment where all I can hear is the muffled fizzing of his Pepsi, and then even that dies out.

Then he says, Let's go upstairs.

Sean's room is tucked into the corner of the second floor, behind a game room with a pool table and next to his private bathroom.

The balcony that overlooks the living room and entrance connects his part of the upstairs with another section that has a guest room and library.

It's a nice house.

The door to his room is almost totally bare, all white

paint on wood except for a small three-by-five photo taped off-center. It's a view from a suspension bridge, looking through one of the gateway supports toward a city skyline in the background.

I say, Is that the Brooklyn Bridge?

I know it from pictures my dad has taken while at conferences.

Sean says, Yeah.

He pushes through the door and into his room. Like his door, the walls are mostly bare and white and untouched. He has a big bed next to a deep red-brown nightstand and matching dresser, vanity, and desk. The furniture all looks pretty expensive. He keeps his room clean, his bed made.

I say, Have you ever been to New York City?

He says, Just once.

It looks for a second like he's going to say more about it, but then just asks, You?

I shake my head. I've been to Wisconsin and Virginia, and then on vacations to California, Florida, Mexico, Germany, and camping in Colorado.

But Dad avoids New York when planning vacations.

Sean falls into a sitting position on his bed, letting himself bounce on the mattress.

I sink quietly into his desk chair, one of those rolling, spinning types they have in offices.

He waits till the bouncing stops on its own, then says, All right.

And reaches down to his backpack and pulls out his French book.

He says, I guess we should get started.

Our project is to create a French magazine.

It has to be at least sixteen pages and have zero English in it. Only 40 percent of the magazine space can be pictures, which sounds like a lot, but it still leaves basically nine and a half pages of pure French text.

The first step, Sean and I agree, is to come up with the type of magazine it is. It can be fashion, culture, food, music, whatever.

Sean says we should pick something that's easy to write about. Like if we made a magazine all about beekeeping or whatever, it would be hard to fill sixteen pages on that topic even in English. But if it's something more broad it's easier.

He says, Why don't we do a travel magazine?

I say, Okay. Or maybe a news magazine.

Because news is always happening, in any part of the country.

I say, All we'd have to do then is find a bunch of regular articles and translate them.

Sean nods to himself, thinking. He's leaning back on his bed, propping himself up with both arms, legs dangling off his bed. The white T-shirt is sort of stretched where his shoulders and arms are. There are a couple hairs on his chin and I wonder how often he has to shave.

He looks at me again.

He says, We could do a dirty magazine. French people are always looking at porn.

I will away the blushing, or try.

I say, I don't think Madame Girard—

But Sean cuts me off and says, Yeah, I'm just kidding.

He smiles a bit and scratches his arm.

We decide to do the travel magazine after all, because that way we don't have to translate a bunch of complicated news stories. We can just make up our own easier articles, and there are tons of travel sites online we can look at.

Plus Sean's mom has a bunch of old travel magazines we can use for ideas. Sean brings them into his room, a big box stuffed full, and we start flipping through them looking for things we could include in our project.

The magazines go back ten years or more and cover everywhere imaginable: Spain, Greece, Argentina, Norway, Egypt, Turkey, Indonesia, China, New Zealand, Zambia. Some of the magazines are even from other countries and feature places in the United States. A couple are in French and we pay close attention to them.

Sean says his parents have been all over the world, sometimes on vacation, sometimes for his dad's work when his mom tags along, sometimes on church missions.

Sometimes he goes and sometimes he stays behind.

I say, What's the coolest place you've been?

He answers quickly: Australia.

I've been to a couple other countries but never Australia. I think about how cool it must be to have all these vacations, but then Sean says,

I try to stay behind as much as possible, though.

I say, Why?

Sean leans back on his elbows again, magazine resting on his lap. It's one of the French ones, opened to an article about Cuba.

He says, It gets old being with my parents for more than a couple days. Dad gets stressed pretty easily.

He stays that way for a second and I'm not sure if I'm supposed to respond, but then he says,

Plus it's nice having the house to myself.

Sean doesn't have any brothers or sisters.

He sits up suddenly and grabs the magazine in his lap and says, Hey, come here and look at this one.

I've been sitting in his desk chair, so I get up and sit next to him on the bed. The mattress bounces a little before I get settled.

Sean puts the magazine half on his lap, half on mine, the two-page spread on Cuba before us. He starts talking about different parts of the article, pointing here and there. Neither of us can make out that much of the French text, but it's the layout he's interested in.

Aside from the article itself and the main photo, there's a sidebar with small pictures and text beside them, high-lighting different points of interest. There's also a shaded

text box with bullet points, probably just listing facts or something.

Sean talks about all these, about which pieces we can use. All told, the article isn't very long because of all the text boxes and photos and the big headline, all of which is pretty encouraging. I can see a picture of our magazine forming itself in my mind.

We're sitting close as he talks, arms sometimes brushing against each other. He leans over to point at something on my half of the spread, and I feel the pressure of his finger through the pages, through my jeans, on my thigh.

We look through a bunch more magazines, putting the ones we like in a pile and the rest back in the box. I stay in my spot to the left of Sean on the bed, each magazine spread out between us in turn. When Sean flips the pages, sometimes his arm grazes my chest.

We work for a couple hours before Sean checks the clock on his nightstand, the blue numbers now reading 7:26.

He says, Hey, we should probably stop now.

I look behind me at the open window, where a faint breeze is pushing the curtains inward. It's dark now, and I realize it probably has been for a while. Dad will want me home for dinner.

I turn back and Sean is looking at me. For the first time I notice little flecks of orange in his eyes, around the inside of the irises. Only a few but they're there, like the first gold leaves in a brilliant green forest, the first gold leaves of fall.

I watch the orange flecks disappear as his pupils dilate, just a little. All at once I realize how close he is.

I think he does too, because he stands up then, putting the magazine we'd been looking at back in the box.

He says, Okay, I'll walk you down.

His voice sounds different now. Sort of tense. Like when he was talking to his dad. I start feeling a bit nervous and I don't really know why.

After a second, I stand up too.

At the front door, Sean says, See you later. Maybe we can work on it again next week.

He's leaning against the edge of the open door from the inside. I'm on the porch, the night behind me. Behind him the house is mostly dark. His parents haven't come home yet.

He seems back to normal now, and I wonder if I just imagined the weird moment upstairs.

I say, Yeah, that'd be cool.

And I notice that I'm looking forward to it.

Halfway down the block a car honks as it passes me. I look and see Mr. Rossini wave lazily out the driver's-side window. I turn to watch and he slows, then pulls into the driveway.

Mom says, Did you get a lot done?

We're sitting at the dinner table. I think Dad's a little annoyed because I came home like a minute before dinner

90

was ready. He looked like he'd been getting ready to be mad, but then couldn't because I ended up coming home just barely on time.

I say, Yeah.

Dad says, Are you going to be over at his house a lot working on this?

I say, Yeah.

He takes a bite of pork and chews and swallows.

He says, Just leave us his number so we can get ahold of you.

I don't have my own phone. Dad said I can buy one with my own money when I'm old enough to get a job, but there's no need for kids to carry cell phones around like they're CEOs or something. That's how he said it.

It's annoying but it also means he can't call me whenever I'm out, which would be even more annoying.

I say, Okay.

Mom says, What kind of magazine are you going to do?

I told her about the project yesterday.

I say, A travel magazine.

She says, Oh, that sounds fun.

I nod and pick at my mashed potatoes, and no one else says anything. Toby and Mom and Dad eat their dinner without looking up, and I do the same.

I think about Sean's open window, feeling the breeze on the back of my neck while I sat next to him.

SEVEN

Victor starts paying attention to me again a couple days later.

I'm in one of the main hallways walking to Biology. There are always tons of kids in this hallway because it connects most parts of the school.

I don't even see him when he passes by. He's walking in the opposite direction, probably to his locker. My mind is somewhere else.

I feel a jarring thump on my left shoulder, hard enough to turn me around a bit and make me drop my book.

I look back and I know my eyes are wide; I'm still not really sure what's just happened, and then Victor turns casually over his shoulder, smirking, and I understand. Tristan and Fuller are with him like always, both grinning.

I stare at him for a second, collecting myself, and then look down at my book lying open, facedown and askew on the ground. I reach down and pick it up, and turn in the direction I was walking without looking back at Victor and his friends.

My shoulder throbs and I'm clenching and unclenching my right fist, but there's a part of me that almost feels relieved.

Like I'm glad he's back to normal or something.

It's Friday and warmer than it should be.

The last couple weeks it's been getting noticeably cooler. Jacket weather. One day was just plain cold.

But today it's back in the upper seventies, one of the last few bits of nice weather before winter comes.

I pick Toby up after school, still thinking about Victor and how weird it is to suddenly have him care enough again to shove me in the hallway.

Toby and I are walking along the main road by the school when I hear a car horn, three quick bursts.

I turn around and it's a pale blue Ford Bronco. Sean's.

He pulls over and leans across to roll down the passenger-side window. He has to do it by hand because they're not power windows but the old-fashioned kind of hand-roll ones.

He says, Hey!

Toby looks at him and then at me.

I say, Hey, Sean.

He says, Want a ride?

Toby raises her eyebrows.

She says to me, My feet are killing me.

I look at Sean through the window and say, Sure, thanks.

He motions for us to get in.

The inside of the Bronco smells dusty but it's comfortable. There's junk all over the floors, especially in the backseat, where Toby gets in. I sit shotgun.

Sean drives fast but not wildly, his right hand flying smoothly from the steering wheel to the gear shift with each turn and acceleration. It's a manual shift, which I didn't even know kids our age knew how to drive.

Mom and Dad both have automatics, and Dad's already told me he's going to teach me on the Corolla next year.

Sean's quiet as he drives. I listen to the sound of the motor, the click of the turn signal, the drum of his fingers on the steering wheel.

Then he says, What are you doing tonight?

I shrug.

I say, Nothing, I guess.

He nods and hangs his left arm out the window. The air rushes up his sleeve.

He says, Wanna play basketball at the park?

Now I nod.

I say, Sure.

From the backseat, I hear Toby giggle a bit.

I turn around to look at her. She catches my eye, then looks away innocently, grinning.

Dad's watching me, not saying anything. I can feel his stare.

The TV's on and he's sitting on the couch, but he watches me as I leave the living room and come back wearing shorts and a T-shirt. I sit down on the carpet to put on my shoes, and he finally speaks.

He says, Where are you going?

Toby says, He's playing *basketball.*

She says the last word like it's something gross. I give her a look.

Dad looks at Toby, then back at me.

Still glaring at Toby, I say, In the park. Gonna play basketball with Sean.

Toby says, It's his favorite sport now.

Out of the corner of my eye, I can see Dad raise his eyebrows.

He says, The one you're doing the French magazine with?

I say, Yeah.

He looks at me a little longer and I can tell he's sort of surprised.

He says, What about your homework?

I stop tying my shoes. I say, I can do it tomorrow. It's just Algebra and Bio.

Dad doesn't say anything for a couple seconds. I can tell he's torn between wanting me to do homework now and wanting me to play sports.

Finally he says, Well, all right. Have fun. Don't be out too late.

I say, I won't.

And I walk out.

It's warm, still light out, but about to turn to dusk.

Dad says there are big Jewish neighborhoods in New York City that have loud outdoor alarms that go off Friday evenings to mark sunset. They sound like air-raid sirens. It's to let the Jewish people know that the Sabbath is starting, and they better get home because they're not allowed to work anymore. I try to picture those neighborhoods now, with the sirens going off and people running home to make it in time.

I have my sneakers and baggy shorts and an old T-shirt and Charlie on a leash. I brought him because he loves going out and he's fun to have around.

He wags his tail this time when he sees Sean instead of howling at him.

Sean squats down to pet him like he did last time.

He says, Guy's got a good memory.

Charlie wags his tail harder, ears flopping from side to side while Sean pets him. He lifts one paw onto Sean's knee and licks his hand, which makes Sean laugh.

Sean looks up.

There are already a couple strong lights shining on the court to keep drug dealers away, so even when it gets dark later, it'll still be pretty well lit. Sean's grinning up at me while Charlie wags and licks and whines in excitement. He's wearing white basketball shorts and a blue Wizards jersey.

He stands up, bringing the ball with him, and now he's eye level.

We're a foot or two apart, Charlie between us. Sean spins the ball in front of his chest with both hands.

He says, Let's play.

We get in place to run the play for the fifth time.

I'm standing at the free-throw line. The basket is behind me.

In front of me, at half-court, Sean dribbles the ball once, twice.

Then he starts toward me.

He drifts to the left, and I follow, keeping him in front. He gets closer and closer, and now I raise my arms in a block like he showed me.

When he's a couple feet away, he turns suddenly to the right. I'm expecting this. He's done it before. I move with him, keeping on him like I'm supposed to, and now he turns around so his back is to me and he's edging backward toward the basket.

My arms are outstretched, keeping him from moving around me.

Sean is inches away. The bit of hair on the back of his head is damp with his sweat, dripping down to his shirt. I can smell it; I can smell him.

He moves the basketball in his own outstretched arm from one side to the other like a crane, looking over his shoulder, looking for a way out.

He finds it like I knew he would, banking hard to the left. Suddenly his hair and his sweat and his arms are gone, and I'm chasing him as he runs toward the basket, dribbling in a steady rhythm without watching the ball.

Sean shoots the ball when he's only feet away, and I have no chance.

He turns, grinning, while the ball bounces hard on the pavement and then lands in the grass. There's a V shape of sweat on the front of his shirt.

My own stain is bigger. I'm doubled over, hands resting on knees. My breathing comes in loud messy gasps while I wait for my heart to stop pounding. Sean doesn't even look winded.

He says, Your left side's always unguarded.

But in a patient way, like a teacher. Kind of like Miss Rayner, actually.

Charlie watches with ears perked, one paw frozen in the air.

I think about how much I like Miss Rayner.

I say, Yeah. For some reason I always think you're gonna go right.

He nods.

He says, Guy with the ball is always gonna go which-ever side is easier. You have more control than I do over which way I go, if you guard one side less than the other. Comes in handy if you wanna trap the guy, like lead him to a spot where another teammate can sneak up on him.

Sean looks at Charlie and grins again.

He says, Like a herding dog with sheep.

I don't think beagles are herders, but I get what he's saying.

He walks over to where Charlie is tied to one of the legs of the picnic table. Charlie watches him the whole way, tail wagging faster as Sean approaches.

Sean bends down to give him a quick pat, and Charlie licks his hand. Then he takes his jersey off.

In the mix of pink twilight and yellow court lights, I can see the muscles on his back moving as he pulls first one arm and then the other over his head to get the shirt off.

Drops of sweat fly off his head. He tosses the jersey on the picnic table. Charlie watches it land on the tabletop. Then he blinks and turns back to Sean, who is now walk-ing back toward me.

I've never seen him with his shirt off. He's lean and defined and looks somehow taller. I glance at his abs and then look away quickly, at Charlie. My heart is pounding.

He says, Wanna go again?

I look at Charlie some more, breathing hard through

my nose. I can feel my nostrils flaring. It's weird and uncomfortable to feel this nervous suddenly, but a part of me likes it.

I nod.

This time I'm better.

A little.

Sean comes at me the same way and I wonder if this is what he does in his games, like if it's his signature move or something.

He has his back to me again and he's trying to creep around left then right, but I switch my focus each time I see him move.

My arms are outstretched. He's inches away, his shoulder blades right in front of my face.

He backs up more and now we're touching, my forearm grazing his rib cage.

Then he bolts right.

But I'm ready, just barely. I move with him and his right side goes into my chest, not expecting me. The ball is outstretched and I make a swing for it, but I'm clumsy and I miss.

He moves it easily but we're pressing against each other more.

Then he breaks left again and he's gone.

I watch him dribble the ball after the shot, both of us catching our breath. I can feel his sweat on my chest, on my face. My heart is pounding in that same weird nervous way, but I'm smiling just a little, smiling because I can't help it.

Sean passes the ball to me and I go half-court.

And then we do it again.

We hang out at Sean's house after. I was worried about bringing Charlie over, but he said it would be fine.

His dad gave Charlie a weird look when we walked in, but all he said was,

Hi, Mike.

I said hi back.

We head into Sean's room. He closes the door after me, walks over to his bed, and slumps backward into it.

He's still shirtless. He stretches while half lying in his bed, his muscles elongating. The bottom of his rib cage presses against his skin. Then he relaxes, hands behind his head, and looks at me, smiling in a kind of sleepy way.

He says, I'm beat.

I'm still soaked. I think about this, about the cool air sweeping over my face, my arms, my legs. I let it wash over me, feel my skin break out in goose bumps, the hairs on my arms standing up. It feels cold, but so nice.

I say, I am too,

and I slide into his desk chair. Charlie jumps up on my lap right away, but I push him back down, wanting to cool off.

But Sean says, Dude, lie on the bed, it's a lot more comfortable. There's room.

I look over at the sliver of bed next to him.

I say, I'm all sweaty.

He chuckles and his stomach clenches, the lines between the muscles growing deeper, abs moving quickly up and down with his laugh.

He says, So am I. Kinda too late to worry about that now.

I look at the beads of sweat on his forehead and temples, the few remaining drops on the light brown skin of his chest. Then I get up slowly, walk over to the bed, and ease myself down next to him. I keep my arms at my side. There's really not that much room. I have to scoot next to him so my left arm doesn't fall off the edge of the bed, which means my right arm is pressing against his side a bit. His skin there is still a little damp but drying. His elbow is touching my head.

I settle in but realize I'm not really relaxing; I'm staying very still and tense and trying not to move. My heart's beating fast now, and I wonder if he can hear it. I can feel his ribs move against my right arm as he breathes, his leg against my leg, the warmth of his skin. There's a bit of a sweaty smell coming from him, but I don't mind.

I try to breathe slowly.

By accident, I just barely move my finger. It grazes the middle of his thigh. I freeze even more, holding my breath. I think I sense him tense too, but then the moment passes.

Then he groans. It startles me.

He says, We gotta find a lot of pictures for this magazine.

102

I relax a bit. He's talking about the project.

I say, That'll be easy. We can find stuff online.

He says, Yeah, but the cover photo has to be something better than just some random thing from Flickr or whatever. Girard said the cover's fifteen percent of the grade.

I think about this for a little, and then about some of the magazines we looked at. Then it comes to me.

I say, I could draw it.

Sean doesn't say anything for a second. Then he turns his head toward me.

He says, You can draw?

I say, Yeah.

He pauses again.

He says, Draw me.

Now I turn to look at him.

I say, Draw you?

He moves his body suddenly, turning so that he's lying on his side facing me, head propped up on his hand, elbow on the bed. His other hand traces a line on his leg.

He says, Draw me like one of your French girls.

I blink.

I say, French girls?

None of the girls in our French class are actually French, I think.

Sean laughs and pushes me lightly on the shoulder. I grab the mattress with my left hand to keep from falling off.

He says, It's from a movie. You've never seen *Titanic*?

I say, Oh. No. That came out before I was born.

He laughs again, but not in a mean way.

He says, So did *Star Wars*. So did *Pulp Fiction*. So did, um . . .

I say, *Duck Soup*.

Sean blinks.

He says, *Duck Soup?*

I say, Yeah, it's one of the Marx Brothers' movies.

Sean looks at me for a long time.

Then he reaches behind him, grabs a pillow, and swings it into my face. It surprises me and I almost fall off the bed, but for just a tiny moment I catch his smell on the pillow.

He laughs and says, You've seen Marx Brothers movies but not *Titanic?*

I'm grinning now. I say, Yeah, because they don't spend three hours on some dumb love story.

Sean laughs again, harder now. I try not to watch his abs clench again.

His laugh turns into a chuckle, and his chuckle turns into a smile.

Then he says,

Seriously, though. You should draw me.

Sean's sitting in the desk chair now, but in a relaxed kind of way, reclining just a bit. I'm on the bed.

He says, How much longer do I have to sit here?

I look at the paper, then at him, measuring in my mind

how much there is left to do. It's dark outside the window behind me.

I say, You wanted me to do this.

He smiles again. I think about how easy his smiles come.

I look over my drawing again. It's just pencil on paper. I'm mostly adding shading now. A little on his jawline, his neck, some under his collarbone. Some around his biceps, in the crook of his elbow. The muscles on his chest, his left side, his belly button. He has just a little bit of hair on the lower part of his stomach, right above the waistband. I move down, adding shading around his legs, between them. My mouth feels dry.

He says, What part are you drawing now?

My ears get hot.

I say, Um.

He giggles a bit and says, What, my crotch?

My ears get hotter.

Sean throws his head back and laughs, and says, I should've had you draw me naked.

My ears are burning.

He laughs again, then stands and walks over.

He says, Lemme see it,

and snatches it from my hands.

His smile fades away as he looks it over. He slowly sinks down onto the bed next to me, then puts the paper down in front of us.

He says, Damn.

I stare at the paper, mentally comparing it to the real-life Sean sitting next to me.

He says, This is great,

and puts a hand on my shoulder and squeezes a bit. The spot where he touches gets warm so quick.

He keeps the hand there for a little while, then brings his other hand up, and massages my shoulders. My neck gets so warm. It feels like stepping into a hot shower on a cold morning. My eyes are fixed on the drawing. I watch a shadow version of Sean massage a shadow version of me on top of the paper.

He says, Jesus, you have some knots up here. You're gonna be real sore tomorrow, bud.

Then he stops massaging and gives my shoulders a little pat.

He says, Can I keep the drawing?

I look up at him and say,

Yeah.

I'm smelly when I get home. But dry now.

There's some World War II special on the History Channel, one of Dad's favorite things to watch. He's looking over his shoulder at me.

He says, Have fun?

I bend down to take Charlie's leash off. The collar jingles. Before it's even fully off, Charlie runs off to his water bowl. A second later I hear his great big noisy slurps

as he laps it up, drinking as fast as he can. I know it's spilling on the floor.

Dad's looking at me in this sort of scrutinizing way
he does sometimes, like he's trying to read something in
my face. Like he's trying to see if I'm hiding something. It
reminds me suddenly of Sean's dad, of the way he looked
at me when I met him.

I say, Yeah. Lots of fun.

Dad smiles after a bit and turns back to the History
Channel.

He says, Great.

EIGHT

Dad zips up a bag.

It's Mom's, old and frayed. It used to be bright royal blue, but it's faded a bunch over the years.

Dad hates this bag. He tries to tell Mom to throw it out every time she uses it, but she always refuses. She's had it for years, since college.

He says, Look, it's got holes in it. Just get rid of it.

They're in their bedroom. Clothes are everywhere: hanging out of the dresser, lined up on the bed, folded in piles on the floor.

Dad's lips are thin and tight, and he has lines on his forehead like Mr. Kilgore does sometimes. He's holding a toothbrush and looking at Mom.

Mom reaches into the closet, takes out one sweater, holds it in front of her, puts it back and takes out another.

She shakes her head.

She says, That's my Wellesley bag.

Dad gives up after a while. He hands me the bag but doesn't say anything. It's lumpy and irregular and kind of heavy.

I take it outside.

Toby is sitting on top of the car, legs dangling over one side. All the doors are wide open, stretching out across the driveway.

I go around back to find room in the trunk. I shove other bags aside to make a spot and I say,

You're supposed to be packing.

Toby shrugs.

She says, I'm mostly done. It'll take like three seconds.

My bags are already in the car. I have two: a big one in the back and a smaller one that I'll keep at my seat. It has my books and iPod and my old 3DS and some other games I can play with Toby.

Toby says, I don't get why they need to bring like the whole house.

I find just enough room for Mom's bag and cram it in. I take a step back and look at my work. I don't know how we're going to fit the rest of our stuff.

I say, Yeah.

Mostly to myself.

Dad told us Thursday night that we were going to go to Grandma's house for Thanksgiving.

We get the whole week off school and he tells us the day before vacation starts.

I mean I guess it's okay since I didn't have a lot of plans anyway. I kind of thought Jared and Ronald and I could hang out a lot at Ronald's house 'cause his mom is so cool and plus she likes to cook, but I hadn't talked to them about it or anything.

Mostly I just kind of wish we weren't going to Grandma's. She's okay but she's old and can be crabby sometimes. And she has a lot of rules.

But really it's because Dad gets weird around her and pretty tense, and gets upset if we do the tiniest thing wrong. Like once Toby sneezed at dinner without covering her mouth, and Dad went ballistic and yelled.

It was gross but not like a huge crime or anything.

Mom said once Dad just doesn't want Grandma to feel too stressed because of her age.

I guess.

Grandma is Dad's mom.

She lives in the western tip of Virginia, a really, really rural place near a tiny town. It's right next to Kentucky.

We've gone there before but always from Wisconsin, which is a super-long drive.

This is the first time we'll be coming from inside the state, but Dad says it'll still take nine hours.

Virginia is a long state.

I stare out the window most of the way. It's the first

time I've been on these roads and it's nicer than I expected. We drive through low mountains covered in orange and red and yellow leaves, all of them dropping and fluttering around our car with the slightest breeze.

Dad says, Lots of kids drive drunk on these highways, Mike.

I look at him, blinking.

He says, When you get your permit next year, I want you to be especially careful on the highways. They may look deserted, especially out in rural areas, but they can be just as dangerous as city roads. Okay?

I say, Yessir.

I look back out the window and watch the mountains roll by. I try to take a picture with my old camera, but I know it won't turn out very good even if it's not blurry.

Pictures never look as good as the real thing.

I glance over at Toby and she's staring out her window, both of us quiet and absorbed in the surroundings. Charlie's sleeping, snout on her thigh.

I end up not even opening my bag.

We pull into a rest stop.

We're only an hour from Grandma's, but Toby really had to go and couldn't hold it in any longer. She opens the door before Dad turns the car off and bolts toward the run-down building that stinks even from here.

Mom gets out and follows her. Dad just stands beside his open door, frowning at the sky. He's annoyed.

It's not twilight yet but shadows are getting longer. This is my favorite time of day.

I look west toward the sun, watch it creep toward the ground. The dried grass and leaves look like fire running up and down the hills. All of it golden.

I squint but I don't really have to, it's not that bright anymore but everything's still screaming colors, pink and orange and yellow.

Behind me my shadow stretches, long and gangly. I reach an arm up and watch my shadow grow, grow, almost farther than I can really see.

Dad mutters:

Jesus,

kind of under his breath but not really.

He looks at his watch and then back at the sky.

Toby comes out of the restroom with Mom, both of them walking slowly through the glowing air.

They get in the car without saying anything, Dad watching Toby until her door closes, and then he sits down.

He says, Get in, Mike.

I get in.

It's almost night when we get to Grandma's, but it's just light enough to see the hills and woods behind her house.

It's an old two-story house, fading yellow paint, long driveway, and a few acres of hilly grassland. Every time we come, Toby and I take long walks with Charlie in the woods. He loves any walk but he really loves those woods.

We can let him off the leash, and he runs and runs, chasing anything that moves, nose to the ground pulling him in every direction.

Grandma used to come with us on the walks but not anymore since her hip's been bothering her.

This is where Dad grew up. He loves the house and the land, but he's uneasy about Grandma being there all alone. It's big for one person and she can't maintain it anymore, and he's afraid of her falling down.

Grandma won't move, though. Dad says she's stubborn about it because she's lived there so long and she doesn't like to think she's getting older. But she is.

I wouldn't want to move either.

Grandma is already outside when we pull up, sitting on a patio chair reading by lamplight.

Mom called her about thirty minutes ago to let her know we were close.

She stands when she sees the car, puts the book down on a table, and walks down the steps to greet us.

Dad's out first.

He says, You shouldn't be out here, Mom.

She waves him off with a hand as she reaches out to hug him and says, I'm fine, Walton.

He says, It's cold.

She gives his back two light pats and says, I'm fine.

And turns to Mom and says,

How are you, Sweet Caroline?

Mom smiles and hugs Grandma and says, Just fine, Martha. It's lovely to see you.

Behind them the porch light turns them into silhouettes.

The house smells musty but good-musty, like old wood. It's the only place I ever smell this smell, but it's always so familiar.

It's dimly lit and cozy and warm.

Me and Toby go upstairs to our room to drop off our stuff. It's the room that used to be Uncle Daryl's when he was growing up, and some of his stuff is still there: old baseball cards and half-finished model airplanes and framed photos. Like someone took a freeze-frame of his childhood from forever ago.

Everything about it is really still. There's no dust because Grandma cleans it once a week, every week.

We put our clothes in the empty drawer, and I know they'll smell like Grandma's house for a while after.

Finally Toby says, I'm so hungry.

I say, Yeah, me too.

I take out some of Charlie's toys I packed with my things and remind myself to bring them down to the garage later. Grandma doesn't like Charlie to be in the house but the garage is fine.

Toby says, How long you think before Dad gets annoyed about something?

The corner of my mouth turns up just a little; I can feel it.

I say, He's already annoyed.

Toby says, He needs a nap.

She takes out her Sunday clothes and hangs them up and says, He always needs a nap.

I smile wider now and she giggles.

I'm keeping Charlie company outside.

In the quiet of the countryside, the crickets are really loud. Charlie's letting me pet him but his attention is out there, facing the darkness with his floppy ears perked as much as they can be.

There's no light except from the house and about a million stars. There are a lot of stars in Somerdale 'cause it's still a pretty small town, but there are even more here, out in the middle of nowhere.

I search through the stars and in just a couple seconds I find what I'm looking for: three stars in a row, Orion's Belt. From there it's easy to find his shoulders and head and bow and arrow.

Once I'm oriented to the right direction, I follow along until I recognize the deep V shape that makes up most of Pisces. It's supposed to look like two fish, but to me it looks more like India. Or like those pictures of sperm they showed us in Health class in middle school.

I turn west and look at the lowest bit of sky I can see. It's late in the month and for a minute I'm not sure I'll be able to see it, but then I catch the tip of it. Capricornus. It's the constellation for my zodiac sign. It's a goat, but the outline is basically just a triangle. I guess the Greeks had good imaginations.

I can only see a little of it. The rest is blocked by trees. But in a week it'll be gone until next fall.

I stroke Charlie's head and neck and behind his ears, and I think about dinner. Pork roast, green beans, potato wedges, gravy on everything. I'm really full, almost to where it hurts, but everything was so good.

In the darkness past the house, I can't make out any shapes. I picture the house behind us the way it must look to someone a hundred yards away: Glowing warm light spilling from the windows, melting into the darkness a few feet out. Boy and dog sitting on the grass at the edge of the light. Complete blackness in front of them. But above the jagged silhouette of the treetops, billions of glittery silver specks, floating outward forever. I'll draw this later.

I say, Come on, Charlie,

and we go in the garage.

Charlie curls up on his mat of old towels and blankets into a little ball surrounded by his own shed fur and closes his eyes.

I go inside.

At night I lie awake a long time, listening to Toby's heavy breathing and the house creaking as it settles.

I think about Sean's house.

* * *

We're in the woods, me and Toby and Charlie. We left right after breakfast because the clouds came in overnight and it looked like it was going to rain soon, and we wanted to beat the storm.

But now it's lighter out and the clouds are almost gone.

Charlie's pulling and I have to hold him back, leash taut. I'm kneeling beside him and he's paying no attention to me, wanting so bad to run into the woods. Toby's watching us.

I unclasp the leash and he takes off, fallen leaves flying in his wake, already barking at something that's probably not there but he's chasing it anyway.

Me and Toby follow after a second, crunching leaves and twigs with each step.

It's cooler today and we both have light jackets on.

We don't say anything for a long time, both of us just quiet and enjoying the woods and then Toby says,

What's up with that Sean guy?

I feel something like a quick jolt and I don't really get why. For a few seconds I'm distracted by that. I must let too many seconds go by because after a while Toby says,

Mike?

I say, Yeah?

My heart's beating faster and I don't get it.

I mean it's just Toby.

She says, I was asking about Sean.

I say, What about him?

She says, He seems kind of weird.

There's a big pile of leaves in Toby's way, and she steps on it on purpose, careful to hit the exact middle to get the most crunch.

Up ahead Charlie's running around still barking, a brown-and-white blur in between the trees.

I say, What do you mean, weird?

I'm facing ahead but I glance at Toby out of the corner of my eye real quick.

She cocks her head in thought as she walks.

She says, I dunno. It just seems like there's stuff he's trying to get at but never says.

I say, What does that even mean? Plus you've only met him once.

She kicks a rock and it hits a tree up ahead and bounces off to the right. Charlie stops and looks back toward the path of the rock, alert, thinking it's an animal. Then he turns and goes on again. Toby nods.

She says, Yeah, I know. I guess I mean it just seemed like he was trying not to give too much away. When he gave us a ride after school, I mean.

I don't say anything. My heart is slowing.

Toby kicks another rock and we're quiet for another minute or so.

Then she says, Sometimes you seem like that too.

I don't say anything.

The weather changes again and the first drops hit just before lunch, when Mom calls us in to wash up.

While we're eating there's a clap of thunder. The rain waits another couple seconds before we hear it above us, building. Another clap and it's pouring.

On the table: sliced ham, turkey, corned beef, provolone, mustard, mayonnaise, white bread, lettuce, tomatoes, pickles, baby carrots, some green beans left over from last night. All spread out before us.

We eat in silence.

Dad looks across the table as Mom and Grandma clear the plates and put away the food, and I know what he's going to say before he says it but I still hold out hope.

But instead Toby says it for him.

She says, Yeah, yeah, we'll get ready.

And stands up.

Dad watches her go, and then I follow.

Grandma goes to church Sunday afternoons.

It's a local Baptist church and she goes for hours, almost until dinnertime and we have to go every time we come to visit.

Upstairs I check Toby's buckle shoes for marks and she makes sure my tie's straight.

Once we're satisfied, we just stand there looking at each other for a minute, neither of us wanting to go downstairs.

Then Toby rolls her eyes and says, We might as well, and we go.

*　*　*

Lebanon Calvary Baptist Church.

It's on the edge of town still in the middle of nowhere, off the side of a small road that curves around a hill, but the parking lot's full. We run in, ducking from the rain.

Toby gasps when the door opens. A gust of humid sticky air hits us. The heater's on and there are so many people, lots of them wet from the storm and the warmth inside.

The preacher's already on the pulpit, talking too closely into a mike, raspy voice echoing, bright eyes, bushy goatee. He's a sweating round man I remember from last year, lots of energy and intense. Right now he paces back and forth and shouts to the congregation.

We find a pew but don't sit. No one's sitting.

People are screaming Amen and Praise Be Him and Tell It and things like that as the preacher goes on and on, no one getting tired.

They sway while he preaches. Eyes closed, most of them.

I look and Grandma already has her eyes closed along with them, head tilted back a bit, smiling, listening but at least standing still.

The door opens and closes, more people come in.

The preacher walks back and forth, back and forth. Some people have an arm or two raised out before them, reaching toward the shouts from the pulpit.

Toby drums her fingers a bit on the back of the pew

in front of her. Mom gently puts her hand over Toby's to stop it.

There are so many people.

Ten minutes into it Dad raises one of his arms. I can barely understand what the preacher is saying through the rasp of his voice and feedback from the mike.

I bow my head and I hope it looks like I'm praying.

It goes on and on.

I love Thanksgiving.

Everything around Grandma's land, the woods and hills, smells fresh and crisp and spicy. It's only ever cool, light-jacket weather, perfect. Now that we're here, I'm kind of glad we came after all.

Me and Toby go exploring with Charlie, taking different routes through the woods.

There's a ravine a mile away and we follow it, pointing out stuff we remember from other trips: a circle of smooth stones in the water; an old hunting stand, half collapsed; a huge oak with a thick branch leading over the creek, perfect for sitting and throwing rocks.

At night we eat delicious food and stay up late playing Uno or reading or talking, though we never say all that much.

Grandma has a ton of old movies and sometimes we watch those.

Dad is tense a lot but not so bad, or maybe we just get used to it after a while.

The leaves keep getting brighter and falling, and Charlie runs through them, never satisfied, and there's nothing to do and I love it.

Thursday morning the house is already full of smells.

I'm having a dream where I'm eating pumpkin pies, one after the other, and I don't stop even when I'm more full than I can handle.

I wake up and for a minute I think I can still smell the pies from my dream. Then I realize I can smell them — they're downstairs.

I walk down in my robe. Toby is already there, inspecting four pies that are sitting on the breakfast table, bent over them with her brow furrowed.

She looks up and says, We have pumpkin and apple, pointing them out as she talks, and that one's gotta be cherry.

She looks at the fourth again, trying to see through the crust.

She makes a face and says, I think this last one's mincemeat.

I like mince pie but I know she doesn't.

Two of the burners on the stove are on, and I can hear bubbling coming from one of the pots. I take a deep breath, sorting through different smells, all of them delicious.

The pot just starts to boil over, lid clattering. Grandma walks in and swats at Toby's hand as she walks by.

She says, Get away from those pies, kiddo,

and lifts the lid of the pot. White foamy bubbles rise up and then fall back under her glare. She looks in a bit longer, then throws some salt in, then puts the lid back on, keeping it open a crack.

She says, Come on now, get out of the kitchen, I got a lot of work to do still. You want to eat all this, dontcha?

Toby nods enthusiastically and says, Ohhh yes.

Mom calls from the other room, Come on, Toby, let's leave Grandma alone.

Dad's voice is louder, booming: Toby, get out of there!

Toby doesn't roll her eyes because she knows Dad can see her, but I can tell she wants to.

Dad pokes his head in.

He says, Why don't you two wash up and then watch TV for a little while? Give your grandmother a break, huh?

We leave and Mom calls after us, Brush your teeth too.

I shower and brush my teeth, but it's the kind of day where you want to stay in your robe so I do.

Toby and me find *Duck Soup* on tape and pop it into the VCR. Grandma's house is the only time we ever use a VCR and I think she's had it like twenty years, so it sometimes doesn't work that great.

Dad's reading a book in the den, some old war history book. Mom tries to help Grandma in the kitchen, but every now and then we hear Grandma tell her not to worry, and finally Mom gives up and joins Dad in the den with her own book.

The tape's already rewound and starts right with the FBI warning.

Toby looks over at me a couple times, jealous of my robe. She already changed into normal clothes.

Groucho Marx comes on and she leans in closer to the TV.

She says, That mustache isn't real.

I say, Of course not, Toby, that's his thing.

She peers closer and says, But it's not even a fake mustache, it's just drawn on! Like with a marker.

I say, You've seen this before, Toby.

She says, I was like eight.

I don't say anything.

Groucho Marx says, I've got a good mind to join a club and beat you over the head with it.

I laugh a bit and Toby giggles.

She looks over at me and says, Maybe I'll change back into my robe.

I say, You can't change back into a robe after you're dressed.

She says, Why not?

I say, 'Cause that's dumb. Plus Dad'll yell at you.

On the screen Groucho Marx blows cigar smoke at Chico.

Toby says, His eyebrows are drawn on too.

I don't say anything.

Dad walks in and looks at the TV and chuckles, barely.

He says, Which one is this?

I say, *Duck Soup.*

He looks over at me and his voice changes.

He says, Jesus, Mike, get dressed, would you?

Toby smiles and sticks her tongue out at me.

I walk back down in khakis and a polo because I know Dad will want us to look nice for dinner.

It's just before three o'clock and I can smell the turkey and it makes my mouth water. I didn't eat any breakfast even though Mom said I should because I wanted to be really hungry for dinner. It's almost ready.

Mom's still in the den. She looks up from her book as I walk by and smiles.

She says, You look nice.

I picked the polo out because it's her favorite. It's striped, light green and blue. She says it's very tasteful.

I say, Thanks, Mom,

and walk into the dining room. Toby's there, setting the table probably because Dad told her to.

Beyond the doorway we can hear voices: Dad and Grandma. But over them the stove exhaust fan drowns out the words.

I look at the embroidered tablecloth: white, lacy,

spotless. The silverware and dishes and glasses shine, all of them reflecting the sunlight coming in through the window.

I'm about to ask Toby if she wants help when the exhaust fan shuts off and Dad's and Grandma's voices turn into hushed words.

Dad says, He's always been like that.

Grandma says, Well, why? Didn't you ever try getting him to join a team or something?

Toby and I freeze.

Dad says, Of course, Mom. He played basketball a few years ago.

Grandma says, Anything since then?

Dad sighs and he doesn't need to say anything after that because the sigh says everything. But he does anyway:

No, not really.

Both of their voices are quiet like they know they shouldn't be talking but not quiet enough. I can feel my pulse behind my ears.

Grandma says, Doesn't surprise me. He just seems a bit soft, is all.

Dad says, He's not that soft, just likes to keep to himself.

Toby is looking at me hard, lips set, firm. She has her fist closed tight around a spoon.

Grandma says, Well, that's soft, isn't it?

I look back at Toby and slowly, very slowly I shake my head once.

Dad sighs again and it's the sigh I hate most.

He says, I'll try throwing the ball with him later. He gave me a Packers football for my birthday, you know. We tried throwing it around a bit before, but it didn't go so well.

Grandma says, Yeah, just keep trying. I just . . .

She stops for a bit, trying to find the words, and Toby and I stare at each other.

She says, I just worry about how he'll turn out, you know?

Dad says, Don't. He'll be fine.

Toby's eyes narrow.

Very quietly, I say,

Don't, Toby.

She looks back at me. Defiant.

Grandma says, Maybe. He just needs a push in the right direction.

Toby drops the spoon she's holding and turns. There's a soft thump as it hits the carpet and I rush into the kitchen behind her hoping to stop her, but I can't and I know I can't and she says,

Mike's not soft and he doesn't need a push in any direction.

Dad freezes, looking surprised and a bit angry, but most of all ashamed. That's the worst part. He looks from Toby to me and we make eye contact and he looks away.

Grandma just looks surprised, and for a minute I don't know if she hears the anger in Toby's voice.

There's a moment where nothing happens, and then Grandma's face relaxes and she smiles a bit at Toby and says,

Dear heart, you'll understand when you're older.

I know right away it's the wrong thing to say.

Toby says, If getting older means being like you, I don't want to get older.

Grandma's face changes and the sweetness is gone, like that. But she doesn't get a chance to respond. Dad takes two steps to Toby and grabs her arm. His face is purple.

From the den, I can hear Mom's voice, quiet, apprehensive:

Is everything okay?

Dad spits, Don't you *ever* talk to your grandmother like that. Don't you *ever*!

Toby yanks her arm out of his grip and stares back coldly. But she doesn't say anything else.

Dad barks, Go upstairs! *Now!*

She turns without a word and leaves the kitchen. I hear her loud stomps on the stairway and, from above, a door slamming shut.

He looks at me, but I turn away before he or Grandma can say anything else, and I walk toward the garage.

Charlie jumps up when I open the door, licking at my arms, legs, anything he can reach, tail wagging like crazy.

I close the door and sit down and let him crawl all over me, and when he's done, he puts his head in my lap and I sit there.

I just sit.

Thanksgiving dinner is tense, almost totally silent.

Toby and Grandma don't look at each other but ask to Please pass the gravy and Please pass the mashed potatoes and they're polite without being nice.

Dad doesn't let Toby have any pie.

I can tell she doesn't care.

Later we clear the table while Grandma rests in the living room and Dad and Mom sit with her and chat.

The dining room is a disaster. We scrape food bits into the trash and scrub the dishes and put them away and wrap leftovers and roll up the tablecloth and bring it to the hamper and wipe down the table.

Toby hands me a plate, arms covered in suds up to her elbows. I wipe it with a towel and put it in the cabinet. I look at Toby and tousle her hair a bit.

I say, Thank you.

Real quiet.

She looks up and flicks a bit of soapy water at me and doesn't say anything, but there's a bit of a smile.

She goes back upstairs after we're done, Dad's orders.

* * *

I walk Charlie through the woods, letting him run around. It's almost twilight and he takes off after every cricket and chipmunk he hears.

The leaves are still falling and it's so nice out. I look around and take a deep breath and listen to the silent woods.

But all at once I don't want to be here anymore, in this middle-of-nowhere part of Virginia near Kentucky where nothing ever happens except at church on Sunday.

I call Charlie and turn back.

When we get back to the yard, I look up and I see Toby watching us from the window of our upstairs room. It's open and she's leaning out a bit and the wind tosses her hair. She's changed into her favorite outfit, an old pair of pink-and-blue overalls.

There was a picture Toby used to have that she loved. Toby and Marla, her best friend from Wisconsin, jumping on a trampoline in Marla's backyard, hugging tight and laughing, their hair flying everywhere. Marla's mom took it.

It was a great picture. Marla gave it to her on the last day of fifth grade. Then it got lost in the move. Toby sulked about it for a long time.

Toby was wearing her overalls in the picture. Now she wears them when she's sad. Whenever she really misses Wisconsin. She doesn't know that I know this.

She lifts her hand in a small wave from the upstairs window.

I wave back.

I put Charlie in the garage and go to the kitchen. Mom and Dad and Grandma are still in there talking, and they pay me no attention.

I open the fridge and cut a slice of cherry pie and put it on a plate with a fork. Dollop of whipped cream on top.

I pick up the plate and then stop and put it down.

In the fridge I find a jar of cherries and take one out and put it on top of the whipped cream. It makes me smile a bit.

I walk out of the kitchen and upstairs, checking to make sure they're still in the living room and aren't looking at me.

They aren't.

Toby is still leaning out the window when I walk in. She turns her head only.

I walk over and put the pie on the desk. The cherry sinks into the whipped cream.

Toby grins.

We leave early morning Saturday. It'll be late afternoon when we get back.

The car trip is mostly quiet, still tense between Toby and Dad.

I think about Mom and what she does when Dad's tense, how she just lives with it instead of doing anything about it.

There's Dad and Toby not talking to each other, and

there's Mom on the side, always on the side, not part of the fight but affected by it.

And I realize I'm the same way.

It's a bit chilly when we pull up to the driveway. My legs are cramped and I stretch them before letting Charlie out, who pulls hard on the leash, happy to be home.

Me and Toby bring the bags in. Dad has a headache so he sits in the living room with the TV off, eyes closed.

Mom goes through the mail, a week's worth of junk and a card from her mother, our other grandma, who lives in Wisconsin.

Toby's grounded the rest of the weekend so she just goes to her room after we're done and starts unpacking.

I go to my room and drop my bags on the floor and go straight to my computer desk. Grandma has a computer but Dad wouldn't let us use it, so I haven't been online in a week.

I check Facebook and I see I have a message waiting for me.

It's from Sean.

I click on Messages and my heart's beating a bit faster than normal.

The one from him is unread and I can see the first few words:

hey just seein what your up to. um i cant remember if you sai...

I click it and it says:

hey just seein what your up to. um i cant remember if
you said you were going anywhere for thansgiving but
anyway. you want to come over sometime? we can work
on the project or not.

I breathe in through my nose, slow, and breathe it out
the same way, slow.
And I smile.

NINE

We're having dinner a few days later.

Beef stew with carrots and potatoes and celery.

Some rice with peas too.

It's good, everything Mom makes is good. Sometimes even better than Grandma's.

Dad says, How'd the paper go, Toby?

Toby had to write a descriptive narrative that was due today. She got it assigned the first day we got back to school from Thanksgiving and hasn't shut up about it, saying how unfair it is to get homework right away like that. But mostly it's 'cause she hates writing assignments, I know.

She says, Fine.

He glances at her before spooning some more stew onto his rice and scooping it up with his fork.

He says, Just fine? What'd the teacher say?

Toby says, She didn't say anything. It was just due today — she hasn't read it yet.

Toby got over being in trouble for Thanksgiving and things between her and Dad are less tense now, but they've never really gotten along that great to begin with.

He says, Well, how do you think you did?

Toby shrugs.

She's quiet for a second but decides that she doesn't want to test Dad so she answers,

I think it was okay. She wanted us to use a lot of adjectives and I wrote a bunch.

Dad nods and goes back to his stew.

Mom says, Well, that sounds promising.

There's more silence for a while except all the sounds of dinner: forks scraping on plates, stew sloshing, Dad's beer fizzing in its bottle after being set down.

I say, Can I sleep over at Sean's tomorrow?

I stare at my stew when I say it and wait a second and look up to meet Mom's eyes. She looks over at Dad and I follow.

Dad puts a forkful in his mouth.

He chews.

He says, Sleep over?

I say, Yeah.

He chews a bit more.

I say, We thought we could maybe work on the project a bit.

Dad swallows, slowly.

He says, What do his parents think?

I say, They're cool with it, he already asked.

I haven't slept over at a friend's house since seventh grade, and I'm wondering if Dad is thinking about this.

Mom just keeps looking at him.

After a while, Dad just shrugs and digs his fork back into his rice and says, I guess I don't see a problem, then. Sure, go ahead.

Jared and I are walking along the edge of the gym.

We have PE together and we both hate it. It especially sucks in the morning because no one's fully awake yet and it makes you so hungry after running and doing exercises and stuff, but lunch is still an hour away.

Today we're supposed to run a timed mile. The coach wanted to do it outside, but it's a bit damp so he's having everyone run a few laps around the gym instead.

He measures out what a mile is and then stands there with a stopwatch, telling us what our times are.

We're supposed to run as much as we can, but we can walk if we get tired. Some kids take it seriously and run the whole thing in like eight minutes and then just sit the rest of the period or play basketball.

But a lot of other kids just end up walking the whole way.

Me and Jared both hate running so we're not even trying, really.

Jared says, What are you doing this weekend?

I say, I dunno. I don't think Dad's gonna make us go to church since we went over Thanksgiving.

He says, Oh yeah. How was your grandmother?

I say, Fine.

I don't really want to talk about Thanksgiving.

He says, Ronald's coming over tonight and we're gonna play Halo. You in, dude?

I say, I'm hanging out with Sean tonight.

He blinks and says, Sean? Why?

I say, We're working on our magazine project.

He says, On a Friday night? That's ludicrous.

I say, Well, we'll hang out some too. He's pretty cool.

I don't say I'm sleeping over because that still seems like a middle school thing to do and I guess I'm a bit embarrassed.

But I am looking forward to it.

Jared shrugs.

He says, Okay, whatever. We'll probably play Halo tomorrow too.

We cross the finish line and the coach is there, but he's kind of lost enthusiasm with the last group of kids and he just mumbles,

Twenty-two minutes and forty seconds.

Shading and lighting in Art.

Dumb stuff I already know how to do.

My drawing is of Charlie and me at Grandma's,

outside, at the edge of the bubble of light coming from her house, sky above full of stars.

It's mostly finished and I have my pencil in my hand, hovering over my paper, but I'm staring out the window, out at the front lawn of the school. Behind it is the road that goes over the bridge and into my neighborhood.

Mr. Kilgore says, Mikey!

I jerk my head, startled. There's a second where I stare at him, blinking, and then he says,

Finish your drawing, Mikey. You can watch the birds outside later.

His voice is cross like always.

The day goes by so slowly.

Sean gets to French class late and Madame Girard is already in full swing, rattling off conjugations while everyone takes notes as fast as they can. I don't get a chance to talk to him until after class.

The bell rings and Madame Girard reminds us that we only have two weeks until the end of the semester when our project is due, but no one's listening to her because it's Friday and the last bell just rang.

I turn around with my books just in time to catch Sean's eye.

He says, Hey, I gotta run to a quick practice, but you wanna come over around eight?

I say, Uh, yeah. Sure.

He says, Cool. See you then.

And then he's gone.

I have my backpack stuffed with clothes for tomorrow, my toothbrush, deodorant, a pack of cards, my French book and notes.

It's seven forty-five and I head downstairs, one strap of the backpack over my shoulder. Charlie is looking at me with his ears perked.

Mom and Dad and Toby are at the dinner table, but I've been excused from dinner because Sean told me his parents are getting us pizza.

I say, Bye.

I have my hand on the doorknob and Dad says,

Oh, I thought I would take you.

I look at him and Mom, and they look back.

I say, He lives just a few blocks away. I can walk.

He says, Well, I thought it'd be nice to meet his parents.

I shrug and say, It's fine, it's not far at all.

Dad's plate is still half full. He looks down at it for a second.

I say, You can meet them some other time.

Dad looks back up and says, All right, have fun.

Charlie watches me as I close the door behind me, still hoping I'll invite him to come along.

* * *

Sean opens the door in his basketball uniform.

Not the Wizards jersey but the school team jersey, black with gold lettering. .

He says, Hey.

I say, Hey.

He moves aside to let me in and closes the door and says, I just got back five minutes ago. Coach made us do like an hour of relays and then we had to run laps. He's been so pissy lately.

He turns to me while I take my shoes off. His hair is a bit damp and I get a whiff of sweat, faint but there.

He says, You mind? I'm gonna take a shower real quick. You can watch TV if you want.

I say, Okay, cool.

Sean walks upstairs and I walk into the living room, which I've never really been in before.

The walls are cream colored, covered in photographs and art. There are some African-looking masks on one of the walls near a photo of Sean's dad and mom wearing khaki cargos and shirts and posing in front of a rhinoceros in the distance. On an end table there are hand-carved wooden figurines: giraffes, elephants, lions. Men with spears.

There's a complicated-looking sound system with speakers spaced out around the room. All-glass coffee table with three African photography books. Cream leather couch to match the walls, windows facing a back-yard garden.

The TV is huge. I stare at it for a while, a big flat

widescreen set into a glass stand with shelves and shelves of Blu-rays. My reflection stares back.

I lean my bag against the wall and sit down.

The remote's on the arm of the couch. I pick it up and press the big red power button, and there's this electric hiss and the image pops in from black: a TV news anchor standing in the parking lot of some mall, talking about Christmas shoppers.

I flip the channel a few times, but I'm not really paying attention to what's on.

Above me I can hear the shower running.

I settle on an old rerun of some show I can't remember the name of and watch that for a few minutes, but then I realize Sean's parents aren't home.

I mean I guess I probably noticed right away, but I just didn't really think about it until now.

I stand up, looking around the living room, listening to TV laughter and the water in the pipes.

Then I look up at the balcony.

I walk back over through the entrance hall, letting my socks slide on the tiles, and toward the staircase. I put my hand on the wooden rail and look up again, listening.

TV music and running water.

I walk up, slowly, not really sure why I'm being so quiet but doing it anyway. The carpet on the stairs is super soft.

From the landing I can see over the balcony into the living room. Straight ahead is the game room next to Sean's room.

I head toward the pool table, but once I'm at the end of the balcony, there's a short hallway to my left leading to Sean's bathroom. The shower noises are a lot louder now, and I realize it's because the bathroom door is partly open.

I can see part of a light green shower curtain, and past it I can just barely make out a shadow that must be Sean. I stop. My heart starts beating faster. The shadow's arms reach up to its head as it turns around under the showerhead. Sean's washing his hair.

Then I turn and walk quickly to the pool table, out of view of the bathroom.

The pool table is already set up for play, like it was the last time I came over. I guess they always have it set up.

I look at the arrangement of the ten colored balls, trying to see if there's a pattern. Pretty quickly I can find one. Solid then stripe then solid then stripe, with like colors next to each other. I wonder if there are rules about this or if that's just the way they do it.

I'm looking at the billiard balls up close and right when I realize I can't hear the water anymore I hear,

Keeps 'em pretty clean, huh?

I jump, heart beating fast, and immediately feel stupid.

Sean says, Whoa, sorry, didn't mean to startle you.

He's leaning against the entrance to the short hallway, light green towel wrapped around his waist. He's still mostly wet from the shower. I look at the drops collecting on his collarbone.

Then I look away and mumble, Sorry, there wasn't anything on TV.

Sean shrugs and says, It's cool. Dad would love to know that his billiard ball polishing efforts aren't going to waste.

I don't really know what to say to that but then Sean speaks again.

He says, You hungry?

I nod and then realize it's true.

He says, Lemme get dressed and then we'll order a pizza. Dad left a twenty.

He turns and as he walks into his bedroom he says, You okay with Papa John's?

I nod again but then realize he's not facing me so I say, Sure.

I don't know what else to do, so I just stand there and wait.

The pizza will take forty-five minutes to get here, so when Sean hangs up we decide to snack on Cheetos and Chips Ahoy. He sits on the kitchen counter, and I grab a seat at the breakfast table.

Neither of us says anything for a while. We just eat.

I start getting a bit anxious for some reason, maybe because of the quiet. One of my legs starts bouncing a bit and I force it to stop.

I say, I brought my French stuff.

The words hang there for a minute. Sean looks almost surprised by what I say, like he's not sure what I'm talking about, and then his face relaxes and he says,

Oh right. Yeah, cool. Sure, we can work on that.

He takes another cookie from the bag and stuffs it in his mouth, two quick large bites.

There's another few moments of quiet and I try again.

I say, So your parents like Africa?

The question sounds weird as soon as I get it out, but Sean nods immediately.

He says, Yeah, they go a lot. Usually on church missions, but they stay a bit longer for vacation. They love the art.

I say, Have you been?

He says, Oh yeah. A couple times to Uganda and once to Kenya. Mom and Dad also went to Sudan once when I was a baby, before it split. Africa's really awesome, just an amazing place. I mean there's a lot of war and poverty and shit, but the land itself is really cool.

I nod. Eat another Cheeto.

Sean is looking not at me but at the wall, lost in thought. I watch him for a bit and then he says,

Haven't been in a few years, but they said we might go again next spring. They always check with the government to see what the political situation is over there and if it's safe to go, and it hasn't really been stable for a few years, I mean less stable than usual, but it looks like it might finally be getting better again. Maybe.

144

I let him speak, just listening, until he stops finally, staring at the wall.

Then I say, So they go on missions?

He looks at me now.

He says, Yeah, with Grace Fellowship. There's a group of churches that sponsors mission trips almost every year, but Grace is ours. Or theirs, anyway.

I say, We go to Grace.

I have never seen Sean there, but it's a big church.

Sean nods. He says, Oh yeah? I don't go that much. Maybe once a month.

I say, It's about the same with me. We've probably just been missing each other.

He nods again.

There's a pause and then he jumps down from the counter, startling me.

He says, Come on, I wanna show you something.

I get up without saying anything and follow him back into the living room.

He walks over to a wall shelf filled with small framed photographs, ones I only glanced at earlier.

I'm right behind him and he goes straight to one with a man and a boy, maybe twelve or thirteen, their backs to the camera, looking out from a hilltop over a deep valley beyond. It's dusk in the picture: pink and orange skies, deep blue mountains barely visible in the background.

He points to the boy and says, Me. Last time we went. And Dad. Mom took it.

I look at the boy, the back of his head, in my mind comparing him with the Sean in front of me. I look at what he's looking at, the sunset over the valley.

I say, That's really cool.

Sean nods, smiling a bit now. He points to a couple little black marks dotting the grassland in the valley.

He says, Elephants.

I look closer and now I can see them, minuscule blurs that look like legs and trunks.

I picture the valley as it must've looked to him, huge and beautiful. Tiny elephant specks moving slowly across the grassland, trumpeting back and forth, barely loud enough to hear from the distance. The breeze, the sunset, the smell of the air.

I say, That's really cool.

I feel dumb saying the same thing twice, but then he puts a hand on my shoulder. Just a pat, real quick. The feel of it lingers and then spreads from the spot to the rest of my back. I can feel the hairs standing on my neck.

He says, Maybe you could come in the spring with us.

After a bit the spot on my shoulder stops tingling and I nod.

I say, Yeah, that would be cool,

but I'm thinking about my dad.

We work on the magazine for only about twenty minutes.

I'm sitting on his bed, him next to me, like last time. We've gotten a couple of the articles written and

146

now we're translating them. It's hard work. We use what we remember from class when we can but usually we end up passing the dictionary between us.

But we get into it and it goes faster than I thought it would.

Sean sits close as we look over each other's shoulders, studying the dictionary and our own notes. Our weight makes the mattress sag a bit, making our legs touch. Sean doesn't seem to care or maybe he doesn't notice.

I frown in the middle of one of the sentences he's dictating. The translation sounds off to me.

Sean stops and looks over at the point where my pencil has stopped, breaking the edge of a lowercase *d*.

I say, Wait, I think that's wrong.

He picks up the dictionary. I listen to the flip of pages as he finds the word. I haven't moved my pencil.

He shows me the page, leaning over so I can see. He puts his arm on the mattress behind me to support himself, the dictionary on my lap.

He points to an entry and says, Right there, you're right. Just copy that word.

I erase the word and start it over, looking back and forth from notes to dictionary.

Sean is close, really close. If I lean back just barely, I can feel his arm against my back.

I finish the word and he looks up at me as I look over.

Suddenly all I can think about is his arm against my back, him leaning into me. His hand is still on the dictionary on my lap. I can almost see his breath as he exhales slowly right in front of me, or maybe he's not breathing anymore.

We stay that way for a second and there is no sound, nothing.

The doorbell rings, crisp and clear and jarring. We're both startled. Sean stands up fast, knocking the dictionary to the ground.

He mumbles, Pizza's here,

and walks out of the bedroom without looking back.

My heart's beating fast now, from being startled but also because I feel suddenly nervous.

I take a breath, calming myself, then leave the room and go downstairs.

The pizza guy is about Sean's age or maybe a year or two older. His eyes flick between us as he gives the box to Sean and waits for Sean to hand over the bills. His face shows nothing, no expression or anything. He mutters a thanks and he's gone.

Sean carries the box to the kitchen. I follow him.

He puts the box on the island and then turns without warning and I almost bump into him.

He says, Do you like beer?

I blurt out, I've never had it.

And then I think maybe that was a dumb thing to say, but Sean doesn't seem to care.

Without saying anything he walks over past the fridge

and through the door to the backyard along a short path that connects to the garage.

I just stand there, not sure what to do. Through the window in the door I can see him disappear into the garage.

He comes out a moment later holding two green glass bottles.

I shift my weight from one foot to the other.

Sean steps back in the kitchen and hands me a bottle. The cap is already bent and loose. I hold it up to look at it. Heineken, something I've seen Dad drink only a couple times. It's warm but fizzy.

Sean says, I got a fake ID but it doesn't really look that much like me. I can only use it at the Citgo because they don't care that much there.

He smiles softly like he thinks it's no big deal.

I say, Cool.

He lifts the cap off and takes a swig.

I look at mine, stalling.

Sean watches me as he sips again, then says,

It's not as bad as you think. The first taste will be a bit weird but you'll get used to it.

I take the cap off slowly and sniff at the beer. I bring the bottle to my lips and don't even realize my eyes are shut tight.

Dad has let me have a sip of beer before just to try it, and it tastes the same as last time, bitter and yeasty like

149

moldy bread. I try not to let it show in my expression but Sean laughs.

Not in a mean way, though.

He says, Sorry it's so warm. I have to hide them from my dad or he'll kill me. He doesn't even drink, himself.

I smile.

We decide to pour the beer into glasses of ice, thinking it will be worth it even if it's kind of lame to drink beer with ice.

This way it's not so bad. It takes longer than I think to get used to it, but when we start our second bottles, the bitter bready taste isn't so jarring anymore.

We drink our beers between slices of pizza, sitting at the kitchen table, talking and laughing about nothing.

Sean got a large pizza but between us we finish the whole thing. I go through two beers along the way. Sean has three.

We stay at the table for a while after the pizza's gone, talking over leftover crusts and five empty green bottles.

Outside it's full dark, has been for a couple hours. There are still crickets this late in the year, and we can hear them as we talk, chirping over us from outside in the backyard.

We talk easily, more easily than I ever have. I look at the empty bottles.

I say, How late do crickets usually last in the winter?

Sean shrugs.

He says, There's not really much of a winter here. They'll be gone only a month or two. You know, they're usually gone by now, but it's been a bit warmer this year.

I mull this over a bit, listening to the crickets, wondering where they'll go when it finally gets too cold.

I say, It's kinda nice not having it be cold all the time. I mean that's all I ever grew up with and I'm used to it. I thought I'd never really care about warmer weather but it's nice.

Sean nods and says, I don't think I could do long winters. What's the point of living next to water if you barely get to use it?

I think about Lake Michigan, which right now is quiet and dark and freezing, surrounded by snow, at the beginning of a long period before it's warm enough to touch again.

Then I think about the ocean, sitting just a mile away, expansive and mysterious.

I say, You go to the beach a lot?

Sean says, Yeah, as much as I can. What about you?

I say, We went a couple times during the summer, right after we moved here. It's all right, just always crowded.

Sean says, Well, yeah, it's better at night. No people, right?

I don't say anything for a second, just go back to listening to the crickets.

Then I say, You've been at night?

Sean raises his eyebrows. He says, You haven't?

I shake my head.

He leans back in his chair, staring at me. Just sits there like that for a minute, then gets up suddenly.

He says, Let's go.

I blink.

I say, Wait, now?

He nods, smiling now, and says, Absolutely. You need to go at night at least once before it's too cold.

I stand, a bit too fast, and brace myself on the table with one hand. I didn't realize how dizzy I was from the beer while sitting down, and it all seems to rush at me at once. But the feeling passes quickly.

I say, Isn't it too cold now?

Sean laughs.

He says, Maybe,

but he's already pulling me toward the door.

We go out the back. Sean doesn't lock the door, just goes, and I follow him through the gate and down the driveway and onto the sidewalk.

He takes long strides and I have to kind of jog a bit every now and then to keep up.

We're covered in the yellow light of streetlamps and the chirping of millions of crickets and a breeze that comes and goes.

We don't need jackets. Even with the breeze it's only a little cool.

We walk for fifteen minutes and then the yellow light

leaves us, and then the crickets leave us too. I can hear the ocean, faint, but I can't see it. Ahead is darkness that is almost complete. The moon shines, then doesn't, covered sometimes with passing clouds, and there are times I can make some things out and times I can see almost nothing past a few feet in front of me except Sean's somehow darker silhouette.

The ground beneath changes and gives. We're on sand.

I look over my shoulder at the fading yellow lights, see the glow from the street fall back.

We walk closer and now I can see the ocean, moon or not, whitecaps crashing on the shore.

Sean stops a few feet from the tide line and again I almost bump into him.

He turns and looks at me. Even in the dark I can see his eyes.

He says, Let's go in.

I can feel myself grinning. I say, It's gotta be freezing.

He says, So?

I say, We don't have swimsuits,

and I'm still smiling despite myself and shivering a bit now too, and he says,

So?

And he turns back toward the ocean. The moon is out full now, a break from the clouds, and I can see him pretty well. He rips his shirt off, flinging it aside.

He kicks his shoes off next as he walks toward the water, and then the jeans, almost tripping over them.

Then his briefs, throwing them to the side, skin shimmering and dark in the moonlight, and then he dives in.

Sean whoops when the water hits him, and he goes under and then back up a moment later, howling at the cold and shaking water from his hair and laughing.

I'm laughing now too. Shivering, not from the cold.

He calls: Come on!

That's all I need. I take my own clothes off, slower than he did and more self-conscious, but I get them off.

I hesitate only a bit before pulling down my underwear and then I run in, and with each step I care a little less about being naked.

The water hurts when I hit it, it's so cold. It's been a warm fall but it's still December. But it's so good too. I yelp, I can't help it, and Sean laughs more.

He splashes me right when I come up for air, and the cold covers me and I yelp-laugh again.

But the more I go underwater, the less cold I feel. The more I want to swim, move, splash.

Sean is nearby, treading water and watching me, and I go to him.

He splashes me and I laugh, wiping ocean water from my eyes. I try to splash him back but he's fast, he dives to the side and underwater.

He comes up behind me and splashes again. Out of instinct I swing my arm back to splash and barely get him. Sean laughs, caught, and tackles me.

His arms lock around my chest and we wrestle, him

154

trying to get me underwater. I'm no match and I go under, holding my breath just in time. The sounds of the night turn muffled and watery, bubbling around me, and I can taste salt water, I can feel his arms across my front, his chest against my back. Out of nowhere I think of my friend Nick from sixth grade, of a summer day in a neighborhood pool. For just a second. Then my mind returns to the present.

We wrestle a bit and when it's clear he's won, Sean lets go, laughing. I catch my breath and I'm laughing too.

Nearby I find a spot where I don't need to tread. The sand is rough below, full of sharp shells, and I imagine crabs and jellyfish, but I stand anyway. The water comes up to just above my waist. Sean is in front of me.

We stand there for a minute, laughing quietly, too close, way too close, and I'm shivering but I'm not cold anymore.

Then I feel Sean put his hands on my waist underwater and I stop smiling. The moon's out again, miles out over the ocean. It bounces off the rippling water under us, making patterns of light against Sean's cheeks, his nose, his chin, his chest, his arms. It dances in his eyes.

Slowly, slowly, I put my hands on his waist too.

He pulls me toward him and I go, I can't help it.

Our faces are just inches apart. His breath comes out in vapor, and I watch it so I'm not looking at him. Then he kisses me.

It's a while before I even think about what's happening.

155

It's a weird feeling. His lips are against mine, really tight, and then his mouth opens. I can feel his tongue and I don't know what to do at first, but then I try to do what he's doing, just move my tongue around. I can't tell if this is really what I'm supposed to be doing, but somehow it feels really, really great.

His chest is against mine, then his waist is against mine. He puts his hands on my lower back, squeezing me toward him. My own fingers move along his skin in a bunch of different directions. He's warm against the cold water.

Sean pulls away suddenly and looks at me serious, and for a second I get scared.

He stays that way for just a moment. But then he pulls me back toward him again.

He kisses me again and his hands slide lower from my back. I almost push away out of instinct, but I stop myself. I look at him a moment.

He's looking back at me. I can't tell what he's thinking from his face.

But I lean into him again, moving my hands all over him. I touch his neck and move down to his chest, sort of rubbing it. I've never rubbed someone's chest before, and I don't even know if that's like a thing, but it feels all right. And plus he's doing the same thing so I figure it's okay.

I touch the little ridges between his abs, shining wet in the moon. The water line comes just below.

I hesitate just a bit then reach down, feeling all around. He gasps a bit.

My face flushes warm and I start to mumble that I'm sorry, but then he reaches down too.

I hold my breath for a second and my heart starts beating really fast.

He's kind of rough and it hurts a little, but it's a good kind of hurt. I try to do what he's doing and after a bit we have kind of a rhythm.

We lean into each other, my forehead on his shoulder, my free hand on his back. I close my eyes for a second, and then I realize my hand is just going up and down his back in one line which seems kind of weird, so I just stop moving it.

My eyes open suddenly and I grunt out a bit without even meaning to make a noise. Against me I can feel his body tense up and then kind of jerk a bit. Then he lets out a breathy sigh.

I'm breathing hard, but it's slowing now. I have the weirdest urge to laugh, and I lift my head up to look at Sean, and as I do, he puts his hand on my arm.

He says, You can't tell anyone about this.

He doesn't look angry or anything, just kind of agitated. Kind of scared. I open my mouth but don't really know what to say, I'm kind of distracted by trying to read his expression.

He says, Anyone.

My mouth is open and I'm not breathing, just staring up at him, and then I say,

I won't.

Nothing happens for a second, and then he lets go and his face relaxes.

He says, Right, okay.

He looks down again and shakes his head.

He says, Jesus,

and laughs softly.

He says, Sorry. I know you won't tell.

I relax again and smile a bit.

He looks around now, at the ocean and the shore, and shivers, and smiles, and says,

Let's get out of this freezing water.

We watch the sunrise at Mill Point Beach.

Black at first. Quiet except the waves, sleepy and dark, moon gone.

Then:

Pink, mostly. Bursts of orange beneath. Hot red, bright yellow. Deep blues racing away, chased by morning. Ocean below, reflecting everything.

Color everywhere, coming slowly out of black, bursting, exploding, breathing, erasing darkness.

I freeze it in my mind, hold it there. So I can draw it later.

We're so tired when we finally get up and walk back to Sean's house.

TEN

Dad wakes me up at eleven o'clock.

He's annoyed. Even half asleep I can tell. Dad doesn't like it when we sleep late, and eleven is about as late as you can get.

I got home three hours ago. Dad was awake, of course. He watched me walk in without saying anything, go straight to my room. I was so tired.

I'm still so tired.

He says, How was the sleepover?

I'm barely there, still half awake, and the colors of Mill Point Beach are running through my mind. I prop myself up on my elbows.

I say, It was fun.

Dad acts like he's been waiting for this word.

He says, Fun? Weren't you two working on a project?

I stare at him, blinking, eyes squinting, dry and crusty. My elbows get tired and I fall back down on my bed.

I say, Yeah, we worked on the magazine a bunch. But it was a Friday; we also just chilled.

Through the slits of my eyes I can see Dad frown.

He says, You should get up.

And he walks to the door.

He pauses with his hand on the knob and turns back and says,

We're going to church tomorrow.

Like an angry threat almost. Then he leaves.

I lie in bed for about a minute, and then I get up.

Like he said to.

Terry sits next to me in the pew, taking in the sermon, quiet like usual. Thoughtful.

Toby is on my other side again, scowling. She protested coming but Dad wasn't having any of it. More family time, he said.

Mom just smiled her thin smile.

I don't see Sean and I'm not really surprised 'cause he said he doesn't go that much. But I'm still a bit disappointed.

After the sermon Dad goes off with Mom to talk to some of the church elders. Me and Toby and Terry watch them from the other side of the social room, where everyone's gathered for refreshments. Lemonade and stale cookies mostly.

I ask, What's that about?

Terry's dad is one of the people in the group talking with Dad while Mom looks on.

Terry takes a bite out of his cookie, shortbread with pecans.

He says, I think your dad wants to get more involved in the church.

Toby snorts into her lemonade and Terry looks at her.

He says, What? I think it's a pretty cool idea.

Toby looks like she wants to say something pretty bad but she sees me staring at her. I don't really want to deal with them fighting right now and I think she can tell.

She finally rolls her eyes and says,

Whatever,

and takes her lemonade outside to wait for us.

I wait a bit and say, What kind of involvement? Like an elder?

Terry shrugs.

He says, Dad's mentioned it, but just in passing. I don't know if your dad is actually looking to become an elder, but I tend to think he wouldn't turn down an invitation.

I nod slowly. Dad as an elder. I think about this for a minute, wondering how I feel. The idea doesn't upset me exactly, but it makes me a bit uneasy and I can't figure out why.

We stand there quiet for a few moments eating cookies and drinking lemonade and watching the adults talk to one another.

Then I say, Do you know Sean Rossini?

Terry nods.

He says, Yeah, I see him here sometimes. His parents are friends with mine. They're right over there.

I raise my eyebrows.

I say, What?

Terry points to the group talking to Dad and, sure enough, Mr. Rossini is among the men. I hadn't seen him before. His wife is nearby, watching the group quietly, but intently. Her brows are bunched a little and her chin is raised just a bit and her mouth is set. I watch her deep brown eyes flick back and forth between the men as they speak in turn.

Terry says, I think they come every week, but Sean only joins them every once in a while. Like you.

I let that go.

I say, Are you friends?

He says, Not really. I don't know him that well. Why?

I can feel myself blushing and hope it doesn't show.

I say, Oh, he's in my French class. We're working on a project together.

Terry nods but I can tell he's still not sure why I brought this up.

Dad and Mom come over before I have a chance to say anything else, though. The Rossinis and Terry's parents walk up with them. Dad looks pleased with himself.

He glances at Terry and then at me and says,
Look who we've just met, Mike.

I nod and hold my hand out to Sean's dad.

I say, Hi, Mr. Rossini.

He shakes my hand and says, Sean tells me you actually got some work done Friday. Impressive.

He's looking at me with that same unblinking stare that doesn't really match his polite smile.

I say, Yessir. We should be done with the magazine soon.

He says, Well, I hope so, it's almost the end of term.

He says it in a joking way but his voice is too loud.

I shake Mrs. Rossini's hand. All she does is nod.

The Rossinis say good-bye and head toward the big double doors. Dad watches them go for a second, then turns to Toby and me.

He says, Terry's father has invited us all to Sunday dinner at their house. Isn't that nice?

Terry smiles, and then so do I.

I say, Cool,

and then remembering my manners before Dad can correct me I say,

Thanks, Mr. Reese.

Terry's dad, already smiling, just nods.

Toby is seething in the car ride over to Terry's house, but she knows better than to say anything.

Sunday dinner after church.

Mom and Dad, me and Terry, Mr. and Mrs. Reese.

And Toby.

I look back and forth between Toby and Mom, between Toby and Mrs. Reese. I think about how different she is, about how much Dad has tried to make her the same.

I think about how much Dad and Mr. Reese are the same. I think about how Terry is like them too. About how I'm supposed to be, and usually I can pass, but sometimes not.

I think about Ronald's mom and what it would be like for her to be here. Almost divorced, dressed in jeans and a sweatshirt, bags under her eyes but easy to smile. She swears sometimes and drinks a bit of wine and has a hard, deep laugh.

She'd be so out of place at this dinner. Like Toby.

The thought makes me smile.

Mr. Reese says, Something funny, Mike?

He's smiling as he says it.

I come to and shake my head slightly.

I say, Oh, no, sir, I was just thinking about something.

He nods and then says, How are you doing over at Somerdale High? Keeping up?

I say, Yessir, I'm doing okay, I guess. High school's not as hard as they made it sound in eighth grade.

He laughs at this, a soft chuckle that comes out evenly.

He says, Yeah, they gotta talk it up so that some of the slackers will take it seriously. But I'm not surprised it's easy for you—you're a bright kid.

I nod. Mr. Reese is a nice man, but talking to him still

makes me nervous and I never get why. But part of it is how careful and polite everything sounds. He talks like someone in a movie from the forties.

Toby groans. It's a low and quiet groan. No one but me hears it. She hates this dinner.

But I don't mind it. I dunno. Maybe I'm not just passing. Maybe I really am enjoying myself.

After dinner Mom helps Mrs. Reese with the dishes, and Dad and Mr. Reese go off to the living room to talk. Terry and I go up to his room. He just got a new Xbox and wants to show me.

He offers to show Toby too, but she asks Mom if she can go for a walk instead. Mom gives her an anxious look. Dad is too far away to ask and Mrs. Reese is watching.

Mom twists her wedding ring around and around and says, All right, Toby, just don't be out too long.

She watches as Toby slips out the kitchen door.

Terry's room is big and really, really clean. He walks over to the TV on the far wall and turns it on, then fiddles with the Xbox. There are a couple soft *bloop*s, and the logo comes onscreen.

He shows me how he can move without controls, and the Xbox will mirror it. He flicks his hand from right to left, and the screen slides with it, like he's flipping a page.

Terry lets me try and I mimic his actions. I get the hang of it pretty quickly, but it still takes a while for it to look natural.

Terry gets bored after a few minutes and then says,

Hey, you know how we talked about that thing last time?

I stare at him. I don't remember.

He says, About porn.

I nod. I remember now.

He smiles a bit, looking at the ground. Then he looks up.

He says, Can I show you something?

I nod again.

Terry walks over to the door, peers out into the hallway, then closes it quietly. He tiptoes over to a trunk he keeps at the foot of his bed and opens it. It's filled with old winter clothes. Heavy coats, scarves, hats, lots of hand-knit mittens.

He digs around for a bit and then pulls a wrinkled magazine from the bottom. The cover shows the face of a naked blond woman. A man is right behind her. You can't see his face but he's grabbing her hair and having sex with her.

My stomach drops a bit. I both like and don't like the feeling.

Terry says, Mom and Dad have a parental control program on my computer, so this was all I could get.

He opens the magazine to a page and shows me the picture. It's the same woman, only now she's lying on her back, while a different man has sex with her. Her mouth is open and her eyes are closed. The man's muscles are tense and bulging, powerful-looking. His teeth are gritted but his eyes are wide and blazing.

I stare at the picture for a long time, taking in every line, every bit of skin.

I say, Wow.

Terry nods, slowly, wide-eyed.

He whispers, She's so hot, right?

My stomach drops again and this time it's only unpleasant.

I don't answer and after a minute Terry suddenly closes the magazine and shoves it deep into his trunk, snaps the lid shut, and sits on it. He looks miserably at the floor.

Neither of us says anything for a while. Now that the excitement has gone, it feels weird to be here looking at porn with Terry.

Finally he says, It's wrong. I just can't help it.

I don't know how to respond so I don't.

He looks up.

He says, Don't you think?

After a minute I just shrug.

Then I blurt out,

Maybe it's not that big a deal. It's just naked people. People have sex all the time and that's not going to change. Maybe not everything the Bible says is really that important, you know? Maybe it's wrong about some things.

The words surprise even me, like I don't know what I'm going to say until it comes out.

Terry stares at me, and then his eyebrows scrunch together.

He says, Let's go downstairs and see if there's any dessert or something.

The car ride home is filled with Toby's sulking and Dad's happy chatter. Mr. Reese offered to recommend him as an elder.

Mom exclaims at the good news. It's wonderful, she says. I tell him congratulations and that it sounds really cool because that's what he wants to hear.

Toby stays silent but her bad mood can't affect Dad now.

After a while I let Dad and Mom have the conversation to themselves. I think about the awkward encounter with Terry and my stomach drops again.

So I think of other things.

The day after that I'm in Art and we are supposed to draw an animal. Any kind of animal is what Mr. Kilgore says. We're learning about drawing living things.

I draw the sunrise at Mill Point Beach.

Mr. Kilgore says, What's that?

I say, It's the sunrise at Mill Point Beach.

He says, You're supposed to be drawing an animal, Mikey.

I say, There's a seagull in it.

He leans in to get a closer look.

He says, Where?

I point to the seagull. It's under the puffy orange clouds. There's even another one nearby.

He says, You've gotta be kidding me.

Like that.

I can hear Victor and Tristan and Fuller snickering now. My ears get hot.

I don't say anything.

Mr. Kilgore says, This seagull is tiny. It's barely even part of the picture. You were supposed to draw an animal, Mikey.

I say, I did, it's just small.

He says, You were supposed to make it the main part of the drawing.

I don't say anything.

He looks at me a bit longer.

Then he walks away.

He tells me I'm getting a zero for the day, but he lets me keep my drawing so I don't care. Plus he always says stuff like that.

I don't care.

On the way to my locker after Art, I hear my name. It's Victor.

He says, Hey, Mikey!

I pretend not to hear and I walk faster.

He says, Hey! Mikeeeey!

He holds out the *eeee* just like that. He does that sometimes.

I'm at my locker now and have it open, and I don't have anywhere else to go, so I turn around. It's Victor, and Tristan is with him. Fuller isn't there because he has a class way on the other side of the building that he has to rush to right after Art. I hear him complaining to Victor sometimes about how he's always late and his teacher gets mad and doesn't care that he has to run. Victor usually tells him to shut up. Victor tells everyone to shut up.

I wish he would shut up sometimes.

He says, Hey there, Mikey!

I just look at him. I can feel my knuckles cramping from holding on to the backpack strap too tightly.

He says, Aren't you gonna say something?

I just look at him.

I know I should say something and maybe that would be safer, or maybe just start putting my Art stuff in my locker and getting out my English stuff, but I can't make myself move.

So I just look at him.

He says, That was a real pretty drawing you did today. Sucks about the zero.

He's got this sort of lopsided grin that he has sometimes. Tristan looks annoyed, like he doesn't really want to be there.

I say, Okay.

He says, Can I see it?

I say, No. I gotta go to English.

He says, Come on. I just wanna see what you drew. It was a sunrise, right? Sounds pretty.

I don't say anything.

He says, I bet it had lots of colors. I bet you like lots of bright colors, huh?

I say, I gotta go to English.

He snickers. His little sideways grin comes back.

He says, I bet you do, Mikey. We'll leave you alone.

Then he walks by, but bumps me with his shoulder when he passes. I guess he hits me pretty hard, and the back of my head slams into the corner of my open locker door.

Some other kids in the hallway see and a few of them giggle.

Like not loud enough so that they want me to hear but loud enough that I know what they're laughing about.

My head hurts a lot but I try not to let it show.

I take my Art stuff out of my bag and put it in my locker. The drawing is in my folder, and I take it out. I sort of look around to make sure Victor is gone and no one's looking, and then I stick it on the inside of the locker door with a magnet.

I like the drawing.

ELEVEN

I leave for school earlier than usual. Today is the last day of the semester and our French project is due.

Sean picks me up in his Bronco at six forty-five with all the materials.

Dad's still home. He waves me a bleary good-bye as he sips on his coffee. I'm much more awake than normal.

We rush to school, Sean speeding and taking turns faster than he should. The neighborhood zips by, still dark and sleepy and quiet. It's finally cold out. There was a freeze last night, and some icicles are still hanging off tree branches and drainpipes this morning, twinkling in Sean's headlights.

Every now and then he rests his hand on my thigh, when he's not shifting gears. The touch feels warmer than

I expected. I watch the crystal neighborhood zoom by, wishing this car ride could last all day, and I smile.

We get to the cafeteria a full forty-five minutes before first period and put the magazine together quietly. There are only one or two students already here. We take a table near the corner and work next to each other. We sit as close to each other as possible.

Sean puts the pages in order while I look them over for last-minute mistakes.

I say, My birthday's coming up in a couple weeks.

Sean pulls a few little binder clips from a box and then makes sure all the pages are even.

He says, Oh yeah? When?

I say, December thirty-first.

He says, Oh cool, New Year's Eve.

I nod. It's actually kind of annoying having a birthday so close to Christmas, but I don't say this.

Sean puts a few of the clips on.

He says, What are you gonna do?

I say, I dunno. We're not going anywhere for Christmas, so we'll probably just be at home.

He nods and says, Cool, we're going to Boston for Christmas, but we'll be back right after.

Sean will be here on my birthday. I don't say anything at this, just watch him put the clips on.

Then he says, We should hang out for New Year's.

He glances up and then back down at the pages and binder clips.

I nod in response, just a little. Shy suddenly. But also excited.

We go our separate ways when the first bell rings.

Sean takes the magazine. We decide that he will bring it to class.

I walk to my locker before first period. The drawing of Mill Point Beach is there on the inside of the locker door, full of color.

I put my body in front of it and look around quickly, but Victor's not around.

I look back at the picture and smile a bit.

Then I get my Geography book and slam the locker closed.

Jared has some notes spread out in front of him at lunch.

He's slurping on a fountain iced tea and flipping through some pages when I reach the table. Ronald's looking at him in this kind of annoyed way.

When he sees me, Jared says, What tests do you have today?

I sit down with my tray. Vegetable lasagna.

I say, I already had Biology. Then Art and Algebra later.

Ronald snorts.

He says, What kind of test are you going to have in Art?

I shrug. Mr. Kilgore will probably just make us draw

something quietly, which isn't much different from a normal day.

I say, What are you studying for?

Jared says, Biology and English. How was Mrs.
Ferguson's test?

Jared has a different Biology teacher, Mr. Howards. I
don't know much about him except that he's bald and fat
and supposed to be really boring.

I say, It was pretty hard. And long. I just barely finished in time.

Jared says, Yeah, but you're slow. Did it cover the
whole semester or was it just the last few weeks?

I say, Just the last few weeks.

Jared nods and says, Excellent. Howards usually does
whatever Ferguson does.

Ronald says, Didn't he tell you whether it would be
over the whole semester or not?

Jared waves his hand and says, He just said to study
the whole semester, but that's what all teachers say to cover
their bases.

I look over at Victor's table, where he's sitting with
Tristan and Fuller. They all look kind of cranky, but
Fuller especially.

I'm guessing he's annoyed about the Biology test.

Most of the other kids took the whole period to finish
it too, which was kind of nice because it meant Victor was
too busy to bother me.

Still, he finished it before me and didn't seem like he thought it was too hard.

Fuller, though, was still working on it when the bell rang. Every now and then I could hear him swearing under his breath.

Victor just sat through the rest of the period, doodling.

When the bell rings at the end of lunch, I find myself hoping Mr. Kilgore gives us a lot of busywork in Art.

He tries to but it doesn't do much good.

When everyone gets quiet after the tardy bell rings, Mr. Kilgore looks around the class with this half smile on.

He says, For your semester exam, you're all going to draw something. Whatever you want. But it has to incorporate all the major elements we've learned so far this year: depth, lighting, shading, color, tone, texture, perspective, and proportion. You will be penalized for any element you leave off, so I suggest you take the whole period. If you think you're finished before the end of class, check again.

He waits, maybe for some reaction, but there is none. So he says,

You may begin.

I roll my eyes when Mr. Kilgore turns around. The big surprise exam in Art class is to draw something. Like we do every day.

I think for only a minute before deciding what I want to draw.

I put a few lines on the paper, adding color here and there. It takes a bit before the shapes start to form:

It's me, from behind. Three years old.

Mom and Dad on either side, holding my hands. Pulling me up just a bit, my feet leaving the sidewalk.

Sunset in Milwaukee, skyline to the left, Lake Michigan to the right.

It's sort of weird because I have to imagine this angle. It's a different perspective from the real memory, the sight of Dad grinning down at me, Mom pregnant and laughing as she helps pull me up.

But it starts to come together, and I think this is what it must have looked like.

Then something soft hits my head and I'm snapped out of the image.

I look around and hear it before I see it: Victor snickering. Giggling softly.

Near my left foot is a crumpled piece of paper.

I look up at Mr. Kilgore. He's walking around, paying no attention.

So I pick up the paper and roll it out.

It's a fat hairy bald man, naked, behind a drawing of me on all fours. It's dumb but I'm recognizable and the detail actually isn't all that bad — I think that's what makes me so mad.

Victor and Tristan and Fuller are all shaking with quiet laughter now, barely controlling themselves.

I don't even think, I just crumple the paper back up and throw it at them.

It misses by several feet and then I hear a hard slap on my desk, so loud I jump.

Everyone looks.

Standing over me, Mr. Kilgore says,

Mikey! What the hell are you doing?

I stare up at him.

He takes the drawing off my desk. Glares at me a bit more, then says,

Since you are apparently so bored that you're throwing trash across the room, I'll assume you've finished your exam. How about I just grade it as is, then?

I say, Victor—

Mr. Kilgore says, Shut up.

From my left I can hear Victor and his friends giggling but I don't look over. My hands are shaking.

Mr. Kilgore glances at my drawing and says,

I can already spot a few elements you've missed. I don't expect this to be a very flattering grade, Mikey.

I glare back at Mr. Kilgore and all I can think about is how angry I am, and before I can stop myself I say,

It's Mike, you dick.

There's silence in the room now.

My words hang there, stopped by nothing.

Mr. Kilgore's lips are tighter than I've ever seen. He stands there, nostrils flaring, eyes piercing into me. Mustache quivering.

Then he turns on his heel and walks to the beige intercom phone by his desk. He picks it up, waits a second, then says,

Claire, can you send an office assistant down with a referral slip? Thanks.

It seems like he's trying to keep his voice from shaking.

Then he turns to me and raises my drawing up before his face. Slowly, he rips it down the middle into two pieces, eyes never leaving mine. He takes the two pieces and rips them into four, then into eight, into sixteen.

Still looking at me, eyes wide, lips tight, he drops the pieces into the wastebasket, letting them flutter down.

He stares at me for a few seconds afterward and says, You will receive a zero on your exam.

I stare back. I don't say anything.

There's a minute of tension before the office assistant opens the door. I stand up as she hands Mr. Kilgore the referral slip. He signs it quickly and practically flings it at me.

I take the slip and my books and leave with the office assistant.

She's a junior or senior. Straight black hair just past her shoulders, dark skin, loose clothes. Careless, sort of clumsy walk. She looks at me kind of funny as we walk down the hall in silence.

Then she says, What'd you do?

I look at her.

I say, I called him a dick.

She raises her eyebrows and says, Damn, dude.

The assistant principal is middle-aged and completely bald and has a beard.

I know that his name is Mr. Whitman but that's all I know. It's a big school so each grade has its own assistant principal. They introduced themselves at freshman orientation, and that's the last time I really heard him speak.

He looks at me across his desk, reading the referral slip again.

He says, You called your teacher a dick. Is that true?

I'm surprised he actually says the word.

I nod.

He says, What were you thinking?

I look at my hands. There's an answer to this, I just don't know if I want to get into it.

He says, I asked you a question, Mr. Matthis.

I say, I dunno.

He says, You don't know.

I shake my head.

He says, You just thought you'd swear at your teacher, is that it?

I don't say anything.

He says, Maybe you did it for the attention?

I look up at him and think about the kids he normally sees in his office, kids who get in fights all the time, kids he knows by name. How he probably thinks I'm like them.

He looks tired and annoyed.

He waits for me to say something, and when I don't, he says,

Well, let's just call your dad and see what he thinks.

And he reaches for the phone.

I miss all of English. It doesn't matter that much because we already had our exam.

I get to Algebra five minutes after the bell rings. Mr. Gardings looks up when I walk in. He looks kind of irritated until I hand him the office slip.

He reads it over, fingering his right suspender strap, then looks up at me. I read the slip on the way to class and I know it doesn't go into detail or anything, but Mr. Gardings will be able to tell that I got in trouble.

But he doesn't say anything, just looks curiously at me through his thick glasses for a moment before he hands me a test and gestures to my desk.

I work through it slowly and finish right before class ends.

Algebra isn't my best subject. But I do okay.

I'm tired when I get to French. I've walked slower than usual so almost everyone's there already. They're all chattering away.

It's the last period of the last day before Christmas vacation and there's no test. The thought cheers me up a little. Just as Sean turns around and sees me and smiles.

He says, Hey,

as I walk to my seat.

I say, Hey.

I sit down heavily in my desk and turn around.

I say, I called Mr. Kilgore a dick.

Sean raises his eyebrows. There's a second or two where he just stares at me like that, and then he grins wide and his eyes light up and he says,

Well, holy shit. Really?

I nod.

He laughs and says, Are you in trouble?

I think about the phone call to Dad. Mr. Whitman didn't take his eyes off me while they talked. I couldn't hear what Dad was saying but I can guess what's coming.

I say, I will be.

We hand in our magazines, and Madame Girard makes us all take a couple minutes to show the class what we did.

After about twenty minutes of this, she lets us talk quietly for the rest of the period. Everyone's excited about the break.

Through the windows we can see the few icicles left on the trees slowly melting, dripping onto the grass and sidewalk below.

When class ends, Sean and I leave together. He stops at the end of the hallway because his locker is in another direction.

He says, So let's hang out during the break. We get back from Boston the day after Christmas.

I say, Sure, that'd be cool.

He says, And then we can do something for your birthday. Maybe you can come over or something.

I nod and smile.

He smiles back.

Then he turns around and walks toward his locker.

And I walk toward mine.

It's too cold to walk Toby home so I take the bus. She has her own bus that she'll take.

The ride home is bouncy and loud and full of kids who can't wait to start their vacations.

I sit near the back, thinking about the next two weeks. Thinking about my birthday.

The kid sitting next to me is some sophomore who lives a couple blocks away. I've seen him a few times but I don't really know him. I think his name is Brendan.

We don't talk.

I get off at my street. My house is pretty close to the stop. I'm still thinking about my birthday when I open the door.

Dad is sitting at the dining room table. He looks up.

He says, What in the world is wrong with you?

I stare. His words cut through the air, surprising me.

He shouts, Answer me!

I mutter something. Probably: I don't know.

Dad's hands are balled into fists, resting on the table.

He taps one foot really fast. I can barely hear the soft *pat pat pat* against the carpet.

He says, That was one hell of a stunt you pulled today.

I don't know what to say. I never know what to say.

He stares for a few moments longer. I'm starting to sweat under my jacket. The heater's turned up high. Mom's doing.

Then he says, You're grounded. For the break.

I say, I'm —

He says, For the whole break, Mike. Until school starts again.

I open my mouth to say something, then close it. Then open it again.

I say, My birthday's on New Year's Eve!

He shouts, Then you should've thought about that before you disrespected your teacher!

I'm breathing deeply through my nose. I'm thinking about Sean.

I say, This sucks.

Dad shouts again. You're goddamn right this sucks! And now maybe you won't act like a goddamn brat!

I stare at him. My hands are shaking.

Quietly this time, he says, Go to your room.

I do.

* * *

That night we go to Toby's school for her choir's holiday concert.

Mom and Dad let me go because they don't realize I want to, and they think I should support my sister. But I've always supported my sister.

Dad seems annoyed that they're calling it a holiday concert instead of a Christmas concert. But Toby points out that one of their songs is about Hanukkah.

Dad taps his thumbs on the steering wheel. I see his eyebrows scrunch together in the rearview mirror.

He says, There are songs about Hanukkah?

Toby rolls her eyes and says, Yes, Dad. Jews like to sing too.

Dad considers this for a minute and then kind of shrugs. He says, Okeydokey.

The holiday concert is actually a big combined concert with both the choir and the band, so there are a million people there already when we pull in. But we're still early.

Toby runs off to join her choir as we walk in. The side entrance to the school opens almost right into the cafeteria, which has been set up with stepped platforms for the band and choir. Folding chairs sit in rows in the rest of the cafeteria for the audience. There are hundreds of people walking around, talking, laughing, hugging. Three sixth-graders walk by with tubas bigger than they are. Mrs. Deringer tries to herd her students together in one corner. She has the same huge bright smile she did the last time I saw her.

We find seats toward the right, closer to the choir side,

Mom between me and Dad to give us a buffer from each other. We sit and wait for the show to start. I look around and watch the chaos.

But I'm thinking about my birthday and Sean. I'm thinking about the message I have to send him later.

The last song to play is "Silent Night," my favorite. It's a pure, slow version that starts quiet, swells, becomes intense and powerful without ever picking up speed, choir and band alternating at times, then together at the end. I close my eyes and imagine the music as something physical, as wind, as something swirling in the air above me, around me, through my hair. I love it.

The Hanukkah song was "Rock of Ages." It wasn't bad.

Mom tells me to go get Toby after it's over.

I find her near the corner of the cafeteria, half in the entrance to the choir room. Her back is to me and she's talking to some other kids in the room I can't see.

She turns right as I reach her. I ruffle her hair and say,

Time to go home, kiddo.

She giggles and says, It's Toby, you dick.

Her classmates gasp and then giggle too, which makes her grin.

She says, Let's go.

My room is quiet and still. Even with Charlie.

He's sitting near the edge of the bed, staring up at me,

186

wagging his tail but being so quiet, waiting for me to do or say something.

I'm sitting on the bed, staring at nothing.

There's my window, closed but with the curtains open. Still bright outside. Neighbor across the street taking the trash out.

There's my dresser, junk covering it.

My wall, light blue, covered with star charts and random drawings.

My door, solid white, closed. A couple old *FoxTrot* comics taped to it.

My computer desk. Junk all over it like the dresser, but pushed to the side to make room for the computer.

I stare at the blank screen, then get up and walk over to the desk. Charlie follows, tail wagging harder now that I'm doing something. He puts one paw on my lap when I sit down, and I pet him without looking at him.

I move the mouse and the screen wakes up. I log on to Facebook and find Sean and click on Message.

Then I stare at the screen for a while longer. Charlie whines a bit.

Finally I type,

Grounded for the break. Can't hang out till after New Year's. See you at school I guess.

I look at the words. More silence. Then I hit Send.

TWELVE

It's cold every day now. It doesn't always freeze, but most mornings there are small icicles hanging on our tree in the front.

Dad still lets me walk Charlie, mostly because he doesn't want to. That's the only time I'm allowed outside the house.

Charlie shivers and doesn't like to be outside as long, but he still runs around enough that he keeps warm.

It's windy, usually. I have a hat and scarf and jacket, but my face gets flushed and cold-burned. I like the feeling. I like leaning against the wind and letting it rush all around me and barely being able to see.

Sometimes I take Charlie all the way to the ocean. We stand there and watch it, watch the waves crashing in, rough now with the wind. The beach is deserted and gray and still.

Then we walk back.

I never see Sean on these walks.

Dad is sitting in the dining room, typing on his laptop. Probably something for work. His reading glasses are close to the edge of his nose. They make him look old and tired.

I walk up to him, and he looks up from his laptop.

I say, I need to get Christmas presents. Can I go to the mall?

He looks at me for a bit and says, For Toby?

I say, For everyone.

He nods and then says, All right, that's fine. See if your mother can take you, though. I'm a bit busy.

Mom fidgets even when she drives. She looks like she wants to say something, wants to talk, but every attempt looks like it hurts her.

She says, Do you know what you're getting Toby?

I say, Not really.

And she winces a bit, as if not sure how to respond.

I have forty-five dollars saved up from allowances and odd jobs I've been able to do, like weeding Mrs. Gunther's garden.

It sucks being fourteen and having no money.

I tell Mom I'm going to get her present first. She tells me I don't have to get her anything, like she always says. I tell her I'm going to no matter what, so she goes off to one of the department stores while I walk into Hartford Books.

It's a small store and it doesn't take long to browse through the whole thing. Some employee asks if he can help me find anything, and when I say I'm just looking, he nods but follows me anyway. Probably thinks I'm going to try to steal something. But I mean if a kid was going to shoplift, he'd probably go to a video game store or something, right? Not a bookstore. Whatever.

I think about getting her a *Garfield* book since I know she likes it, but then figure that's kind of lame. Then I see their religion section.

They have a bunch of Christian theology books and then a small section of Bibles. I look at these, and pretty soon I see a big navy one with gold lettering and a velvet green page marker.

Mom has tons of Bibles but none this nice. I look at the back and it's twenty-five bucks. Kind of a lot.

But Mom will love it.

I don't let her see the bag when we meet up. She follows me into a music store to look for Dad's present.

Dad loves classic rock but already has a million albums on iTunes. But then Mom points to a section of vinyl.

She says, I'm going to get your father a record player,

190

because he's said he misses his old one. Why don't you get him some records to start his collection?

This is actually a pretty good idea, so I look over at their vinyl section. The records are really cheap, like five bucks. I pick out two: Kansas and The Who.

All that's left is Toby's present. I was telling the truth when I told Mom I didn't know what I was going to get her. I have about ten bucks left, and as we walk through the crowded mall, I look left and right at the stores for inspiration. But I can't imagine her wanting anything from any of these places.

Then we pass by an art store. I love this store. Sometimes I go there to get drawing supplies. And suddenly I get an idea.

Mom's eyebrows draw together when I lead her into the store, but she doesn't say anything.

I already have a bunch of supplies, so I only end up picking out a small canvas and a couple tiny tubes of paint. Still, it comes out to like fifteen bucks.

I look at Mom.

I say, I'll pay you back. I promise.

She still looks unsure, but takes out some bills and pays the cashier the difference.

She says, Don't tell your father.

I don't have much to do when we get home, so I get some wrapping paper and tape and scissors and old newspapers and go upstairs with my stuff and close the door.

I wrap up Mom's Bible and Dad's records. I'm not really good at wrapping presents, so they end up looking kind of messy, but whatever.

I put those in the closet and then lay out the canvas and paint tubes on the newspaper that I've spread out on the floor. Then I add some of the stuff I already have: more paints, a paintbrush, a pencil, and a paint palette.

I sit down in front of my supplies and look them over. And then I think about Toby's lost picture. Toby and Marla, on the trampoline, sun in their hair, laughter frozen on their faces. Toby's pink-and-blue overalls.

It's been months since I last saw the picture, but I can still remember it pretty clearly. I'm good at that kind of thing. And I think I can remember what Marla looks like.

The canvas is about the size of a book. Not big. I don't paint that much at all, mostly draw, but if I outline it in pencil first and paint over it, I should be okay.

I do it as light as I can. I have to erase a lot. But after an hour the shape is there and it looks really familiar.

Then I start mixing paints. Pink and blue for Toby's clothes. Marla had some kind of yellow shirt and purple pants. Light brown hair for Toby, red for Marla. Blue sky, no clouds. Green ferns in the background, dark brown fence, reddish lens flare from the sun.

The faces are the hardest, especially with this small a canvas. You have to keep changing the colors, because of light and shadow, and then you have to have a really steady hand with the details.

I do my best, and when I think I'm finished, I look away. I stare at the door for a full minute, letting the white of it wash over my eyes, getting the image of the painting out of my head.

Then I look back at the painting.

It's not bad. I can immediately recognize Toby. Marla's okay too. I can tell what they're doing in the picture. I can see them laughing, I can tell what's hair and what's leaves and what's sky.

It's done.

Toby wakes me up on Christmas. It's six thirty in the morning and she pounds on my door.

I start, sitting up in bed. She opens the door and Charlie bounds up to her, excited by her excitement.

She yells, Wake up, Mike! Christmas!

Then slams the door. I can hear her running down the stairs, singing.

I get up.

Mom and Dad make themselves some coffee, and we gather around the tree. It's just light outside. Everyone's in their robes. Charlie walks from person to person, licking whatever he can reach.

Dad smiles, eyes tired, and says, Toby, why don't you go first?

We take turns selecting presents and handing them to each other.

Dad opens Mom's record player first and his eyes light up, suddenly not looking that tired anymore. His next present is mine, and he laughs when he sees the albums.

He says, This is great, Mike! Thanks.

I nod.

Mom gets a *Garfield* book from Toby, which makes me glad I didn't get her one. She hugs Toby thanks.

When she opens my Bible, her smile fades and she inhales quickly but quietly, almost a gasp. She runs her fingers over the gold lettering, tracing the grooves.

She says, Oh, Mike, this is beautiful. Thank you.

I get a computer game and some Blu-rays and a new star chart from Mom and Dad. Toby gives me an art book, which is really cool because it has a lot of Albert Bierstadt paintings. I love his landscapes because he uses color in a way that makes it look like the paintings themselves are lit.

Toby opens my present last. I can tell she has no idea what it is when she picks it up, probably thinking it was a book before she felt how light it was.

Then she unwraps it and gasps.

Mom says, What is it honey? and leans over.

Then she gasps too.

Toby looks up at me and her eyes are wet.

She squeals, Mike!

And looks at me for another moment, trying to think what to say, and then she just throws her arms around me and hugs me really tight, almost knocking me backward.

Mom says, Mike, that is really wonderful.

Dad leans over to look at it and whistles. He looks up at me and smiles.

I smile back. Just a little.

We go to church later in the morning. It's packed for Christmas. Toby doesn't mind so much today because her choir is singing. Plus it's Christmas, and it's hard to be upset on Christmas, even for Toby.

I see Terry but he and his family are sitting a few pews over. We talk for a bit after but not much.

Mom makes Christmas dinner in the early afternoon. Ham, potatoes, corn, biscuits, cheesy broccoli. Just the four of us. It's delicious.

I go up to my room after. I'm getting kind of stir-crazy because I haven't been out except to walk Charlie and once to the mall.

But also part of that I think is because Sean hasn't written back yet.

When I log in today, though, there's a message from him waiting for me.

My heart's pounding for no reason, and I open it.

It says,

which window is yours?

I blink a few times. For a moment I'm not sure what he means. Then I look out my window at the street below and understand.

I write back,

Second floor, closest to the street on the west side.

I think for a minute, looking at the window.
Then I add,

The electric meter's right below it.

And hit Send.

A few hours later, there's a new message:

stay up late on your bday. look outside at 11.

The week between Christmas and New Year's is long and slow.

I get more and more stir-crazy. I hate being in the house so much. So I end up walking Charlie more often, to the beach when I can. I lean into the cold, letting the ocean wind blow all around us both. Sometimes we stay·for the sunset.

I don't see Sean, but one time I see Victor.

He's near the park when I walk by. Standing near a bench, shaded by trees, smoking a cigarette.

He brings the cigarette to his lips between index finger and middle finger, takes a drag, pulls it away between thumb and index finger.

196

He watches me. I pretend not to see him.

But when I'm close enough he yells out,

Have a nice Christmas?

Charlie looks up at the voice, curious.

I don't answer.

Victor yells, What'd you get? Dollhouse? Easy-Bake Oven?

I don't answer.

But I glance back, just once.

He's not grinning like he normally does. He just looks pissed.

He takes another drag and watches me walk off.

On my birthday there are three presents waiting for me at my place at the kitchen table.

Everyone's already up by the time I get downstairs. Mom is making breakfast. Dad's reading a book. Toby looks up and grins when she sees me.

Mom has put a little cupcake at my spot with a single candle in it. When she sees me, she smiles and takes a matchbook out from the drawer and lights the candle.

She and Toby start to sing "Happy Birthday." Dad lowers his book and watches.

I blow out the candle.

I'm fifteen now.

I try to smile but don't. It's my birthday but I'll be inside. I think about tonight and wonder what Sean is planning.

* * *

This year while I'm fifteen:

- • I can get my learner's permit.
- • I'll start sophomore year.
- • I can lead a junior prayer group at church.

I make this list on a sheet of notebook paper and stare at the three bullet points. This is all I can really think of, though.

Plus I doubt I'll ever lead a junior prayer group. It would make Dad and Mom really happy, but I don't think they'd pick me.

It'll be cool to get the permit. Dad says he'll start teaching me after the holidays. Just in parking lots and stuff so I can get a feel for the car. I have to wait until six months after my birthday to get the permit, though. That's the law here. Just like Wisconsin. It's kind of weird.

It's cool to be fifteen, I guess, but there's not much that is going to happen now that I write it out.

I'm making this list just to give me something to do. It's late evening. We already had dinner, and Mom and Dad are just downstairs watching TV. Probably they won't stay up for the new year. They never do.

My room is quiet and dim. I keep checking the red numbers on my alarm clock.

9:35.

9:58.

10:11.

Just before ten thirty there's a light knock at my door. I can still hear the TV downstairs.

I look up and Toby pokes her head in.

She says, Hey, come downstairs. I wanna stay up till midnight and watch the ball drop in Times Square.

Toby has tried to stay up till midnight for three years in a row, but she always falls asleep.

I say, I dunno, Toby, I'm kinda beat. I'll probably go to bed early.

She frowns at me. She never hides her disappointment.

She says, Okay,

and starts to close the door.

I say, Hey, Toby.

She looks at me.

I say, Are Mom and Dad still up?

She says, No, they went to bed a few minutes ago.

I say, Okay.

Toby leaves.

Ten minutes to eleven, I'm just staring at the clock nonstop. I get up a couple times and look outside the window, but there's nothing there.

The TV's still on downstairs.

I'm sitting on my bed with my sketch pad and pencil to pass the time. Not really sure what I'm planning to draw, but it takes shape pretty quick.

It's Charlie, or a quick sketch of Charlie, running away from the viewpoint. I scribble some rough trees around him. Leaves on the ground and trailing in his wake. Hills and a creek.

Charlie running in the woods at Grandma's house.

I stare at the sketch for a moment, then look up at the alarm clock just in time to see it switch from 11:01 to 11:02.

I sit for a half second, then scramble up off the bed and hurry to the window, sketch pad still in hand.

There's a figure standing in the shadows by the side of the house. My heart starts beating fast.

Sean waves when he sees my silhouette.

Slowly, I lift my free hand and wave back.

He makes a gesture and I realize he wants me to open the window. So I open it.

He whispers and in the silence outside his voice carries easily to me.

He says, Come on down.

I shiver in the chill breeze coming in from outside.

I say, How?

Sean is holding a bag, which he puts down before he walks up to the outside wall. He climbs on top of the outside fan for the air conditioner, just below my window.

He points to the electric meter, just to the right and a little above him.

He says, Climb down on the window ledge, and put your feet on that.

I look at him.

He says, Don't worry, I got you.

I look at him for a bit longer, shivering, then break out into a grin.

I say, Okay. Let me get my jacket.

I rush to find it, trying to be as quiet as possible. Once I have it and put my shoes on, I start toward the window, then stop.

Very quietly, I tiptoe to the bathroom, grab my toothbrush, and go back to my room. I close the door and turn off the light, and head to the window.

Sean is still standing on the air conditioner fan, looking up.

I climb out of the window feet first, heart pounding. I know I'm clumsy and I'm kind of scared of heights too. But Sean steadies my legs.

When I'm finally dangling from the window, I feel for the meter with my legs, Sean helping me, and after a moment I'm standing on it, facing the wall.

Slowly, I turn around.

The grass isn't that far below me. I jump and hit the ground at a roll. I hear Sean jump down from the fan as I get up, and suddenly he's standing in front of me, grinning.

I grin back.

He says, Happy birthday.

We walk through the neighborhood, whispering only sometimes. Most people's lights are on, but hardly anyone's outside even though it's not that late. Whenever a car comes by, we hide.

No one knows we're here. I'm shivering a bit, but not with the cold. Sean puts his arm around me as we walk.

I turn my head in every direction, looking out for anything or anyone. Every now and then we see a distant car or person but mostly it's just us.

Still in a whisper, I say, What's in the bag?

Sean's still carrying it in his free hand.

He says, Rope. I didn't know how easy it would be to climb down from your window.

I nod, and he holds me tighter.

Then he smiles a bit and says, And some other stuff.

But leaves it at that.

I'm about to ask what else is in the bag, but I think I hear a noise behind us.

I turn around in time to see a figure far off crossing the street. But he's a ways back. I turn around and we keep walking.

It's like before. Streetlamps, turning us yellow in their light as we get near and then leaving us in darkness when we pass.

It's colder now but lighter. The moon is out now, no clouds to cover it. A breeze pushes against our backs then slows, then pushes, blocked in part by my jacket but more by Sean, his arm always around me, leading me and holding me.

No crickets now. The only noise is:

Us. Our quiet steps.

A car every now and then.

The wind in the trees. Rustling branches.

We're heading toward the beach again. It's our place, something that belongs to us. I like this thought and I smile.

The sand makes the ground unstable, and I step higher as I walk, spraying it in all directions. Sean too. I look back once at our scattered messy footprints.

We go to a spot just in front of a small sand hill, facing the ocean. Behind us are low bushes and scrub and drift-wood blocking out the neighborhoods.

The ocean is stronger tonight, waves and whitecaps crashing with more force, drowning out the only sound there might've been from behind. Out here it's easy to pretend we're alone for miles, far away from houses and people and yellow streetlamps.

The breeze is stronger too and it's colder by the ocean. Sean holds me more tightly as we sit, so tight I can feel his heartbeat through our clothes.

He looks up.

He says, Kind of crazy how many stars you can see on the beach.

I look up too.

I say, When's your birthday?

He says, May eleventh.

I say, You're a Taurus, right?

He says, Yeah.

I scan the sky, and then point at a spot a little to our right.

I say, See those five stars close together in a small V formation?

He looks where I'm pointing. After a while, he finds it and says, Yeah.

I say, That's your constellation. Taurus.

He says, No shit?

I say, Yeah. There's more to it, but that's the bull's head.

He laughs and says, That doesn't look like a bull's head to me.

I say, I know, you kind of have to use your imagination.

I point a little ways away and say, That one's easier to make out. It's Orion. The three stars are his belt, see? Then the two stars above on either side make up the shoulders. Then two at the bottom to make up the corners of his tunic thing, and then over there are his arm and his bow and arrow. He's shooting at your bull.

Sean laughs again.

He says, You know your stars.

I say, Yeah, I'm kind of into it.

Normally I think I would be a bit embarrassed by this. But this time I'm not.

Sean just holds me and we look up at the sky.

After a long time, his watch goes off, sending out tiny beeps.

He says, Oh shit, we only got a minute.

I'm confused for a second but then I understand. He reaches into his bag and pulls out a bottle of wine, a corkscrew, and two wineglasses. He works quickly, taking the cork out and pouring first one glass, then another.

He says, I couldn't get champagne.

He hands me a glass and looks at his watch. After a moment he starts counting down.

He says, Five! Four! Three! Two! One!

At zero, he smiles at me.

He says, Happy New Year.

We clink glasses and take a sip.

Sean holds me tight again and we watch the ocean for a few moments. Far behind us we hear firecrackers popping every couple minutes.

Then he turns to me. I look back.

He leans in and closes his eyes and kisses me, and I kiss back, tasting the wine on his lips. It feels less weird this time, a bit less clumsy. My hands go under his jacket, around his chest and back, feeling everything.

Sean runs his hands through my hair, holding the back of my head.

Far away some car horns blare.

He pulls away for a second, breathing harder now.

Then kisses me again, pushing my jacket off my shoulders. His too. And then my shirt, lifted over my head, and I help him with his.

It's cold and that makes us hold closer together.

We kiss longer and longer, hands running over each other, and then I hear another voice from nearby, deep, gravelly, so close my heart stops.

It says: Sean.

* * *

Sean pushes away from me, hard, knocking me back. I scramble to my feet looking for the voice, trying to get my balance on the soft sand, Sean already standing.

There's a figure just a few feet away, around the corner from the short sand hill. In the low light I don't recognize him at first, but then I do and my stomach drops.

Sean says, Dad!

His voice almost cracks. He's already putting his shirt on. I just stand there, cold now, staring, mind blank.

Sean's dad looks at him with an expression that makes me shiver.

Sean says, Da—

Mr. Rossini says, What are you doing?

Low, almost a whisper.

Sean pulls his jacket on.

He says, I'm not—we're not doing—

Mr. Rossini says, Didn't look that way to me.

Sean says, No! Dad! It wasn't—

Mr. Rossini says, Shut up.

Sean walks toward his father.

He says, Dad, listen, we weren't—

Mr. Rossini swings out of nowhere. His fist hits Sean square in the jaw, and Sean goes down, letting out a small cry. I jump back.

Mr. Rossini's eyes are flaring now as he looks down at Sean in the sand at his feet. Sean's lip is cut and bleeding, but he just looks up at his dad.

206

His dad says, I know what I saw.

Sean says, We didn't —

Mr. Rossini says, I said shut up!

It's the first time he shouts.

He reaches down and pulls Sean up by the arm easily, bringing him to his feet.

He says, We're going home. Now!

Mr. Rossini looks back at me for just a second. I step back from that look, from those eyes that are so like his son's every time I've seen them except now.

He drags Sean away. I can hear Sean's voice fading as they disappear behind the bushes and into the yellow light of the streetlamps.

I stand there for what seems like hours. Just staring.

This is what I see:

• Patterns in the sand where Sean fell.

• Wineglasses knocked over, one of them broken.

• Bottle on its side, still dripping wine into the sand.

My shirt is still off and I'm freezing now, shivering hard. Slowly, I reach down and get it, shaking out the sand, and pull it over my head.

Every now and then there's a sound like popcorn off in the distance. Kids setting off firecrackers.

Then I hear someone laughing, very nearby.

I jump again, looking around.

There's some movement in the darkness of the bushes,

and then Victor steps out. He tries for a second to keep it in but he can't, and just lets it out, sort of bent over, laughing really hard.

I stare at him.

He catches his breath after a minute and says, Hey, Mikey!

Sort of in between gasps.

He straightens up. Takes a deep breath, still grinning.

He says, Man! Look at you.

That sets him off and he laughs again.

I stare at him, shivering so hard it makes me sway a bit.

He says, Sorry to ruin your New Year's. I just saw you two heading down the street and followed you. Just 'cause you seemed a little close.

Victor steps out a bit more into the moonlight. I can see his phone in his right hand.

He laughs a bit more and says, Anyway, yeah, I called Sean's dad and told him his son was making out with some dude at the beach. Jesus! Didn't think he'd actually punch him, but that was something else, right?

Something in my stomach gets hard.

He says, Goddamn, all those times I called you a queer, I didn't *really* think . . . I mean, I could sorta see it, but damn.

My hands close into fists by themselves, slow.

Victor shakes his phone and says, Got it all on video. This is, like, YouTube gold.

I take a step toward Victor.

He says, Oh, hey, maybe your dad wants to know too. Should I give him a call?

I stop, and the hard spot in my stomach loosens.

Victor laughs again. Easy, like he just heard a joke.

I run.

I run past him, through the bushes, into the street. I run as fast as I can, houses blurring by.

I feel nothing, hear nothing. At some point I remember my jacket, still lying on the beach, but I don't care. I'm just thinking about getting home.

The streets pass by and I turn here and there without thinking.

I start to think of Sean but see only his head snap back as his father hits him, his legs giving out under him, blood streaming from his lips, and I shut it out.

I slow down on my block, and now I can feel the cold again, hear my panting, feel my sweat dripping down my forehead. My lungs itch from the cold air. At the front door I stop, catching my breath, wanting to be quiet. It takes a minute. My stomach cramps.

Slowly, I open the door.

Mom and Dad are sitting at the dining table. They look up as I walk in.

Mom puts a hand to her mouth, lets out a small noise like a whimper. She wants to say something but won't. So instead she lowers the hand and wrings it with the other. She looks helpless. It is the worst feeling, watching her look helpless.

Dad's stare is blank and dead.

He says, Go to bed, Toby.

Toby is in the living room. She gets up immediately, walks out of the room, glances at me only once. She looks scared.

I look back at Dad, listen to Toby's steps as she walks upstairs. The close of her bedroom door. Then just silence.

Dad says, I got a call from a boy at your school.

I was waiting for this but still hoping for something else. My stomach drops. I want to throw up.

Dad doesn't say anything for a while. His mouth works but no words form. He stares into space. Finally he looks back at me and says, quietly,

Why don't you go up to bed too?

I say nothing. I just go.

I'm in the bathroom, staring at the counter. My toothbrush isn't in its usual place and I can't figure out why. I stay that way, almost totally still, staring helpless at the empty toothbrush holder for almost ten minutes before I remember I brought it with me to the beach.

Then I turn and leave the bathroom and head back to my room.

We don't talk all of New Year's Day, or the day after. I stay in my room the whole time.

I think about the night before.

Sean holding me tight on the way to the beach.

The sound of the wine bottle opening.

His dad's voice. Sean pushing away from me, hard.

Victor's laughs.

Just that, over and over.

School starts the next Monday.

Dad tells me the night before that I'll be staying home. He's going to write me a note.

I know it's not for me; it's for him.

I sleep in. Half awake I can still hear Mom and Dad moving around, getting ready. Then Toby.

Then after a while it's quiet.

I wake up fully and walk downstairs.

Mom has left a note: She went to run some errands. Bank, shopping for new reading glasses for Dad, taking Charlie to the vet for his annual checkup and shots. There's Frosted Mini-Wheats for breakfast and she left a sandwich in the fridge for lunch.

I pour myself some cereal and milk and eat it at the dining table.

The only sound is the crunch from the Mini-Wheats.

I don't really do anything all day.

I watch some TV, but there's nothing on 'cause it's during the day.

I can't take Charlie out because he's at the vet. I don't really want to go out anyway.

It's pretty boring.

And when I get bored my mind wanders, and I start thinking about New Year's Eve.

Or worse, I think about what's happening at school. Victor's probably told everyone by now. Tristan and Fuller and his other friends. Has he shown them the video? Who else knows about it? What about Ronald and Jared? Or Mr. Kilgore or Miss Rayner or Mrs. Ferguson or Madame Girard? What's Sean doing? Did he skip too? It kind of makes me anxious, knowing that stuff has happened but not really knowing what.

So I try not to think about it. But it's really hard.

Finally I can hear a car in the driveway. Mom. And she probably picked Toby up on her way home.

I go upstairs before they get inside and close the door to my room.

I turn on the computer for the millionth time and go to Facebook.

I have a message.

It's from Victor. We're not friends but you can message anyone on Facebook.

The message has no words—it's just a YouTube link.

My heart starts beating, but I click on it anyway.

The video is really dark. You can't see much, and for a second I'm almost relieved.

But then it zooms in a bit and the light shifts, and it's me and Sean making out. It's hard to tell, but it's definitely us.

212

Then Mr. Rossini's voice: Sean.

Sean saying, Dad!

The sound of one of the glasses breaking as he gets up.

Sean and his dad talking back and forth.

Very quiet but very close, muffled laughter. The camera shakes a bit.

Then a sharp smack and a cry: Mr. Rossini punching Sean.

Quietly:

I know what I saw.

We didn't—

Then loudly:

I said shut up!

Some movement, then:

We're going home. Now!

Mr. Rossini pulls Sean up into the moonlight, and then they both get out of the frame.

The camera tries to follow them a bit, and then it swings to the right.

It's me, standing still, staring after them, my shirt off.

My shoulders are slouched and even in the dark you can see how wide my eyes are. I look really stupid just standing there. I hate it. I think I hate that part the most.

The muffled laugh gets a bit louder and then Victor stops trying. There's just a split second of loud, hard laughing and then the video ends.

I lean back in my chair and stare at the screen.

The video has 124 views. I tell myself that's not a lot for YouTube. I don't really know, though.

After a while I turn off the computer.

I don't go to school Tuesday either.

Wednesday.

I'm sitting at the breakfast table. Dad and Mom are sitting across from me.

Lying in front of them are a few pieces of paper, which Dad now slides over to me.

They are printouts from some website. At the top is a blue banner with the word INNERPEACE next to a small picture of a tree. Below that is a heading that says ALL TRUTH RESIDENTIAL PROGRAM, and then a few paragraphs.

I look at this, then up at Dad.

He says, It's a one-month program.

I don't say anything.

He says, You'll be just outside a small town a little ways west of here. You stay there the whole time, in the dormitories they have. You can't have visitors during the program, but it's not that long when you think of it.

I look at Dad during all this. He speaks in a flat voice. I try facing Mom for a while, but she looks like she's about to cry and that's worse, much worse, so I look at Dad.

Dad says, It'll be like camp.

I don't really think so but I don't say anything.

He says, Your mother and I have decided that we

won't make you go. It's your decision, but you need to think long and hard about this.

His voice is a bit firmer for the last part.

He says, You want to change, don't you, Mike?

I think about this for a while. Dad waits.

I say, Yeah.

I know that's what I'm supposed to say.

I go upstairs.

I'm leaving tomorrow and I need to pack.

I hear Dad's question in my head again. You want to change, don't you?

I've never really thought about it. It sort of makes my heart beat a bit faster, so I try to put it out of my mind.

I open my closet door and look at it. There are a few jackets and nice clothes. A small luggage bag tucked away in the corner, the same one I packed for Thanksgiving.

I stand that way for a while, just staring inside at nothing.

Then I close it and walk over to my computer.

Without really thinking about what I'm doing, I log on to Facebook.

There's another message for me, and for a second I think Victor sent something else. But it's from Sean.

I blink a couple times and open the message.

It says:

**hey. mike. jesus. im sorry about yr birthday. im so
screwed, never seen dad like t his. don't know what to**

215

do. can i see you? i can get out if i need to but if you cant thats fine, i can just go to yr window. whatevr. i just want to see you.

There is a blank line after this and then:

im sorry i pushed you.

I lean back in my chair, staring at the last line. At the period at the end of it.

I think about Dad's question again.

I think about Victor, about getting my shoulder slammed in the hallway or my books knocked out of my hand or the drawing he did and threw at me in Art.

Pastor Clark's sermon, and Toby arguing about it with Terry.

Grandma whispering with Dad in her kitchen.

Sean pushing me away.

Mostly I think about the video, the sound of the breaking glass and the muffled laughter and me standing there, just standing there without a shirt on looking really dumb, and how much I hate it.

I lean forward again and put my fingers up just above the keyboard. They hover there for a second.

Then I type out a message and hit Send before I look up to read it.

THIRTEEN

I hug Mom and Toby good-bye in the driveway. Both of them are crying a bit.

Dad drives. We don't talk much. I ask about school and he says I might be able to make it up in the summer so I don't have to repeat the year. I hadn't thought of that before, repeating the year.

I think about Ronald and Jared. How weird it would be for them to be sophomores and for me to be stuck in freshman year again with everyone younger than me. All because of what happened at Mill Point Beach.

But other than that we don't talk much.

Mostly I just sleep.

Or I pretend to.

*   *   *

We take the highway through Suffolk and Franklin along the bottom edge of Virginia. It's a long drive; winding, twisting roads toward the end, flat but pretty woodsy.

It's kind of nice, really.

We drive forever and then suddenly we turn off the highway and onto a back road. We come to a large campus of buildings tucked away in a cleared section of forest.

There's a big marble slab at the entrance to the campus that says INNERPEACE in the same blue as the website.

Dad parks and we walk up to the main building and into what looks like a reception area.

There's a sign for registering new arrivals. We go there and Dad gets some paperwork from the lady behind the desk. There's no one else.

I kind of zone out, just looking around.

Everything seems clean and really still. Like it was just scrubbed and polished.

I say, I gotta go to the bathroom.

The lady behind the desk points down the hall to the right.

She says, Just down there, first door.

She smiles and I mumble, Thank you, and walk to the restroom.

Everything is clean and sparkly in here too. There are big dividers between the urinals. Bigger than they really need to be. I look at this and then I see that there are no doors to the stalls.

I pee and wash my hands with soap and dry them on a

paper towel. Every noise I make sounds a lot louder in the silence.

When I come back out, there is a man talking to Dad. He looks a bit younger than Dad, maybe in his thirties or something. Sandy hair, kind of wavy. Light skin. Khaki jacket and gray pants.

I stop and look at them, and then the man sees me and smiles. Dad turns around.

He says, Mike, this is the youth pastor, Mr. Landis.

Mr. Landis smiles wider and reaches out to shake my hand.

He says, Good to meet you, Mike. I lead the program for teens and kids, so we'll be spending a lot of time together.

I nod but don't say anything.

Dad looks strained, especially next to the cheerful Pastor Landis.

Dad says, Okay, you're all checked in. I'm going to head back.

He puts a rough hand on my shoulder and says,

I'll see you in a month.

And then he leaves my bag at my feet and turns and walks out.

I watch Dad head back to the visitors' lot. He doesn't turn around.

Then Pastor Landis says,

Why don't I show you up to your room?

* * *

219

These are the rules at InnerPeace:

There's no contact with the outside world. No visitors and we can't call or write anyone.

We can't go into town. We have to stay on campus for the full month.

We have to do everything the camp administrators say.

No Abercrombie or Calvin Klein. No dyed hair. No sports bras for girls. No cologne for boys.

Twenty minutes per day in the bathroom, total.

No keeping a journal and no drawing.

That's it but that covers a lot.

There's a strict daily schedule for each day. Lights on at six o'clock. Morning prayers, Bible studies, sermons. Youth Group counseling, Small Group counseling, One-on-One counseling. Private Reflection. Supervised Outside Activities. Breakfast, lunch, dinner. Lights out at nine thirty.

They searched my bag the first day to make sure I didn't have a phone, computer, anything that would connect me with the outside.

I didn't. Dad read the brochure carefully before we left.

My dorm room is small and bare. Two beds on either side. Two small dressers. Two closets. Two desks. Wooden walls and floor and furniture. There's a small suite bathroom that we share with another room.

My roommate is Timothy. He's two years older than me. From somewhere in Michigan.

220

That's all I really know about him. He doesn't talk much and neither do I. He has short cropped blond hair and small-frame glasses and a medium build. He wears polos tucked neatly into khakis.

I told him when I first met him that I used to live in Wisconsin on the other side of the lake from Michigan. He mumbled something and went back to reading.

He reads a lot.

I'm in a small classroom, no windows but bright fluorescent bulbs all over the ceiling.

Sixteen foldout chairs arranged in a circle, all of us facing one another.

On my right is a girl about my age, short hair, slumped in her chair. To my left is another girl but a bit older, longer hair, stony expression.

Timothy is almost directly across. Polo, khakis, glasses. Eyes downcast.

The person speaking isn't Pastor Landis but one of his assistants, Jesse, who leads our Small Group.

I don't know Jesse's last name. He's just Jesse.

He's talking to the girl on my right, Liz. Polite and cheerful but firm, like always. Liz is sort of the troublemaker in Small Group. I mean it's not like she misbehaves or anything, but she questions everything.

Jesse never gets annoyed. He doesn't tell her she's wrong; he tells her she's misguided. He doesn't get angry; he gets disappointed. He tells her he understands.

Liz looks back at him as he speaks, letting him finish, but her foot is tapping pretty fast under her chair.

He finishes and she says, Fine, but you still haven't said what the harm is. That's what I don't get and what no one will tell me.

Jesse nods as she speaks, then looks around at all of us.

He says, Does anyone want to take a stab at Liz's question?

Jesse does this a lot, makes sure everyone's involved.

No one answers and his eyes fall on me.

He says, Mike, what about you? Do you know what harm acting on homosexual urges can cause?

My face is warm. I stare at the ground and mumble a response.

I say, I dunno.

Liz glances over at me and I look at her and I see the faintest smile. She thinks I'm defending her.

Jesse looks between us two for a minute and opens his mouth, but then Timothy cuts him off.

Timothy says, The harm is that you're more likely to contract sexually transmitted diseases. Practicing homosexuals are also more likely to suffer from depression and drug abuse, and their relationships are at least twice as likely to fail as heterosexual relationships. According to studies, it's also not an ideal environment in which to raise children.

He speaks low and fast, eyes still downcast. Body rigid. Everyone looks at him, and there's silence when he

222

finishes. This is the most I've heard him speak, the most any of us have heard him speak.

Jesse smiles.

He says, That was very eloquent, Timothy.

Timothy's eyes flicker up for a fraction of a second and then back down.

Liz is scowling at him.

The Youth Group is divided by age. There's a College group, a Mid-Teens group, Early Teens, and Pre-Teens.

I'm in the Mid-Teens group but barely. It's for fifteen- to seventeen-year-olds. I think I'm the youngest.

We do everything together: Small Group, Bible studies, morning prayers. Everyone has a roommate in their same age group. Even meals and outdoor activities are with the other Mid-Teens, except the other Youth Group ages are also with us for those parts.

Most of us in the Youth Group are in high school. There aren't that many Pre-Teens. The ones that are here all look scared, all the time.

Even though we see other Youth Group kids, they keep us separated from the Adult Group. I mean sometimes we see them walking around campus but that's it.

At lunch I sit with the other Mid-Teens.

Timothy and Liz. Rebecca, the girl who was sitting on my left in Small Group. Then there's also Gerald, a junior who always acts nervous; Patrick, who has a buzz cut and ears that kind of stick out; Kelvin, a Vietnamese kid who doesn't speak that much English; and Benny, the oldest kid in the group, who turns eighteen in a few weeks and barely talks to anyone.

Then a few other kids whose names I haven't learned yet, all guys. Liz and Rebecca are the only girls in the group.

We're all at one big table, sitting close but not really talking.

Not too far away are the tables with Early Teens and Pre-Teens. Off in the corner by themselves is College.

I count and there are forty-eight of us in Youth Group.

Forty-eight kids eating lunch and it's almost totally quiet.

Then Liz says, Do you have any STDs, Timothy?

A couple kids look up. Timothy is still eating his mashed potatoes like he didn't hear anything. Liz looks at him a moment and then around at the rest of us.

She says, Do any of you have an STD?

No one says anything and she looks back at Timothy.

She says, No one? Funny, isn't it, Timothy? Fifteen of us and not one case of AIDS.

Timothy looks up at this.

He says, It's not a guarantee. It's just statistically proven that homosexuals are more likely to contract HIV.

Liz says, Yeah, more likely. Isn't it also more likely for black people to have AIDS than whites? Should black people stop trying to be black, then?

Timothy looks back at his plate and sculpts his mashed potatoes with his fork.

He says, HIV is just one aspect. It's one negative. Like depression and drug use and relationship instability. There are all of these negatives when you're a practicing homosexual; it's like everything is working against you. There are all these obstacles to being a homosexual already, and that's before you even consider that it goes against the obvious purpose of sex. I'm just saying that maybe the natural world is trying to tell you something, and maybe you should listen.

His voice is low and controlled and a bit nasal, almost like Jared's. But Jared usually sounds relaxed and bored when he talks. Timothy sounds a little tense.

Liz points her fork at him.

She says, How do you listen? You talk about nature and you know what? Nature is telling me that I like lady parts. I can't help—

He says, You think you can't, but that's tempta—

She yells, I know I can't!

Rebecca says, Liz.

Everyone gets quiet and looks at Rebecca, the tall girl with the strained face. Liz whips around to face her.

There's a moment and then Rebecca says, Let's just eat.

Liz turns to Timothy, who is staring at his plate but not moving. As if waiting for an explosion. Then she takes another bite from her plate.

After a moment, Timothy goes back to his mashed potatoes.

Rebecca is the only one Liz listens to.

Outside it's chilly and brisk but sunny. We're in a courtyard in the campus interior, where we go a couple times a day for Supervised Outdoor Activities.

There's a basketball hoop where several Mid-Teens play a game of Around the World. None of them look like they're really into the game. Nearby is a set of gymnastics bars and some benches along a short running track.

I'm walking around the perimeter of the courtyard like I always do.

I'm thinking about school.

I mean school back home, not here at InnerPeace.

I'm thinking about Ronald and Jared eating lunch without me. About Victor and Mr. Kilgore. About Sean.

I don't know if any of the kids at school know where I am or why I'm not back, but it makes my stomach hurt when I think about it.

I don't really miss school, but I still wish I was there instead of here.

While I'm thinking about this, I look up and see Liz walking near me. I don't know how long she's been there.

She's not looking at me so I don't know if she walked up to me or if she just happened to be there, but then she says,

You worried about AIDS?

It comes out fast and jerky.

I say, I don't know.

She snorts and looks up at me, then back down at the ground. Walking with me now, hands stuffed in her jacket pockets.

She says, AIDS has got nothing to do with Timothy's worries.

I don't say anything.

She says, People like him don't like being queer to begin with. Then they look for reasons that fit. To pretend that's where their thinking comes from. Don't believe it.

I don't say anything for a while.

Then I say, What makes them not like it in the first place?

Liza shrugs and says, Religion. That's why I'm here. Not mine, I don't care at all about being a dyke, but my parents are just *allll* about Jesus.

She jerks her head in Timothy's direction. He's off on the other side of the courtyard, walking by himself.

She says, That boy is going to end up married to some poor woman. She'll give him a couple of kids and he'll congratulate himself on turning straight, and then one day he'll wake up old and full of regret.

I don't say anything.

After a while Liz grumbles, See ya.

And then walks off.

* * *

Nine thirty. Lights off.

Timothy goes into the bathroom to change into his pajamas. Then I do the same.

One of the rules is that you have to wear a shirt at all times, even while sleeping.

He gets into bed and turns off the light, and then it's dark and I'm staring at the ceiling.

I wait for a few minutes, just staring up.

Then I say, Is that true? What you said in Small Group today, about AIDS and drugs and stuff?

My voice sounds weird to me in the dark.

I hear Timothy rustling in his bed, turning over to face me.

Then he says, Yeah. There are lots of statistics about it.

I don't say anything for a while, then I say, What did you mean when you were talking about all those negatives and stuff? At lunch, I mean.

Timothy says, There are a lot of consequences to being a practicing homosexual. It makes sense to assume that those consequences are nature's way of telling us that homosexuality isn't viable. So it's logical to listen to that and lead a life that avoids the actions that cause those consequences.

I let this sink in for a while, thinking again about how formal he always sounds.

Then I say, Nature?

I turn my head and can see just a bit of light reflecting off Timothy's eyes. He's turned on his side, looking at me.

He says, Yeah. Or God.

I say, Is it really all those reasons that make you think homosexuality is wrong, or is it God?

He doesn't say anything for a long time.

Then he says, I could never be a homosexual because of my faith. But even if I was atheist, all those signs from nature would make me reconsider my desires.

I don't say anything, and after a while he turns back over, facing the wall.

It's quiet and then finally I say, Have you ever been able to make those desires go away?

There's no answer. After a while I decide he's asleep.

I turn over and face my wall.

As we get ready in the morning, Timothy ironing his khakis and me brushing my teeth, he suddenly puts the iron down and looks up at me standing in the bathroom over the sink.

He says, Not yet. The desires, I mean.

Then he goes back to his ironing.

FOURTEEN

I think about Dad yelling.

I think about Victor.

I think about having to go to church.

I think about Mr. Kilgore and his annoying voice.

I think about Sean pushing me away, about his dad hitting him in the face, about how stupid I looked standing there with my shirt off.

I think about these things most mornings to keep me from missing home.

It works.

But sometimes I let myself think about the pink and orange and yellow, the red all across, the deep blues fading to black. Sometimes I think about the sunrise on Mill Point Beach.

* * *

Jesse looks pained as he speaks. Serious, concerned. Eyebrows scrunched.

He says, You may have noticed there's one fewer chair here this morning.

No one says anything.

He says, Liz has left the program.

There's a moment where everyone looks at him, waiting for him to continue. Liz's absence was the first thing we noticed at breakfast this morning.

Jesse says, This was the decision of Pastor Landis. Liz clearly had issues with being here, and we all felt her presence would end up being a distraction for the rest of you.

He looks around at each of us. I keep my eyes on the carpet.

He says, This program works, and it works well, but only when you want it to. Liz didn't want it to, so it made little sense for her to continue when she might create obstacles for her peers.

I glance to my left, quick. At Rebecca.

She looks strained like always, but there's more of it today. Like she's just barely keeping it in.

She's kind of on her own now. I look away.

Jesse hands us all thick bright blue rubber bands.

He says, Put these on your wrists.

We do.

Then he says, I want you to keep these on you at all times from now on. When you sleep, when you shower, always. Do not take them off until you leave this campus when the program is over, and even then I encourage you to keep them on.

We all look at each other.

Gerald's eyes dart quickly between Jesse and the other kids. Kelvin just frowns at his rubber band like he expects it to do something.

Rebecca doesn't seem to care. She just stares ahead at no one.

Jesse says, These are your Accountability Bands. Every time you have an impure thought — every time — you are to snap the band against your wrist.

Timothy frowns but keeps looking at the floor.

Jesse says, The minor pain is to remind you where your thoughts should be. You will be training yourself not to fall back on these thoughts, but to keep your minds and hearts focused on God, and what God wants.

Jesse looks all around the room at us. No one says anything.

He says, This is all on the honor system, of course, but I want you all to hold each other to this. If someone is neglecting their Accountability Band, you should tell them. If they continue to neglect it, you should tell me. Do you all understand?

A few of us mumble, Yes.

But most of the kids just stare.

* * *

Pastor Landis speaks with his arms, raising them up, bringing them wide, slamming them down.

He speaks with lots of energy, never stopping. He reminds me of Pastor Clark back home.

I listen but only kind of.

Behind him are windows facing the courtyard where we have Supervised Outdoor Activities. Sunlight streams in and hits him from behind, covering him completely, reflecting off the pulpit, making long shadows.

I stare hard as he speaks. Light shines through the blond hairs on his arms. It almost looks like his body is glowing.

My eyes move along his arm, across his bicep. Up to his shoulder, where it meets his neck. Farther up to his ears, where his sandy hair turns gold in the sunlight.

My heart's beating faster and I realize I'm thinking of Sean.

I look away, fast. At a point on the pew in front of me.

My hands find the rubber band on my wrist and I pull on it, as far as it will go, and snap it. And again. And again.

Timothy is next to me. He looks over at the sound and then back to the front just as quick.

I stop and rub my wrist, still looking at the pew, now hearing nothing of what Pastor Landis is saying.

When I finally look down, I see the small welt on my wrist.

It's nothing. I'm fine.

I'm fine.

* * *

Jesse says, Have you had any incidents since yesterday?

He asks this every day. Always the same word too.

Incidents.

I look down like I always do, picking at my nails.

We're in a small room, just the two of us. One-on-One counseling. Our two chairs are in the middle, facing each other. A dozen more are stacked against the wall behind him. The carpet is light blue. Thin and plain, but new and clean.

He says, Michael?

I look up. He's only called me Michael a couple times and it sounds weird, but I don't think he means it in a mean way. Like when Victor calls me Mikey.

I blink and I feel my ears grow a bit warm at this thought of Victor.

Jesse's still looking at me.

I say, Yes.

Quietly but it still sounds loud.

Jesse only raises his eyebrows, just a bit.

Then he says, When?

I say, At sermon last night.

He says, Who were you thinking of?

I take a breath and I say, Sean. From back home.

Jesse's eyes flick to my wrist. Just a quick moment, less than a second. Without thinking I move it away.

He says, Sean's the one you . . .

He pauses for a moment, trying to think how to say it. I shift in my seat.

He says, . . . the one your parents found out about.

I say, He was the only one. There wasn't anyone else.

It comes out quick, defensive.

Jesse only nods.

He says, What were you thinking of right before Sean?

I say, I was watching the sermon. Watching the sun shine through the window behind Pastor Landis.

Jesse frowns.

He says, Why would that make you think of Sean?

I shrug, looking down again.

I say, I don't know. It was shining right behind him and I could see his outline and just suddenly I was thinking of Sean.

There's a long wait this time. Jesse looks at me, just looks. I'm still looking down, but I can feel the stare.

When it's gone on so long that I almost can't stand it anymore, he says,

Mike?

I don't look up but I'm still, really still.

He says, Do you want to stop having these thoughts?

Before I even think about it I say, Yes.

The word hangs in the air.

But then I do think about it and realize I mean it.

Jesse nods again. But then he smiles.

Just a bit.

He says, Let's get Pastor Landis in here.

* * *

The door makes a loud, satisfying click when it shuts. Through it I can hear Jesse's footsteps getting softer and farther away.

Pastor Landis sits in the other chair now, facing me, hands clasped in his lap. I look at the gold hairs on his wrists surrounding the bands of his watch.

He says, Hi, Mike.

I look up and see the small friendly smile he always has.

I mumble, Hi.

He smiles a bit more, then glances at his clasped hands for a second before looking back up.

He says, I'd like to try something with you.

I say, Okay.

He keeps looking at me with his small friendly smile, and I start wondering if he's expecting me to say something.

Then he says, We're going to practice hugging today.

There's a beat and then I say, Hugging.

Pastor Landis chuckles and leans back, holding his palms out to me.

He says, I know, I know. It sounds weird. But hear me out.

He leans forward again and says, It's based on the theory behind something called touch therapy, which has actually been around for a while.

I say, Touch therapy?

Pastor Landis looks at me for a bit, as if he's trying to decide how to explain this.

Then he says, Mike, do you know why you have same-sex attractions?

I think about this for a long time. I guess I can't remember the first time it happened, but I can remember the first time I noticed.

It was back home in Sheboygan Falls, in the summer between fourth and fifth grade. My friend Nick and I were playing around in our neighborhood pool, and we were both trying to dunk each other, and Nick grabbed me from behind and fell backward into the water, putting all his strength into it. All the laughter and screams and splash sounds cut out as we both went underwater. And then I felt his chest against my back, and suddenly I stopped fighting against him. I just stopped, feeling him pressed against me. It only lasted a moment. Then it was over and we both were above water and went back to playing around.

When I got home after, I sat quiet in my room for a long time. I started remembering other times, started thinking for the first time what it meant. Mom came in at one point and asked if everything was okay, and I just said, Sure, Mom.

I think of it now and it makes me think of Sean, of Mill Point Beach, of that night before the sunrise.

I look up at Pastor Landis and say, I don't know. It's been that way for a while.

He nods and says, That's the case for most of us.

Then he looks into my eyes and says, Are you close with your father?

The question's really unexpected and I'm not sure how to respond.

I say, What do you mean?

He says, Well, do you get along easily?

I say, Sometimes.

I pick at my nails.

I say, Not really.

He nods again and says, Is he a bit distant?

I say, Distant?

He says, Emotionally.

I think I know what this means, but I don't really know how to tell if Dad is emotionally distant because I don't know what that would look like or not look like. I think about Terry's dad, who is nice and polite and easy to laugh but still seems kind of like he's faking it. Then I think of Ronald's mom. I know she's a mom and not a dad, but she and Ronald are pretty close. Close in a way Dad and me aren't.

Pastor Landis probably sees that I'm having a hard time with this because then he asks,

Okay. Do you see him laugh a lot?

I say, Not really.

He says, Is he affectionate?

I blink. I say, No.

He says, Do you wonder whether he loves you?

I say, No. I know he loves me.

I clear my throat.

He says, How do you know?

I shift in my seat. These questions are weird.

I say, I dunno. He cares how well I'm doing at school. He's my dad, he loves me.

Pastor Landis nods. He says, And he brought you here, which shows just how much he really does love you. But does he tell you that, regularly and often?

I blink again. I say, No. Not really.

He nods more, like he was expecting this.

He says, And does he hug you?

I say, Not . . . not a lot.

Pastor Landis leans back again. He says, Touch is very important to a man's development. I know it may sound odd, but we all need affection and direct love from our fathers when young in order to fully develop and grow into healthy adults.

I just look at him.

He says, As children, especially very young children, we naturally crave that touch and affection from a father figure. And without it, we never learn how to process touch from a man, how to differentiate between nonsexual and sexual touch. So our adolescent minds become confused. And once puberty hits, we're still craving that touch, but now there's a sexual component to it. That's what's happening with you now, and that's what we're here to fix.

I don't say anything.

He says, All right, let's stand up.

Pastor Landis rises, swinging his arms a little as he does it.

I hesitate a bit, but then get out of my chair slowly.

He says, What we need to do here is teach you to accept nonsexual touch from a man, and hugging is a great way to learn it. It's a natural, platonic form of affection, and it's something that can be shared between men without awkwardness. And it makes you feel good!

He chuckles a bit at this last part.

He says, Okay! Let's try it out.

He holds his arms out, waiting.

I take a moment, then reach out, moving slowly toward him. I bring my arms around him, and just when I realize I'm trying not to touch him, he closes his arms around me and pulls me forward. I wait a second, then slowly press my arms against his back.

We're hugging.

He's a bit taller than me, so my face is pressed to the side against his shoulder. I catch a faint whiff of shaving cream. His sweater is itchy and a bit warm, made warmer by the heat coming from his body. Through my shirt I can feel his hands moving very slowly up and down my back. I try to picture what it looks like from the side, and I think of the way people hug when they haven't seen each other in years, or when someone dies.

I'm extremely aware of every point where our bodies are touching and realize I'm not moving at all.

He takes a deep breath and lets it out through his nose. I feel it on the back of my shoulder.

Very quietly, he says, Good, good. Concentrate on the

feeling of being in another man's arms. Concentrate on the platonic nature of the hug—how it could be a close buddy or a family member. Close your eyes and imagine it's your father giving you this hug. It feels different than a hug from your mother—stronger, more powerful, more masculine. A different kind of affection, but still a parent's love.

I'm barely breathing.

He whispers, I'd like us to hold this position for a few minutes.

And we do.

Only a couple minutes into it, my arms are tired from holding them still against his back. My feet ache from standing in place. It's hard to breathe from having my face against his shoulder, and my neck is starting to cramp. I feel every one of his breaths against my left shoulder. My nose itches.

It goes on forever. I don't know what I'm supposed to be feeling, but all I can think about is how I want it to stop.

And then, after about five minutes, Pastor Landis whispers,

Okay, I think that's good for now.

I let go right away. My face and arms feel cool suddenly as the air hits a thin layer of sweat. I take in a large breath.

He says, That wasn't bad for a first run.

I say, First?

He nods and says, I think we should have a few more of these, once or twice each day.

I stare at him. I don't want to do this again. All I want is to get out of this room.

Pastor Landis says, It's going to take some practice for your body to react to this kind of touch in the appropriate way, out of habit. Remember, we're trying to get you to unlearn behavior that's been with you for years.

I don't say anything.

He says, We'll try again tomorrow, and try to go for longer with each one. I want you to be able to hug for at least twenty minutes, uninterrupted.

I can't imagine doing this for twenty minutes. I'm trying to think of what to say.

He puts a hand on my shoulder and rests it there.

He says, We can beat this, Mike.

He leaves his hand on my shoulder and smiles.

I just stare at him.

We stand there like that for a while.

Then the thumb of his hand rubs into my shoulder, lightly. He just smiles.

My heart starts beating a little faster.

He smiles a bit wider. Just a bit. He doesn't take his eyes off mine. His thumb just rubs my shoulder, right at the base of my neck.

Neither of us moves for a few more moments. I notice I'm holding my breath.

Then Pastor Landis's smile starts to fade. He pats my shoulder and then glances away as he lets his arm drop.

He says, Why don't you get down to Outdoor Activities. I'll see you again, same time tomorrow.

He walks to the door, opens it, and leaves.

I stand there by myself for a few seconds, staring at the door. My heart is still pounding. I realize I'm breathing a bit deeply, through my nose.

Then I open the door and walk out.

But I head right down the hallway, instead of left toward the courtyard.

I don't really know what I'm doing or why, but a moment later I walk into my and Timothy's room.

I close the door behind me and walk over to Timothy's bed and sit down.

There's a minute where I just sit like that, looking at a spot on the carpet. I don't even know if I blink. But I guess I probably do.

Then I get up and walk back to the door, and then I just stop.

My hand is on the doorknob. I'm supposed to go to my group.

But something keeps me there, and a minute later I'm pulling my clothes out of the dresser, putting what I can into my backpack. Not really looking, just grabbing the few things I have here and stuffing them all in.

There's too many clothes for just the backpack, so most of my stuff stays in the closet. But I don't really care.

I shove the backpack into the corner of my closet, then take one last look into the mirror. I look normal enough. I try to smooth down my hair, then head out.

No one seems to think much of me being late to Outdoor Activities. The counselors know I was with Pastor Landis. I wonder if they told the other kids.

Timothy gives me a look from across the courtyard. I can't read his face.

I spend the time walking around the fence. Shoulders hunched against the wind. Head down.

Timothy leaves the bathroom in his pajamas and I go in to change.

I keep my regular clothes on under my pajamas and look at myself in the mirror.

I look a bit bulky but not too bad.

Just in case I turn off the light before I leave the bathroom, so it's dark as I get into bed.

Timothy says, Good night.

I pull the covers up over me and say Good night back. It's hot but I wait.

It's a while but finally Timothy's breathing gets deeper and deeper, longer pauses between each one.

I wait another thirty minutes to make sure. Staring up at the ceiling. I worry about falling asleep but I'm too nervous to sleep anyway.

Finally I pull the covers down.

Slowly.

I sit up in bed and swing my legs over. My feet find the floor.

I stay in this position for a minute, totally still, listening.

There's no change to Timothy's breathing so I stand up. I take my pajamas off, and am in my shirt and pants, and put my shoes on. Then my jacket from the closet.

I put the backpack on.

Before I leave I look at Timothy. He's still breathing deep.

Quietly I open the door, slip out, and close it behind me.

I look up and down the hallway. The lights are on, but there's no one there.

I don't know what kind of security they have here. I mean I know there's always someone at the front desk of the dorm building and I think sometimes counselors keep an eye on the hallways, but I don't know if they have cameras or alarms or anything.

But there's no one here right now, so I walk quickly to the stairwell at the end of the hall and down a couple flights.

I peek through the small window of the stairwell door on the first floor. I can sort of see part of the lobby. I wait awhile and I don't see anything, so I crack the door open and listen.

I can't hear anything.

I open the door and slip through.

The guy at the desk can't see me from his position.

He has his head resting on one hand, but I can't tell if he's asleep or not.

I wait a long time and there's no movement. I try walking a couple steps.

Then he suddenly moves and I freeze.

He shifts his head to his other hand, then he's still again.

I don't know what to do.

But a minute later, he stands suddenly and walks off and into the hallway on the other side that I know leads to the bathrooms.

I stare at the hallway as he disappears into it, my heart hammering. I hear a doorknob click open, a pause, and it closes.

Then I run.

I run through the front door and outside. There's no alarm.

I keep running.

FIFTEEN

I don't know how long it'll take for them to realize I'm gone.

I think about this a lot while I walk down the highway.

Timothy never really wakes up during the night, but he does get up earlier than me. Like five thirty.

So I guess that'll probably be when they notice.

I'm walking along the highway in the direction I know is home. I know it's home because I remember coming this way when we drove in.

But also because I passed a sign saying this was U.S. 58 East, and east means home.

It's almost one in the morning now. I've been walking for more than two hours. At a pretty good pace too, which means I guess six miles or so.

The math worries me a bit. It took about an hour and a half to drive to InnerPeace from home. That's like ninety miles.

And I'm going three miles an hour.

It's pretty cold out. And I'm tired.

Finally I stop. Just on the shoulder of the highway and listen.

A car passes by going the opposite direction.

I look off to my right, into the trees, and shiver. It's dark and cold, and I wonder if it's safe to sleep there. But there isn't any shelter anywhere and I'm tired. I start thinking about how long it'll take to walk all the way home, with no food or money and then what if it starts snowing or something?

While I'm thinking about all this, I hear the car that passed by slow down. I glance over my shoulder.

It does a wide U-turn across the short grass median and gets into the rightmost lane, and starts driving slowly toward me.

I turn toward it but back away, toward the trees. I wonder if the headlights ever caught me.

Red and blue lights start flashing from the top of the car, and my heart skips.

I say, Shit.

To myself.

Another light turns on, bright and white and solid, from the roof. It turns toward me and holds me in place. My eyes sting. I blink and shield my face with my arm.

The police car pulls up beside me. On the side in big letters, it says VIRGINIA STATE POLICE.

I just stare at it, through the open passenger-side window into the space where the driver would be. I can see the silhouette of a man wearing a wide-brimmed hat.

Nothing happens for a second. The silhouette doesn't move. Behind him the asphalt glows red then blue then red.

Then the man says, Well, hey there.

I jump, just barely. The voice is higher and louder and more chipper than I was expecting. The officer has a pretty thick southern accent. For just a second I think about Ronald, then I mumble,

Hey.

The man opens the door and steps out, taking his time, and walks around the front of the car to my side of it. He keeps his eyes on me and his right hand on the butt of his gun. When he's a few feet away, he stops. I can only sort of see his face.

He says, Can't sleep?

I blink twice.

He waits a bit, then sighs.

He says, How old are you?

I say, Eighteen.

He says, How old are you?

I glance away and say, Fifteen.

He nods.

He says, What are you doing out here in the middle of nowhere, son?

I say, Going home.

He says, Going home.

He says it back slowly, like he's thinking about what it means or something.

Then he says, Okay. Listen, I'm gonna pat you down a sec. Just for my protection, you understand?

I nod. He still sounds kind of chipper.

He says, You're not gonna give me any trouble, are ya?

I say, No sir.

He says, I'm not gonna find any weapons or controlled substances, am I?

I say, No sir.

He says, All right. Put your arms out at your sides for me.

He walks over slowly, keeping his eyes on mine.

His hands pat gently along my arms, then my sides and waist, then down each leg.

Then he takes a step back and seems to relax a bit. He takes his hat off, and for the first time I get a good look at his face. He's younger than I thought. Maybe Jesse's age.

He says, I'm Trooper Manske.

I nod but I don't say anything.

He says, What's your name? You can put your arms down.

I let my arms drop. I say, Mike.

He says, Mike what?

I open my mouth, wait for a second, and say, Pilsner.

I don't know why I pick Ronald's last name, but I don't want to give him my real one.

He says, Had to think about that, huh?

I don't say anything.

He says, You have any identification? Learner's permit, maybe?

I say, No, I only just turned fifteen a couple weeks ago.

He says, Happy birthday.

I mumble a thanks.

Trooper Manske turns his head and looks down the highway as another car passes by. Then he turns back to me.

He says, So you're going home, huh?

I say, Yessir.

He says, You're a ways from the nearest town.

I don't say anything.

He says, Where is home?

I glance away and say, Somerdale.

Trooper Manske looks down and lets out a long, slow breath through his nose.

Then he looks up.

He says, What are you doing out this far?

I'm not sure what to say. I don't want to mention the camp because then he'll just take me back. But I can't think of another reason to be out here that sounds believable.

He says, You run away, son?

I look up and say, Yes. I ran away.

He says, How long ago?

I'm stuck again. I couldn't have made it this far away from Somerdale on foot.

Then I say, A couple hours ago. I hitchhiked.

Trooper Manske raises his eyebrows. He just looks at me for a few seconds.

He says, You hitchhiked?

His voice is a little clipped.

I say, Yeah.

He says, Who picked you up?

I say, I don't know. Some guy.

He says, What did he look like?

I say, I don't know. Medium height I guess. Brown hair. Not too old. Like my dad's age, maybe.

I'm wondering if my voice is steady enough and if Trooper Manske can tell I'm lying.

He says, What was he driving?

I say, Um, a pickup.

He says, What color?

I say, Blue.

He says, What make and model?

I say, I don't know. I wasn't really paying attention.

He says, Why'd he drop you off?

I blink a few times.

I say, Um, I asked him to. I didn't want to go any farther.

He says, Why not?

I say, I . . . changed my mind. About running away.

He says, What accent is that?

I say, What?

He says, Your accent. You didn't grow up around here, right?

I say, Oh. No. We moved from Wisconsin.

I try to cover my accent and am glad when I don't hear it in the last few words. It comes out sometimes when I'm nervous and I don't really like it.

Trooper Manske nods, then leans back against his car door.

He says, Look, son, what you did was just incredibly dangerous. I haven't been doing this long and I've already heard horror stories about what's happened to some hitchhikers, 'specially kids. You don't wanna know what some crazies are capable of, okay? There are some real messed-up folks out there.

I nod.

He says, You gotta never do that again, no matter how bad things get at home, okay?

I nod.

He gives me sort of a sideways look.

He says, How bad are things at home?

I don't answer.

He says, You're not gettin' hurt or anything, are you?

I say, No.

He says, Why'd you run away?

I don't know what to say. Then it comes out:

My dad left. It's just me and my mom and my brother.

I think about Ronald and his mom and feel awful. But I didn't know what else to say.

Trooper Manske stares at me awhile longer with that sideways look.

Then he says, Okeydoke. Let's give your mama a call.

I say, No.

I blurt it out.

He raises his eyebrows at me but chuckles.

He says, Son, I gotta call her and let her know you're all right. And then I'm taking you home.

I just stare back at him.

He pulls a cell phone out of his belt clip and says, Now, what's your home number?

I take a deep breath, and I give him Ronald's number. I know it by heart.

He says, Area code seven-five-seven?

I nod.

He dials really slow, then puts the phone up to his ear and turns a little to the side. I hear it ring for a good while. My mouth is really dry.

The fifth ring cuts off in the middle, and a tiny voice comes through the speaker.

Trooper Manske says, Sorry to disturb you so late at night, ma'am. Am I speaking to Miz Pilsner?

He pauses.

He says, Ma'am, this is Trooper Gil Manske with the Virginia State Police. I don't mean to alarm you, but I have your son Mike in my custody. Now, he's not in any harm and has not been arrested. But I did find him walking along the side of the highway a good ways from Somerdale.

He says he hitchhiked out of town about two hours ago. Runnin' away from home. Were you aware of this?

There's a long, long pause. My heart is beating really fast. I'm trying to imagine what Ronald's mom is thinking.

Then I hear the tiny voice again. I can't make out what she's saying.

Trooper Manske glances at me, then says, Yes'm, that's right. He's completely unhurt, but I have to say that's a heck of a lucky break for you both.

Another pause.

He says, No, that's fine, ma'am. I'm going to bring him home now. Seems he was headin' that way anyways.

Pause.

He says, All right, ma'am. Sorry again to wake you.

He looks back at me as he pulls the phone from his ear and hangs up with his thumb. The phone lets out a little beep. I realize I've been holding my breath and let it out slowly.

He says, She was still asleep, so didn't have a chance to be worried out her mind. Good for her.

I nod. I'm trying not to look nervous or give anything away, but I end up just blinking a lot. Trooper Manske looks at me a bit longer, then shakes his head.

He says, All right, get in.

I've never been in a police car before.

There's a small laptop sitting on a built-in platform thing. It's open now and swiveled toward the driver's seat.

Under it are a bunch of controls and then a radio. From the radio I can hear a dispatcher talking in codes every now and then, and then crackles from other officers' voices. It's kind of neat, I guess.

Trooper Manske drives faster than I really expected. He doesn't have his lights or siren on, though.

He speaks into the radio every now and then, but I don't really pay attention to what he's saying. After a bit he turns it down.

He glances over at me and says, Are you hungry? When's the last time you ate?

I say, Uh, I guess. Yeah. Dinner was at like six o'clock.

He waves his right hand at the dashboard in front of me and says, There's some granola bars in the glove. Have a couple.

I open it. There are papers and a car manual and a small can of pepper spray and a bunch of granola bars all stuffed in. I take one out. The wrapper says OATS AND HONEY.

It's crunchy and a bit messy, but I try to be careful not to leave crumbs. It's not bad, and after I finish it I reach in the glove compartment and take out another. My mouth is a little dry afterward but I feel better.

I say, Thanks, Trooper Manske.

He waves the thanks away.

We sit in silence for a bit. I listen to the crackles over the police radio and think about Ronald's mom. I don't know if she's going to be pissed. I'll probably get to their house after two in the morning. It's Friday night, but

256

Ronald says sometimes she works on Saturdays. I hope she's not going to work in the morning.

But she did play along and pretend to be my mom. She lied to a cop for me. The thought makes me smile just a bit. I like Ronald's mom.

I wonder what will happen when I get there. Will she let me stay over or just take me home?

That thought makes my stomach a little uneasy and I shift in my seat. Dad's going to be pissed no matter what. And there are still a couple weeks left in the camp, so he'll probably just take me back. I'll have to go back to Small Groups and sleeping in a dorm with Timothy and probably more of those hugging sessions. And Pastor Landis.

But maybe Mrs. Pilsner will just let me stay at their house for two weeks. Then I could lay low and only go home when it's too late for the camp.

Then I remember that the camp counselors will notice in the morning that I'm gone, and they'll probably call my parents. And the police. And then I wonder if I'll get in trouble for lying to a cop. And then wouldn't Ronald's mom get in trouble too? Like would they arrest her?

I'm thinking about all this when Trooper Manske says, So, Somerdale, huh? You know that kid?

He says it slowly, in a low voice.

I blink a few times, trying to think what he could mean, and turn to him.

I say, Huh?

He glances at me a second, then looks back at the road.

He says, From over the weekend.

I blink again, not sure what to say.

He glances over at me again and says, You did hear about it, right? It was all over the news. They musta mentioned it at your school.

I cough and say, Oh. Yeah, I heard about it. Um, what was his name again?

Trooper Manske shakes his head and says, Don't remember. A few in our unit responded to it. Happened actually just a little ways up. But I was patrolling farther out west.

I say, Oh.

I look outside the window for a while, then turn back to the front.

I say, Um. So what happened?

I hope it sounds casual enough. Trooper Manske flicks another glance at me.

I say, They didn't really go into detail at school.

He nods and says, Yeah, not surprised.

He pauses a bit, and his voice gets lower again.

He says, Couple of squad cars were called to an accident on the westbound lanes of Highway 58, about twenty miles outside of Suffolk. Not long after one o'clock in the morning. Pretty clear right away that the vehicle had been going very fast when it spun out of control.

He's driving with one hand on the steering wheel. He brings the other up to his mouth and coughs lightly, then continues.

He says, There were some tire track marks at the scene that showed the driver had veered into the grassy median, then turned sharply right to correct his course. But he overcompensated, which caused the car to flip over several times.

I look out the window again.

He says, During the flip, the roof of the car hit the trunk of a tree so hard that it bent the car nearly in half.

I watch the silhouettes of trees zipping by and try to picture a car hitting one hard enough that it actually bends in half. Wouldn't the tree break? But if the trunk was thick enough, maybe it wouldn't. I shudder a bit, just barely.

Trooper Manske says, They found a bunch of empty cans of Heineken in the car and scattered around the crash site.

My heart skips a beat. I look over at the trooper.

I say, Huh?

He says, Heineken beer. Eight empty cans, I think, still wet. Handful of others that were leaking, having been punctured during the crash. Seems a pretty sure thing the driver was intoxicated at the time of the accident.

My heart starts beating faster.

He pauses and says, Quite intoxicated.

I stare at him, waiting for him to go on. My mouth is really dry. When he doesn't say anything for a while, I say, So what happened?

Trooper Manske takes a deep breath and lets it out in a sigh.

He says, The kid's parents reported that he had been having some sort of trouble in his personal life the last couple weeks and seemed depressed. They were not aware that he had access to alcohol and didn't keep any in the house themselves.

I'm breathing pretty fast through my nose, but I'm trying to do it quietly.

I stare at the dashboard for a few seconds. There's a bit of dust buildup in the air-conditioning vent. I reach forward and run a finger between two of the slats and hold it up to my face for a few moments. Then I roll the gray fluff into a little ball and flick it away. I put my hand back on my thigh.

I say, So what happened? To the kid?

It comes out rushed.

Trooper Manske looks over at me again, then back to the road.

He says, The driver was thrown from the car during the accident, most likely while the car was flipping. He was not wearing his seat belt. Officers found him just on the shoulder of the highway, ninety feet west of where his car came to rest.

I blink once. My elbow sticks to the leather seat and I pry it off, then rest it back in place.

He says, It appeared that his head struck the road with some force. There isn't an autopsy report yet, but he probably died instantly.

I notice I've been holding my breath. I let it out slowly, through my nose. I look carefully at the curvy shape of the side-view mirror and think about how there are no straight lines. In the reflection I can only see bare shadows, trees gliding by, too blurred to make out.

I say, Died.

He says, Oh yes. It woulda been real difficult to survive an accident like that, especially with no seat belt.

I dig my fingers into my thighs. I count each point of pressure from my nails, going right to left and then back. There's a lump under my chin. My eyes feel dry and I keep blinking.

He says, It's lucky there wasn't anyone else on the road at the time. It's awful, but coulda been much worse with the drinking.

I'm barely aware that his voice is back to normal. I dig my nails farther into my thighs. A small crumb of granola bar resting on the inside seam of my jeans falls in between my legs.

I say, And you don't remember his name?

Trooper Manske shakes his head slowly. He says, Nah. I'd probably recognize it if I heard it again, but otherwise I'd have to look it up.

He waves his free hand at the laptop.

He says, Just don't wanna do that while driving.

I look at the back of the laptop, at the rounded corners and flat gray casing. There's a Dell logo imprinted in the middle. I look at the upturned *E* of the logo, and tilt my head a bit until it becomes a blocky *W.*

My heart's beating fast. I think about what would happen if I said a name out loud and jogged Trooper Manske's memory.

I open my mouth slowly. The dryness makes my lips stick together just a bit. I lick them.

I turn back to the front and stare at a spot on the windshield where some dried crud has collected outside the reach of the wipers. Through it the road looks a little bit darker.

I want this moment of not knowing to last a little longer, but my heart's beating too fast.

So I ask.

SIXTEEN

I'm three. It's summer in Milwaukee and the day has been hot and dry and long, all ending now. The sunlight comes in at a slant, shining from Big City to my side and crashing into the lake on my other side. It looks like fire.

I know it's Lake Michigan, that's what Daddy says, but we're not in Michigan so I don't get why it's not Lake Wisconsin.

I think about this and then look up at Mommy and Daddy, both of them holding my hands, and I say, Do it, pull me up! You both now!

Daddy grins down at me and counts, and I count along because I learned how, it's one, two, THREE, and they both pull and my feet leave the ground, I'm Superman and I'm flying now and laughing, and they're laughing too.

* * *

I'm seven, sitting on the swing at recess.

I'm just sitting, not swinging, not 'cause I'm scared —
I'm not scared, I just like to sit sometimes.

Travis is running around the blacktop playing tag. I'm
watching him, his light blond hair and green eyes. We're
okay-friends. He invited me to play, but I wanted to sit
and watch them and not swing.

But I only watch Travis.

I'm ten and it's summer in Sheboygan Falls.

The pool opened yesterday and it's crowded today, all
the kids from town are here, and there's a game of Marco
Polo going on but me and my friend Nick, we're not
playing.

We're standing in the main part, not the deep end.
The water's four feet and it comes to my chin.

Nick splashes me and I splash him back and he laughs
and disappears underwater while I wipe my eyes.

I look around for him and then I know what's coming
right before it happens. He grabs me from the back in a
wrestle hold.

I laugh-scream and fight against him but it's no
use, he's stronger than me and I hold my breath right
before he pulls me under.

For a second he's holding me there underwater and I
can feel his heartbeat on my back, and for just that second
I stop fighting against him.

Then he lets go and we both go back to the surface and I splash him right as he comes up.

I'm twelve. The church vents blow cool air over us, a break from the summer outside.

Another major heat wave washing over the Midwest, over one hundred degrees. News stories every few days about an old couple dying in their homes, Mom shaking her head and clicking her tongue at each one.

The preacher talks about hellfire, and I can feel it trying to get in from just beyond the great double doors, the windows, the heavy stone walls.

He talks about hell and how to get there, this place where you have no family or friends, no love, no happiness, nothing but the rest of eternity before you, on and on forever, and for the first time I wonder where I'm gonna go when I die, if I'll be with Toby and Mom and Dad or on my own.

For the first time the preacher's words aren't just words but something that makes me uneasy.

The heat rises from the asphalt as we walk back to the car, making everything shimmer, the fire from below coming to get me, trying to break out of the earth and reach me, grab me, pull me down, claim me.

I'm thirteen and in Green Bay again, just me and Dad. First game of the season. He's taken me once a year for the past few years.

We're right in the middle of the field in one of the first few rows. They're about the best seats in the whole place. Dad's told me a hundred times.

I look around and around at the huge stadium, at the thousands of people all dressed in green and gold, not really paying attention to the game.

Then I look back down at the sidelines, at one of the football players who's running off the field.

He takes off his helmet and wipes sweat off his head, but his hair is still wet and stuck together. It's hot to be running around.

He sits on a bench. His jersey clings to his shoulder pads and back, bare arms shining with sweat, biceps bulging as he wipes his face again with a towel.

Dad shouts and stands up suddenly with the rest of the fans, startling me. Something happened in the game and I try to follow along. But after a minute or two, I look back at the football player.

I'm fourteen and me and Toby are sitting on the couch, listening, Dad with his serious face on, Mom wringing her hands nervously.

We're going away from Wisconsin to live on the East Coast—it's Virginia and there's a beach near our new house and won't that be nice?

I think about my friend Nick. Nick who I probably won't see again.

There are other friends I have, better and closer

friends, friends I hang out with all the time, not just once every few weeks or sometimes months like Nick.

But it's Nick who I'm thinking about, not them.

I'm almost fifteen and it's not summer anymore.

It's a late fall night in Somerdale, Virginia, unusually warm, and the wet wind is blowing in from the Atlantic, forming small dunes on Mill Point Beach.

I'm sitting in front of one of these dunes and I can't see anything. I can feel the wind and hear the water and that's it.

Then the first crack of light: blue.

It keeps coming as the sun rises, colors coming in one after another, running into each other, carving out the land around us from black to light, and now I turn and I can see his face finally, light brown skin reflecting the orange and red and blue and pink and pink and pink.

Sean looks back at me and now, in that whirlwind of colors, the green of his eyes is the strongest, brightest, clearest.

He smiles and his hand closes over my fingers.

Trooper Manske taps my shoulder and says, Hey.

I blink and look over at him.

He says, You're home, son.

I turn my head to the right. The car's stopped. There are lights on in Ronald's house. I can't remember the last few minutes.

The front door opens while we're still walking up the porch. There's a bit of a cold breeze. My hair waves in it and tickles my forehead.

Ronald's mom steps outside. She's wearing white sweats and a light blue hoodie that's too big for her. She hugs herself tight as we walk up to the door. Ronald is behind her.

Trooper Manske spins his hat in his hand. Mrs. Pilsner's arm snakes around my shoulders. She squeezes tight and nods while he talks. I don't really listen but this is what I hear:

side of the shoulder

hitchhiked

so relieved

kid's lucky

I know it

dangerous

keep an eye

won't file a report

thank you

okay, thank you

I stare at the police car behind the trooper, at the dark street behind the car, and I don't say anything.

He taps my shoulder again.

I look up but it's not Trooper Manske.

I say, Ronald.

Ronald is looking at me, but I've never seen his expression like this. His eyebrows are scrunched together. There

268

are two small vertical lines between them, like a sideways equals sign.

I say, Where's Trooper Manske?

Ronald says, He left a few minutes ago, dude.

He says it quiet, not like his normal voice.

I notice that I'm sitting at Ronald's kitchen table. I look down at the surface. It's a light orangey wood color. There are no place mats. Right near my hand is an old ring mark, fat on one end, almost a full circle. Next to that is a glass of water. A drop of condensation makes its way down the side, slowing and then speeding up. I watch it.

For just a second, I get an image in my head: me at the computer, my fingers hovering above the keyboard, thinking how to word what I want to say. I push the thought out of my head as fast and hard as I can. The last thing I see before it goes is the N key partly covered by my thumb.

I look back up. Ronald's mom is standing in the doorway of the kitchen. Just past her I can see the front door, closed.

I say, Did you get in trouble? For lying?

She looks at me a bit before she shakes her head once.

I reach out for the water and take a long sip. It's just barely too cold.

I say, Sorry to make you get up. Do you work tomorrow?

She hugs herself tight again and nods.

I say, The police car was neat.

She says, Mike.

I say, The inside, I mean. It had a radio where we could hear the dispatcher. And a whole laptop. And there was a can of pepper spray.

She says, Mike.

I say, Are you going to call my parents?

She pulls at the sleeve of her hoodie.

She says, Not tonight.

I nod and say, Cool. Thanks. I heard about Sean.

No one says anything. Then the lights flicker for just a second as the heater turns on. I listen to the hum of the fan as it picks up speed and trace the water ring on the table with my finger.

Mrs. Pilsner walks over and sits down at the table near me. She looks at me for a while. I'm watching the tabletop.

She says, Mike.

I say, What.

She says, Mike, do your parents know where you are?

She knows the answer already so I don't lie. My eyes are on a fixed point, a turn of the grain in the wood, when I shake my head slowly.

She says, When did you leave the . . . the place?

I didn't know how much she or Ronald knew about where I've been, but I can tell by the way she asks this that they know something. I'm not that surprised. I mean I haven't been at school for a couple weeks.

I say, Ten thirty.

Barely a whisper.

She nods, waiting a second, hesitating.

She says, Hon, I'll have to tell them you're here. The place will call them when they see that you're missing, and your parents will be out of their minds worrying.

It's like she's pleading with me, asking me to understand. I feel a rush of affection for her and glance up just for a second.

I nod.

She says, But we'll do that tomorrow morning. You sleep here tonight, okay?

I nod.

She looks at the clock and says, It'll only be a few hours, I know. But better than nothing.

She turns back to me. She looks like she's about to say something, trying to decide how to start.

Finally she just asks, Are you hungry?

I nod.

She says, Okay, babe, we made some spaghetti tonight so I'll heat some up.

I nod.

She doesn't get up.

Ronald is still standing to my side. She looks at him a second and then says, Mike.

I say, Yeah.

She says, Sean . . .

I stare at the wood.

She takes a breath and then says, I'm so, so sorry about Sean.

I don't say anything.

She says, And I'm so sorry you had to find out about it the way you did.

I run my finger over the wood again.

She says, There is nothing—*nothing*—about this whole thing that is fair, or right, or even remotely okay, and what you've been through and what happened to that poor kid are the worst parts.

I don't say anything.

She says, Listen to me, Mike.

I stop moving.

She says, Listen to me.

I look up. She's leaning forward a bit, looking right at me.

She says, You did nothing wrong. Ever, in any of this.

I blink.

She says, Do you understand? Sean's death is . . .

She stops. She looks down at her lap, lips pressed.

She looks back up at me.

She says, Sean's death is on his parents. Not on you.

I blink a few more times. My hand is shaking a bit.

She says, And what you've been through, all that bullshit shame and that—that despicable place they sent you, that is on *your* parents. Okay?

I can feel the first tears, white-hot and silent, burning.

She says, Mike, listen, at some point you have to tell them this yourself. It sucks and it's unfair, but people like your parents will keep shaming you until you stand up for yourself. There's only so much the rest of us can do.

272

I don't say anything.

She sighs. Then she says, But that's for tomorrow. For tonight, I just . . . I need you to understand that you have done nothing wrong.

I try to keep from crying. There's another flash in my mind, my thumb covering the N on my keyboard.

She says, Do you understand?

My hand is shaking harder. Mrs. Pilsner looks almost angry.

She says, Mike. Do you understand?

And she reaches out her hand and puts it over mine to stop it shaking.

I lose control and start crying harder. I nod.

She smiles for the first time. It's small but there.

She says. Okay. I'll heat up some spaghetti.

I sleep three hours.

It's still more than I expected.

At six in the morning there's a crack in the door to Ronald's room, light spilling in from the hallway around his mom's silhouette.

She whispers, Hon, it's time to get up.

I sit up in bed and blink a few times, letting my eyes and my brain adjust. Ronald is still totally asleep, stuffed in a sleeping bag on the carpet next to me. He let me have the bed.

I swing my legs over the side and get up.

* * *

Mrs. Pilsner waits until I'm done eating breakfast before she calls my parents. She says she wants to make sure I have time to eat, but I know there's more.

She takes the phone into her bedroom but I can still hear her voice, not quite a shout but something more than a calm conversation.

When she comes back out, holding the phone against her shoulder, the sweatshirt puffy and soft, she reaches out a hand, stops, then runs it through my hair. Her fingers are warm.

She says, I tried, baby, but they wanted to come get you right away. I can't blame them.

She turns and puts the phone in the cradle. As she walks back into her bedroom, she adds,

For that.

Ronald is next to me at the kitchen table. He hasn't said anything and I haven't looked at him and I don't know if I want to.

But then he says, Hey.

His voice is croaky and deep and he clears his throat.

He says, Are you coming back to school now?

I say to the table, I dunno. Maybe.

He lets that hang for a bit.

The clock on the wall ticks a few seconds.

He says, I'm sorry, dude.

It comes out so quiet I'm not sure I heard it. I look up.

For the first time I see the cut above his right eye. It's nearly healed.

Ronald's looking at me with the same weird expression he had last night, and suddenly I realize what it is. Because I saw it in his mom's face. They have the same crease in their brows.

I don't know what to say.

So I say, What happened to your eye?

He says, Victor.

I blink. I haven't heard the name in a long time and it takes me by surprise.

Then he says, I hit him first.

The serious face breaks just barely, enough for a bit of a smile.

Ronald raises his right fist.

He says, Knucks.

I stare at him, not understanding. Or maybe I do understand but pretend not to because it's such a dumb thing to say.

He says, Come on, dude. Knucks. We're bros, right?

Serious again.

I smile, slowly, for the first time in weeks, and then I fist-bump Ronald.

I step outside with Ronald's mom.

Mom and Dad are standing near the car, but they don't move. The engine is running.

I stare at them for a few seconds before I realize they're not looking at me; they're looking next to me. At Ronald's mom.

I turn my head slowly to look at her too. She's glaring at them, not hiding it.

I watch her for almost a minute, then turn back to my parents.

Dad's expression is almost as angry.

But Mom's is harder to read.

They don't say anything in the car on the way home.

Dad is angry, dangerous angry, I can tell by his silence.

Mom is crying so quietly into the arm of her cardigan.

I'm not thinking about either of them. I'm thinking about the house on Hyacinth Court, the red-brick house with the mound of weeds and shrubs and the blue Ford Bronco in the driveway.

Dad tells me to go to my room as soon as we get in. It comes out short and clipped, and I know he so badly wants to say more.

I turn to go without hesitating but then he stops me.

I look back around at him and his mouth is working. He's tapping his foot. It looks like he can't help unloading after all.

It comes in waves. The words start flowing together. I don't listen to any of it.

In the middle of a sentence, I just turn around again and walk up the stairs.

Dad's voice trails away but he's too surprised to react,

and before he can I close the door to my room, shutting him and Mom and everything out.

There's a light knock.

I know the knock, it's the same way she does it every time, so I don't ask who it is, I just open it.

Toby says, Hey.

Softer than her normal voice.

Then she rushes forward and hugs me. She holds tight.

She whispers, I'm so sorry.

And pulls back again. She lets her arms drop at her side.

I don't say anything, just look at her.

Toby says, I'm so glad you're back.

She looks at me for a while. Then turns and walks toward her room.

I watch her until she's inside, yellow light all around her.

She closes her door, and I close mine.

SEVENTEEN

Dad has gone back to talking as little as possible. Lunch on Saturday is silent.

Mom shoots quick glances at one or the other of us between bites, like she's wishing she could somehow fix what's broken.

I don't really care, though, and maybe that's what's so broken.

When I'm done I carry my dishes to the sink and go upstairs. I know Mom watches me go, I can feel it. I know Dad makes sure not to watch me, I can feel that too.

Back in my room. Sitting on the bed. Christmas vacation all over again.

Only not really. The window stays empty, no one left to wait outside. I don't look at it.

In my room I can feel something that's not really happy or even that okay, but at least isn't the empty dread I feel everywhere else. It lets me feel like everything is still controlled and contained.

My computer's sitting on my desk, monitor blank but not off, humming, waiting for me. I ignore it. When I look at it, all I think about is that last message I sent to Sean. So I don't look at it.

I don't leave my room until dinner, where all four of us act the same way we did at lunch. But I don't care.

I don't care.

Sunday morning feels exactly like Saturday morning.

I wake up on my own, sunlight pouring in.

It looks like this:

Old foggy light fixture. Two black smudges from light-bulb heat. Tiny specks, the shadows of dead dried-up bugs.

Four fake-wood fan blades stretching out, inch of dust at the tips, some strands dangling, about to drift away.

Metal beaded string hanging straight down, too high for me to reach anyway.

Ceiling. White, rough.

Perfect straight lines where it hits the walls.

All in that order.

That's kind of what I see every morning.

Mom and Dad are dressed up at breakfast. This morning is church. Dad in his suit as usual, Mom in a mostly black dress, which is unusual for her but still okay for church.

Dad didn't invite me and I'm not going to ask.

Even if he told me to go, I'd say no.

But he's not going to do that because there are friends of his there, lots of them, elders and deacons and the pastor. Everyone who by now has to know where I've been, why I'm back. Why Sean is —

I grip my spoon tight, tight, making the thought go away, breathing in deep through my nose and then out. I breathe carefully. After a second or two I'm back to normal.

My grip relaxes. Eyes flick to Toby and hers flick down, but I know she saw.

But she doesn't say anything and Mom and Dad don't notice and breakfast is as quiet as all of yesterday.

Toby isn't dressed, so even before they say a quick goodbye I know she's not going with them.

I'm still sitting at the kitchen table. Toby's standing at the entrance to the kitchen, watching Mom and Dad leave.

I breathe out but the breath back in doesn't come easy.

It's being outside my room. I want to get back.

Past Toby I can just see the tail of Dad's overcoat brushing the tile before the front door closes and he's shut out.

Before I can even stand up, Toby turns sharply around and looks at me.

She says, They're going to Sean's funeral after church.

She says it rushed and strong and a little defiant, like

she's daring the words not to come out but they don't even put up a fight. Her eyes are bright, satisfied.

I look back at her, letting what she said register.

Then I say, How do you know?

She says, They told me they'd be home late and they told me why. They told me I couldn't tell you.

That satisfied, defiant voice again.

I say, They?

She says, He.

My breaths are coming quicker now. The numb feeling is gone, or at least held back, replaced now by something much better, something that makes my heart beat fast.

I say, What time? Did they say?

She says, Just right after church.

I think this through quickly:

Service starts at nine o'clock. Over by ten. Chatting for about fifteen minutes but maybe they won't do that. Ten-minute drive to Forest Park Cemetery.

So to be safe, just a few minutes after ten o'clock.

Right now it's eight forty. Dad always likes to leave early.

Suddenly I have a lot of energy. The last thing I want is to be holed up in my room.

I stand up and run to the closet, grabbing my jacket. The cemetery is the most important thing in the world now and I'm hurrying, not able to stop myself but not wanting to anyway.

I mumble a quick thank-you to Toby and open the

front door wide and love the sound it makes when it slams behind me.

She watches me go but doesn't say anything because I'm being driven by this new in-charge feeling, and she knows it because she feels the same thing every day.

It's finally cold, not just chilly but sharp cold.

I mean the walk from the InnerPeace camp felt cold but only because I was outside for a long time. Now it's actual cold.

I love it. I tilt my head back, I take it in. It makes everything feel more real.

The cold outside and the energy inside both make me want to walk fast, but I'm already going to get there early.

Forest Park Cemetery is the only cemetery in town. The only place for Sean to go.

I try to walk slow.

But I can't. I'm there just a little before nine thirty.

And I wait.

By nine forty-five I'm glad I left early. There's a car, black, with little white flags attached to it, driving slowly into the park.

I jump up from where I've been sitting, on the edge of the actual cemetery in between a couple bushes.

Church must have let out early for the funeral.

The car is creeping into the cemetery along the

winding path. Then there's another, right behind it. A procession. Which means —

And there it is, the third car: black, too long, curtains in the windows. I guess it's supposed to look elegant, but it just looks creepy and kind of gruesome.

It makes me shudder, hard.

But I watch.

The cars stop in a little parking area or else on the curb of the wide lane, and people slowly climb out.

Pastor Clark is in the first one, a shiny dark blue thing that looks like he washes it every day. He takes his time walking around, facing the cars behind him as others approach.

Sean's parents get out of the second one. Their arms are at their sides. His dad looks at his mom. She looks at the hearse.

Even from this far away, I can see their sadness. For some reason it surprises me.

Men in black climb out of the hearse, but they move differently than Pastor Clark or the Rossinis. More quickly, like they're not affected by everything around them. Professionals. They open the back and are joined by a few others, who help them ease out a sleek mahogany coffin. I look away.

In my head I count backward and forward, backward and forward, one two three four five four three two one two three four five. Up and down, staring at the dirt on my shoes.

* * *

The bushes are just outside a low wrought-iron fence at the edge of the cemetery.

Behind me a few steps is the sidewalk and then the road, but the bushes are big enough to hide most of me. If someone really looked from the road, they could probably spot me.

No one looks.

The funeral has been set up farther along, maybe a hundred feet from where the little parking spaces are. It's a big crowd, bigger than my field of vision through the leaves.

But I can see the middle of it, the coffin, the folding chairs right next to it where Sean's parents must be, the portable podium where Pastor Clark is now speaking.

His voice carries but the wind covers most of the words. I only catch a few of them:

call

dust

Heaven

Lord God

loss

young

taken

love

love

love

Something about that word gets to me, and for a second I forget myself and stand up.

When I do, I move past the leaves and can see the

whole crowd, and there are Mom and Dad, sitting a couple rows back on the opposite side.

I get back down really fast, quicker than I knew I could move. But in that bit of a second, I thought I saw Dad looking in my direction.

I hold my breath. Wait. And then, very slowly. One leaf at a time. I peel just enough of them back so I can see the spot where they sit.

Dad is facing Pastor Clark, all attention on the speaker.

I breathe out slowly, a long, wheezy sigh that comes from the bottom of my lungs, and realize I'm a little disappointed.

Pastor Clark is done for now. He steps aside as a very old black woman climbs up to speak.

Her voice sounds like rustling leaves and I hear none of it.

When she finishes, Pastor Clark says something quickly, an instruction, and everyone stands.

The coffin starts sinking into the earth, and it takes everything in me to stop myself from getting up, from running over and stopping it, from keeping Sean above the ground.

Sean's parents are the last to stand, but they alone move once they're up. They walk slowly to the hole with the mahogany coffin. His mom holds out her hand in a fist and even from here I can see it shaking.

She opens her hand and spills dirt onto the coffin and

there's a sound like a low, rising wail. It takes me a second to be sure it's her making it, it just sounds so awful and different from any sound I knew a person could make. Some of the tension leaves my body.

One by one, others come forward with their own clumps of dirt.

I sit back down, closing my eyes. Just for a break.

In my own dark I can still hear the rustling of movement, chairs being pushed aside, mutterings of consolation, the horrible sounds of Sean's mother.

Then footsteps, too close to be part of the funeral.

I open my eyes and Dad is striding toward me, Mom behind, and I can feel the heat of his anger on me like a radiator.

He's still a few feet away when he hisses,

What the hell are you doing here?

like he can't get to me quick enough.

I say, I'm here for Sean's funeral.

The words are out before I know I'm thinking them and I'm surprised how strong my voice sounds.

Dad is right up against the fence. He holds the top with both hands tight, really tight.

He says, You need to get out of here. Now.

I say, No.

He says, Don't you tell me no! Turn around and walk home now, before anyone sees you.

Mom is looking back and forth at us. Her eyes are wild.

I say, I'm staying.

Dad says, Goddamnit, Mike,

and his hands shake a little,

Do you think Sean's parents want to see you?

Dad's voice rises unsteadily like he can't control it, like he's trying to shout and not shout at the same time. Over his shoulder I can see a few people looking at us.

He speaks through clenched teeth:

Now get. Your ass. Home.

A couple people are moving toward us, slowly, but I keep my eyes on Dad.

I say, I'm going home after I see his grave.

Dad breathes deeply through his nose, nostrils flaring.

He says, If you don't turn and walk away right now, buddy, you'll be back at that camp again. For the rest of the school year.

His voice is just above a whisper. I can't remember when I've seen him this angry.

I glare at Dad, neither of us blinking.

I think for a second about staying at that camp for another four or five months. I think about all the rules, about Pastor Landis, about the other scared, sad kids. I think about repeating ninth grade and being a year behind all my friends, and how much I would hate that. And I can't help it, it almost makes me change my mind.

But I think about what Ronald's mom said.

I open my mouth to say no, I'm staying and I don't care what happens, and then my eyes flick over his shoulder.

Sean's mom is a few feet away, walking toward us

cautiously, like she's not sure what she's seeing. Behind her is Sean's dad, keeping his distance, watching his wife helplessly. He looks so old.

This close I can see the details of her black dress, her veil that doesn't quite cover the puffy red eyes. Those eyes are the saddest thing I've ever seen, but there's something just behind them, mostly blocked by grief but still just visible: something hard that scares me.

Dad follows my eyes and turns around right as Sean's mom says,

What's the matter here?

Her voice is raspy, dried out from sobbing.

Dad is quick:

I'm so sorry, Mrs. Rossini, Mike was just leaving.

She says, Leaving.

In a kind of distracted way. She glances at me, and I suddenly realize what the look in her eyes is. It's the same thing I see in Toby sometimes.

Dad says, Yes, of course, we weren't planning on bringing him. He walked from home.

She looks at me just a bit longer, then back at Dad.

Dad says, I'll drive him home now. I'm so very, very sorry for the disrupt—

She cuts in, What disruption?

Dad raises his eyebrows but doesn't know how to answer.

Sean's mom says, Is he back from that camp now?

I blink. The question is so unexpected. Dad seems taken aback too for a second, but he recovers quickly.

He says, Just for now, yes.

She says, Then he's going back?

Her voice changes with this, becomes lower. Out of nowhere I think of Madison, my friend Kris's cat back in Sheboygan Falls. Madison really liked Kris's mom, rubbing up against her legs and meowing softly whenever she came home. But she hated Kris. Kris didn't really like her back and would pull at her tail until Madison's meows would get lower and lower. Like a warning.

Dad senses it, too, and hesitates before he says, Yes, probably for a longer time.

Sean's mom glances back at me just for the quickest fraction of a second, but I see it again: the something else in her eyes, the something harder taking over and covering the sadness.

She says, My son is dead.

Her voice is almost a whisper but still it's the only sound, cold and powerful.

She says, I would . . .

She trails off and looks away. We all watch her.

Nothing happens, and I think she's just going to leave it at that. But then she whispers:

I would trade anything in this world for him to be here.

She looks up, turns her gaze to Dad, then to Mom. Mom shrinks back from that look.

She says, And you, you still have your son. What for? You could spend as much time as you wanted with him, but you're going to send him away instead.

She speaks every word slowly, carefully, quietly. Mom looks back, terrified.

Mrs. Rossini says, Do you know what I would do if Sean were still here?

Mom and Dad look back, frozen.

She says, I would love him.

There's just quiet after this. Then she turns and walks back toward Sean's dad. He reaches out an arm to put around her shoulder. She shoves the arm away and walks past him without a glance.

His face sags as he watches her go. He stands that way a long, long time.

Then, slowly, he walks after his wife.

Mom stares after him with an expression I can't read.

Dad looks lost. He gazes at nothing for a moment, then seems to notice the people at the funeral. Almost everyone is watching us now.

Dad's face turns red and he mutters, Jesus Christ.

Mom turns around at his voice slowly, as if coming out of a daydream.

Dad says, Okay, let's go.

He starts to move.

Mom says, No.

Her voice is small, quiet.

Dad stops and stares at her. I look at her too. Neither of us knows what to say. Mom still has that unreadable expression, something I've never seen before.

She says, Mike hasn't gone to see the grave yet.

Dad's eyes widen and his face turns redder.

He says, Are you joking?

Mom says, No.

And her voice is a little stronger now. She looks back at Dad steadily, but there's still fear in her eyes.

He glances back at the crowd by the gravestone.

Dad says, They're watching—

Mom says, They're watching us make the same mistake Sean's parents made.

Dad winces a bit.

He says, But they all . . . they all know, Caroline, they'll all say—

Mom takes a step forward right up to Dad, eyes still on his so she has to tilt her head back a little and says,

Fffffuck—What they have to say.

It comes out like that, pushed out through all those *F*'s so that it pops at Dad, at all of us, the rest of the sentence not spoken but hissed with more force than I've ever heard from Mom even in her angriest, and her eyes are so intense and wild, and the fear is there even more.

And I realize that fear isn't of Dad but for me.

Dad stares back, mouth barely open, breath held.

Mom says, Mike is going to see Sean's grave.

And something in Dad gives. I can actually see his face and shoulders sag, hopeless, helpless. His breath lets out slowly in a low moan.

He tries to say Okay, but no sound comes out.

Mom turns to me.

She says, Come on, Mike,

and holds out her hand.

I realize I'm shaking.

I climb over the fence in a kind of clumsy way and jump to the ground on the other side, feet making a soft thud on the mushy grass, and I take Mom's hand.

Mom leads me toward the grave site. Her steps are quick and regular.

Mine are halting at first, but then they fall into rhythm with Mom's.

There are still a few people there. I don't look at them. Sean's grave is ahead and I look at that.

Mom pulls me along by my hand, and for just a second I remember what it felt like when she lifted me with that same hand into the breeze from Lake Michigan and the Milwaukee sunset.

Then she stops, still several feet from the grave and the black rectangular hole in the ground.

She stands behind me, hands on my shoulders.

She whispers, Okay, sweetie. Go ahead.

And I feel the gentlest nudge.

I stand there for a second.

Then I walk forward.

The hole gapes wider as I get closer. The gravestone is fresh, clean, white marble.

It says SEAN MARCUS ROSSINI.

I trace each letter with my eyes, taking in each curve in the engravings. I think about the years of wind and rain and ice and heat that will smooth out the sharp points, fill the letters with hardened dirt, make cracks that snake across the words and eventually crumble and destroy this thing that looks so solid and unbreakable.

But right now it's fresh, the gravestone and mahogany casket and the sweet smell of the earth and perfect angles of this rectangle hole, everything's fresh except the only thing that matters.

I look down into the hole, at the wood that's still visible under a few clumps of hand-dropped dirt.

And I say good-bye to Sean.

LAST

School isn't so bad.

Everyone knows everything, I can tell as soon as I get there Monday.

But I already knew they would.

A few kids snicker when they see me. There are whispers too, trails of them that I can just hear when I walk past.

A lot of kids stare at me in the halls or in class, kids I don't even know, and for the most part I ignore it. I ignore a lot about school, because it's easier just to think about nothing.

But sometimes I do look, and what I see in the eyes staring back at me isn't always bad. There's some curiosity.

And, just once, a faint smile. Just enough for me to notice.

Ronald seems different.

It's Tuesday. He's walking with me down the hall to Biology.

He did the same thing yesterday, with some of my classes too. I mean we used to walk together if we were going in the same direction, but since I got back he's been doing it even when his classes are in some other wing. Right now I know he has PE and the gym is way at the other end of the school. I don't ask him about it, though.

He says, You think it's going to be hard catching up in Ferguson's?

I say, I guess.

I'm kind of distracted though. Victor was out yesterday, and I haven't seen him yet today. But if he's here today, he's in my Biology class.

Tristan and Fuller were here yesterday, but they both ignored me the whole day. I didn't mind.

Ronald says, Cool.

It takes me a second before I realize his response doesn't really make sense. I glance over, and he seems kind of distracted too. He's looking around, but not at me. Like he's expecting something. He's been doing this a bit lately.

While still looking at him, I say, But she told me after class yesterday that she'll let me do the tests I missed as homework.

Ronald says, Yeah.

We pass a couple older kids in the hall and Ronald clenches his books tightly. He relaxes his grip when they're past us.

He says, Okay, well, good luck.

I was still watching him so I hadn't noticed that we arrived at my class. My heart kind of skips a beat, which makes me feel a little dumb.

I'm not afraid of running into Victor. I just really don't want to see him.

But Victor's not there.

His lab stool stays empty the whole period.

Fuller sits next to it. He never looks over at me.

I relax a bit and go back to thinking about nothing.

Jared acts like I haven't been gone. At lunch he talks the same as he always did, and there are a couple times while I'm eating that I almost forget I was even away.

I catch Ronald sneaking looks at me, his mom's crease in his forehead. He tries to act natural if I look his way, but I still see it.

I look over at Tristan and Fuller eating by themselves at their usual table.

I say, Is Victor Price sick?

Ronald raises his eyebrows.

He says, Dude, you don't know?

I look at him.

Jared takes a sip of his Arizona Green Tea and says, Victor was suspended indefinitely.

I put my sandwich down.

Jared says, The school board had an emergency meeting last week after the accident. The YouTube video Victor posted was a large part of it. He took it down pretty soon, but of course everyone had already seen it.

Jared unwraps his Kit Kat and flattens the wrapper, creasing it neatly. He breaks the chocolate into the four long sticks, then takes his knife and chops each stick into five square-sized pieces, arranging them in a grid on top of the wrapper. He takes the corner square and pops it into his mouth.

He says, The board voted on a new zero-tolerance bullying policy, effective immediately. There were a couple news stories about it.

I just stare at Jared, who alternates Kit Kat pieces with sips of tea. I don't know what to say, so I look at Ronald.

He has a bit of a smile on his face. I look up and see the faint cut above his eye.

I tell all this to the counselor.

We're supposed to meet a couple times a week, just a few minutes before school starts. Her name is Miss Dobbs-Shannon, hyphenated like that. She's kind of young, has long straight hair, barely reddish but mostly brown. She's all right.

The counselor was Principal Huston's idea. That's the

main principal, not the assistant principal, Mr. Whitman, who's kind of an idiot.

Mrs. Huston called me into the office my first day back. I was in Art again, and it was the same office aid girl who came and got me when I called Mr. Kilgore a dick.

Mr. Kilgore just stared at her when she knocked and walked in, dressed in loose clothes again, glossy lipstick, hair dyed red this time, and told him she had a referral to bring me to Mrs. Huston's office.

Then he sort of threw a hand into the air and said, Knock yourself out.

On the way there she asked me, You call someone else a dick?

Principal Huston's a large woman with bushy black hair and a carefully pressed black pantsuit. I'd never been in her office before. She got right to the point: she talked to my parents and thought it'd be a good idea for me to meet with a school counselor for a little bit because of the incident.

That's the word she used, incident. Like Jesse from camp.

She said my parents agreed and I was to start the next day.

I said, Which parent did you talk to?

I just sort of blurted it out and for a second I thought it probably sounded rude.

But she said, Your mother.

* * *

So Wednesday morning I tell Miss Dobbs-Shannon that school's not so bad.

She says, What about the rest?

I say, The rest?

She says, Home, your weekends, hobbies, anything else you do aside from school.

I think about this.

I say, I guess it's fine.

She says, Fine?

I say, Yeah.

She says, Does everything feel normal?

I say, No.

She says, Are you sleeping?

I don't say anything.

She says, Is that a no?

I say, I'm sleeping a bit.

She says, But not enough?

I say, No.

She leans back in her chair and studies me a bit. She does that sometimes. Usually it means there's something she's going to say that's important and she's thinking about how to word it.

She says, Michael, you went to a conversion-therapy camp for two weeks. When you get back, you immediately find out Sean has died, and right away you come back to school. And you've only been back a couple of days.

I look at the ground. Blank hard no-color carpet, cheap stuff they fill schools and offices with.

She says, You've been through a whole, whole lot in a very short amount of time. And everything's "fine"?

I breathe out through my teeth and lean back.

I say, This is stupid.

Miss Dobbs-Shannon doesn't react to that. She looks at me a bit and then says, Maybe you're still numb, Michael. Maybe that's why school isn't so bad.

I don't say anything.

Maybe I am numb.

I spend a lot of time at Ronald's house.

It's not really on the way home from school, but I just take the bus with him and we hang out for a couple hours, mostly just eating snacks and watching TV.

His mom comes home and always smiles when she sees me. There's something behind that smile, a kind of searching look. The first day I came over, she smiled at me and asked,

How are you doing?

but low, almost under her breath, not like a regular greeting but like she really wanted to know.

Ronald said, Mom.

In a kind of warning tone. She just smiled at me again and walked off into her bedroom to change.

Sometimes Jared comes over too.

He still acts like everything's normal but that's just Jared. Nothing really fazes him.

The only time he said anything about what happened the last month, besides telling me about Victor getting suspended, was at lunch in the first week. Not on the first day but maybe like Wednesday.

I'd just sat down and he was already there. Ronald was still in line getting Salisbury steak.

Jared says, Do you have to repeat the year?

I look up, blinking. It takes me a second before I figure out what he's saying.

I say, No. Mrs. Huston says I can do most of the makeup work during the year, but I'll probably have to come for a bit of summer school because the district has some rule about attendance.

Jared says, Oh. That's dumb.

I don't say anything, just nod. I'm going into myself again. I can feel my mind drifting off, thinking about nothing.

Jared takes another bite of his sandwich and says, Did you want it to work? At the camp?

I'm already pretty deep in my own head and Jared's voice sounds far away, not important, but some part of me registers his words, and the question is so unexpected it draws me back, like waking from a dream because someone calls your name.

I look at him hard and for the first time he seems very alert and attentive, even though he's not quite looking at me. He's stopped chewing.

I say, Yeah. I did.

Jared chews again, slowly.

I say, I really did.

Jared chews. Pauses. Swallows.

He says, I don't think that kind of thing ever works. So don't sweat it.

I just look at him and watch the alertness sort of fade away until he's back to his usual unfazed self.

That was the only time he brought it up.

Miss Dobbs-Shannon says, You look tired again, Michael.

I say, Can you call me Mike?

She says, Of course, Mike. I'm sorry. You look tired.

I say, I have to wake up early for these sessions.

She says, You haven't been sleeping anyway.

I stare at the table.

She says, There's something you haven't been telling me.

I stare at the table.

She leans back in her chair and looks at me.

She says, When you're ready.

Dad doesn't speak much.

It's not like before, right after New Year's when he seemed too angry to know what to say.

This time it's more sad. Deflated. Like at the funeral, after Mom said what she said.

When Mom or Toby says something to him, he just

mumbles without meeting their eyes. Or sometimes he doesn't respond at all.

I don't say anything to him. But sometimes I watch him.

Mom speaks for both of them now. Just everyday stuff, like Time for dinner or Can you turn the TV down a bit? or How's everything at school?

It's strange having her suddenly in charge, but she picks it up as if she's been doing it forever, and after a few days I sometimes forget it's different now.

But Mom still shoots Dad a glance every now and then, reading his face, looking for signs of his old self.

I don't really know if I want his old self to come back.

I feel a bit relieved when Mom looks away, disappointed.

I still pick Toby up after school.

I open the door to the side entrance because it's closer to the choir room, and I hear her voice from a distance. She's up ahead, talking to someone out of view around the corner. I can only see her pink backpack.

This is about two weeks after I'm back at school.

I'm about to call out to her when I hear her say,

I'd rather have him as my brother than you. I feel bad for Casey.

Another girl says, Hey! Leave me out of this.

I keep walking toward them, a bit faster now.

There's a laugh and then a third voice, a boy, says, You mean, your sister. At least Casey has a real brother.

The girl who must be Casey says, Colin, let's just goooo.

Colin says, Fine. 'Bye, Toby, say hi to your sister for us. And you look stupid in that backpack, by the way.

Toby says, You don't even need the backpack to look stupid.

I get to the corner a few seconds later, right as Toby turns around.

She says, Hi, Mike!

A little too brightly. She smiles like nothing's wrong. I stare past her at Colin and Casey, who are almost at the end of the next hall.

We're crossing the bridge over the creek that separates our neighborhood from the school.

I ask Toby who those kids were.

She doesn't want to say.

I ask again.

She hesitates for a few seconds, kind of swinging her backpack side to side while she walks. Then she tells me. Casey is another girl in choir. Colin's her brother who's in eighth grade who comes to pick her up sometimes.

We take a left after the bridge.

There's a sinking feeling in my stomach suddenly. It never occurred to me that everything that's happened in the last month could've affected Toby too. That kids at her school could be bothering her.

I wait for a few moments, then I ask how she's been since New Year's.

She doesn't hesitate this time. She says, I'm fine, Mike. Firm and quick, but not annoyed.

I don't say anything. I'm thinking about Colin.

Miss Dobbs-Shannon says, Your teacher says you haven't really been paying attention in class.

I look up. The corners of my eyes are really dry, and I can almost feel them creak as I try to keep them open.

I say, Which one?

She says, Miss Rayner.

English.

I think back on what we've been studying in English the last couple weeks and realize I can't really remember much of it.

She says, What do you think about when your mind drifts in class?

I say, Nothing.

She says, Mike—

I say, No, I mean I think about nothing. Like I just let my mind go blank.

Miss Dobbs-Shannon raises her eyebrows just a bit. She looks at me that way a moment and then says, in a quieter voice,

People often do that as a way of avoiding other thoughts.

I don't say anything.

She says, It's understandable that you don't want to think about the accident.

I don't say anything.

She says, But escapism is just a means of putting off the inevitable. At some point, as painful as it will be, you will have to allow yourself to think about Sean's death in order —

I say, It's not the death.

Miss Dobbs-Shannon pauses.

She says, I'm sorry?

I say, It's not the death I don't want to think about. I mean I don't, but that's not just it.

She says, Then what is it?

It's a couple days after New Year's. Last month.

I'm at my computer desk, thinking about Dad's question.

You want to change, don't you?

Sean's message is in front of me. He wants to see me and he can get out of the house and be at my window and all I have to do is tell him to come and he will.

But Dad's question is there, bigger than Sean's note, bigger than Sean.

And then I read the last line again:

im sorry i pushed you.

And I make myself think about this and forget the rest. I think about the actual push, about falling on the sand. I think about the last taste of wine leaving my mouth dry. I think about standing there without a shirt on and looking dumb.

I make myself think only about this, over and over again, while I type out a message to Sean.

Miss Dobbs-Shannon doesn't speak at first. I know she's waiting for me, but I'm not speaking either.

Finally she says, What did your message say?

My breath catches before I answer her:

I don't care what you do, just stay away.

It comes out louder than I expected, and awkward, every word hurting. I rush through it to get it over with. My voice cracks a bit on the last word, and I turn it into a small cough, clearing my throat against the silence that comes.

It's not that I didn't want her to know. I just didn't want to say it out loud.

Miss Dobbs-Shannon leans back in her chair.

She clicks the pen in her hand.

She writes down a quick note on her pad.

She looks up and says, Mike.

I say, What.

I'm looking at her pen and trying not to move. I'm sort of sitting on my hands.

She opens her mouth, then looks to the side and closes it.

Then, slowly, she says, I think we have our next steps laid out for us.

I frown.

I say, What are you talking about?

I know it sounds rude but I'm really anxious talking about this and I wish she'd just say what she means.

She says, We need to get you to understand that you're not responsible for Sean's death.

I sort of freeze.

She says, Mike, I'd like to speak to your parents about th —

I say, No.

She stops. I'm still looking at her pen. I can feel her eyes on me. I can hear her breath coming out slowly through her nose. The clock above and behind her ticks seven times.

She says, I won't without your permission. But, Mike, listen to me.

I wait.

She says, You've been miserable for weeks, and I think this will help.

I wait.

She says, I just want to talk this over with them. I want to tell them about your message to Sean.

My fingernails dig into my thighs.

She says, I think you need to hear it from them. I think that's what's been missing.

I don't say anything.

I breathe slowly, timing it with the clock. Three ticks for each inhale, three for each exhale. Miss Dobbs-Shannon waits again for me to say something. I try to imagine her talking to my parents, telling them what I just told her, and it makes me feel a little sick to my stomach. I hold on as long as I can, putting off the moment when I have to answer her. But then I hear myself saying it anyway.

I say, Just Mom. Not Dad.

When I look up, she smiles, just barely.

She nods slowly and says, Just Mom.

Jared and I are at Ronald's house playing Halo.

Jared and Ronald are talking every few minutes, but not a lot. I'm not really listening. Mostly the only sounds are gunfire and explosions and the voice on the TV saying, Double kill! and Reinforcements! and Killing spree!

Over the noise we hear the front door open and close, and then Ronald's mom call out, Turn it down a bit, would you?

No one really moves.

I follow the sounds of Mrs. Pilsner walking into the bedroom, dropping her purse onto the bed, the jangle of keys as she tosses them onto the end table, her footsteps on the carpet and then back on the tile near the front door.

She says, Ronald.

Ronald grabs the remote next to him and turns the TV down four notches.

The game says, Betrayal!

Ronald says, Goddamnit, Jared.

Mrs. Pilsner says, Ronald, come on.

Jared says, You walked into my line of fire.

Ronald says, I wasn't even moving.

Jared doesn't say anything back, and there's just more gunfire.

But then I realize I haven't heard Mrs. Pilsner move and think she's probably standing in the doorway, and right when I think that, she says,

Hi, Mike.

I jump a bit, and my character dies.

I turn around while it restarts my life. Ronald's mom is looking at me with the same smile she's had the last few weeks. Thin-lipped. A little sad. But still kind.

I say, Hi, Mrs. Pilsner.

She looks at me a bit more and then says, Jeri.

I say, Hi, Jeri.

I watch her sad smile widen, making creases around her eyes. Then I turn back to the game and hear her walk out of the room.

I get home a bit late. We didn't have pizza at Ronald's, so I was supposed to be back for dinner. I'm barely in time. Everyone's already at the table.

No one says anything. It's just leftovers.

I finish eating first and pick up my empty dishes and carry them to the sink and rinse them and put them in the dishwasher and walk past the dining room table and upstairs to my room.

I have Algebra homework due tomorrow. It's not hard but it's a lot so it'll still take a while.

I'm on the fifth problem out of forty when there's a knock at the door. Not Toby's knock, Mom's.

I say, What.

She opens the door quietly, but it still creaks. She walks in and sits next to me on the bed, smoothing down the thighs of her pants and then putting her hands in her lap. She's looking at nothing, at the carpet.

She stays that way for a few moments, then clasps her hands together and says,

It's not your fault.

I say, What?

But my heart skips a beat.

She says, I spoke with your counselor today. We talked over a few things. She told me what you said to her. And I wanted to let you know that it wasn't your fault.

My mouth is open just a bit and I'm breathing as slow as I can.

She says, Mike.

I say, No, wait—

She says, Mike.

I shout, No!

She stops and looks at me. Calmly.

I take in a breath.

I say, He just wanted to see me. All he wanted was to get out and come over and talk through the window. I told him to stay away.

But she's already shaking her head before I finish.

She says, He's dead because he drank eight beers and got in a car and drove. He's dead because he didn't get the support he needed from his family. He's dead because his father made an awful, awful mistake—

Mom starts fighting back tears here, and it makes me start to tear up.

—An awful mistake, and his mother didn't know enough to stop it from happening. He's dead because everyone around him failed him, but you were not one of those people, Mike. You gave him what he needed and you were the only one to do it, the only one who did it right and the only one with an excuse to get it wrong, and I'm sorry, Mike, I'm so, so sorry that your father and I nearly made that same awful mistake with you.

I just stare at her, trying to breathe normally.

She looks back at the carpet and clears her throat. She brings a thumb up and wipes her eye.

Then I say, Would he still be alive if I had told him to come over?

Mom looks back up. She looks at me a long time before she says anything.

She says, I don't know.

My breath catches.

She says, But that's not the same as fault. You did what your father and I would have wanted you to do.

She smiles grimly, but she doesn't look happy at all.

She says, It's just that we were wrong in wanting that.

Then she stands up and turns to face me and looks at me.

She says, Mike. No argument now. You didn't cause this.

She kisses my forehead and turns and walks out.

I watch the empty space on the door while I cry, as quiet as I can, for ten minutes.

That night I have a weird dream:

Jared and Ronald and Terry and I are building a house. All four of us even though in real life Terry's never met the other two.

It's a house in the middle of nowhere, and we finish building it and realize this, that we're surrounded by trees and plains and nothing, no people.

So we build a city just so we have somewhere to live. We do this only because we're afraid that if someone wants to send us mail, they won't know where to address the envelope.

We build a city hall and a school and a mall and a fire department, and a lot of the dream is taken up by us arguing about where to put the library. Terry wants it up north because he has some friends up in that area who like to read, but everyone else wants it in the south because it's closer to downtown.

It's a dumb dream that means nothing. I wake up right as we're about to strike a compromise on the library.

And walking to Geography the next day I realize that this was the first silly stupid dream I've had in a long time. The first one that wasn't about everything that's happened in the last month.

Mom picked Toby up today, but I walk over to the middle school anyway.

Colin's hanging out near the choir room, looking at his phone, waiting for his sister. I wasn't sure if he'd be here but I'm glad he is.

I walk up behind him. He doesn't hear even though I'm not trying to be quiet or anything.

I say, Colin.

He jumps a bit and turns around, stares at me.

He says, Who are you?

I say, I'm Toby's brother. Mike.

His eyes widen just a bit. Just enough for me to know.

I say, You need to leave my sister alone.

Colin says, Or what? You'll try to kiss me too?

I start to take a step toward him. He jumps back a little and trips, but doesn't fall or anything. I snort-laugh.

I say, If you see Toby, don't talk to her. Don't even look at her. Or I'll know.

I kind of think the threat sounds weird and wish I'd thought of something better. But he still looks a little freaked out. He doesn't say anything, just stares at me.

I say, Leave her alone, douchebag.

And walk away.

A couple weeks later Charlie and I are hanging out with Toby in her room.

We used to do that a lot when we were kids in Wisconsin. Especially on Friday nights. I'd go down the hall to her room, and we'd hang out and talk until Mom or Dad came in to tell us to go to bed. I haven't done it in ages.

I'm sitting cross-legged on the floor, watching Charlie toss his squeaky toy in the air and pounce on it when it lands. Toby's on the edge of her bed, playing with an old lump of Silly Putty she found in her drawer.

She's telling me about a boy in the band who has a crush on her.

She says, He was there when we had our Christmas concert, that's how we met.

I say, Holiday concert.

Toby gives me a look.

I say, So what's wrong with him?

She rolls her eyes and says, He told me he loved me from the moment he first laid eyes on me.

I laugh.

She says, He said he couldn't hear the percussion

section over the beating of his own heart. Like he actually said that.

I laugh. Charlie looks up at the sound, then dives at his toy again. I scratch him behind his ear.

I say, I thought you liked it when guys are into music.

She says, He plays the bassoon. It's like the dorkiest instrument in band. And band is already full of dorky instruments.

I say, I don't even know what a bassoon looks like.

She says, Kind of like one of those T-shirt cannons they have in stadiums.

I say, That sounds pretty cool.

She says, No, it's way too big for his body. He's like smaller than me.

Toby giggles.

She rolls the Silly Putty into a ball, making it as perfectly round as she can. Then she says, When do you think Dad's gonna stop being such a tool?

I laugh again. Partly because it comes out of nowhere, and partly because I've been wondering the same thing.

I say, I dunno, Toby.

She sighs and falls backward onto her bed.

She asks, Is he angry at you?

I say, Who gives a shit?

It comes out kind of annoyed.

I say, I don't think so, though. I think he's just . . . thinking stuff over. He's been in his own head.

She says, Well, he needs to get out of it.

316

I look up from watching Charlie. I can't see Toby's face, but her arms are stretched out in the air above her. She pulls the putty into a long thin ribbon until it droops onto her stomach.

I think about Ronald's mom again. About what she said.

I say, He does.

I close Toby's door behind me. Walk past my room, down the stairs, through the living room, into Mom and Dad's bedroom.

Mom's in the attached bathroom. I can hear the water running. Dad is in front of me, hanging up his shirt.

He turns when he hears my footsteps and stops what he's doing.

I say, Hey, Dad.

It comes out casual, much more casual than I feel. I'm actually a little nervous. It's the first time I've spoken directly to him for anything important since I got back from the camp.

He looks at me. He's still wearing his slacks, belted over a white undershirt. He looks tired and a little uneasy. But he doesn't say anything, just waits for me to talk. And suddenly I'm not nervous anymore. I'm just annoyed again. It makes the words come out easier.

I say, You've had a few weeks. You're making Mom do everything, and everyone has to pretend everything's okay. It's getting old.

The arm that was hanging up his shirt lowers slowly to his side.

I say, I don't know what you need to do to snap out of it, but I wish you'd figure it out already.

He stares at me. I'm about to turn to go, then I say, That camp was awful, and you shouldn't have sent me there. And I know you hated that I was at the funeral, but it was worse for me having to be there. This will always be harder for me than for you, so get over yourself.

I turn to leave and say, Good night,

and walk out and through the living room and up the stairs and into my room.

Two days later I'm watching TV and Dad comes into the living room. I can hear him walking up, but I'm watching so I don't turn until I feel his hand on my shoulder. He looks at me and opens his mouth like he wants to say something.

After a second he looks down, gives my shoulder a small pat, and walks out of the living room.

I turn back to the TV.

Then sometime in March.

We're at dinner. It's quiet like it has been for a long time.

Mom's still shooting her glances at Dad, but the disappointment there has become something else now. Almost like anger.

Mom says, Toby, what time does your choir concert start?

I know for a fact Mom already knows it starts at seven thirty tomorrow, that Mom is saying this just to have sound and conversation at dinner because that is what dinner should be like. Because she still hasn't stopped trying after six weeks.

Toby says, Seven thirty.

Mom says, What are you singing?

Toby pokes a fork into her salmon.

She says, A bunch of southern spirituals.

Mom says, Southern spirituals?

Toby says, I dunno, Mrs. Deringer likes that stuff. Like a lot of old slave songs, I think.

Mom says, Well, that sounds interesting. What songs?

Toby chews slowly. I can tell she knows what Mom's doing and doesn't like being a part of it.

She says, One's called "O Won't You Sit Down."

Toby almost sighs it out, trying to make it as clear as possible that she doesn't want to talk about it.

Mom says, Well, how does it go?

Toby chews. Swallows. Takes a sip of milk. Swallows.

She half sings, half mutters:

O won't you sit down? Lord, I can't sit down.

She stops. Mom looks at her expectantly.

Toby rolls her eyes and opens her mouth to sing the next line.

Dad half sings, 'Cause I just got to Heaven, gotta look around.

Toby stops. She blinks, forgetting to look annoyed.

Dad looks up, also surprised.

Then his blank, deflated face turns into the faintest smile.

He says, I used to hear that one on the radio growing up.

Everyone frozen.

He says, Jeez, it must be decades since the last time I heard that.

He barks out a laugh, awkward, like he's forgotten how.

Mom smiles, slow. I watch it spread over her face.

Toby starts giggling, and something in the room, some heaviness I've gotten so used to I don't notice it anymore, lifts away, just for a moment. Dad chuckles a bit, his fork held out, speared piece of fish forgotten at its end. I watch a little juice drip off it right before Dad looks at me, smiling through his tiredness, eyes meeting mine for two seconds. Most of me doesn't want to smile back, but it's already there, familiar in the way things are even after missing them for so long.

And maybe that's what starts it.

Dad and I don't talk about it, not directly. At least not yet. And as the weeks go on, I think about how we still have a long way to go. How it might be a long time before we're totally okay.

There are days I wake up angry, days where I don't want to let go of that anger. Days where I can see Dad is nowhere near where he should be, where I don't want to be around him and can't wait to get out of the house for good. Those days we just sort of avoid each other.

But other days I can tell my anger is going away a little bit at a time on its own. Just a little.

Maybe it's that small bit of normal at a dinner in March that starts it, that spreads to the rest of me, makes me less tired, less numb.

But the next time I'm at Ronald's after school and his mom comes home and turns her searching eyes toward me, she finally seems to find what she's been looking for.

Her smile grows wider this time, and she walks into her bedroom without a word.

I'm walking to my locker after French.

Madame Girard seemed to take Sean's death pretty hard. Not because she knew him, really, but I think because she doesn't know how to react to one of her students just dying.

I sit at his desk now. The first day back I walked toward my old desk, then just dropped my books down on his instead. Madame Girard looked up right as I sat down slowly into his chair. She blinked twice, eyelashes brushing her reading glasses, then looked back down at her papers. No one said a word about my new seat.

The room looks a little different from this point of

view. I like thinking that this is what Sean saw every day.

My old desk is empty and abandoned.

I'm walking back to my locker and the halls are filled with kids rushing to get out, a different kind of rushing than the kind that comes during the day, when they're just going to their next classes.

They still hurry during the day, but hurrying because you have to feels different from hurrying because you want to.

Right now there's a real energy to the place: kids want to get out of here and go home, hang out with friends, whatever.

But I'm not in a rush.

I open my locker and put my French book in. I'm looking at the other books, thinking which ones I have to take home for homework, and then my eyes just turn themselves to the inside door of the locker.

Sunrise on Mill Point Beach. I stare at the drawing for a long time, the ocean mirroring the sky, the bursting clouds, the colors blending into one another, the two seagulls that got me a zero for the day in Art. I'm lost in this picture when I realize there's someone standing a few feet away, facing me. I turn.

Victor doesn't react or even say anything at first. He just looks at me.

He came back to school yesterday. He was already in Biology when I walked in. My heart skipped but I didn't slow down, just walked to my stool, watching him. He never looked up at me as I walked by. I spent the period burning a hole into the back of his head with my eyes.

I stare back now and raise my eyebrows slowly. There's no fear anymore when I see Victor. There's only a low sort of anger, still there but unshaken, like the stuff that settles at the bottom of a bottle of dressing. My ears feel normal.

Finally he says, Hey.

I say, What.

He winces, just a bit.

He says, I didn't think you'd be at your locker right now.

I don't understand what he means by this and I don't know what to say. So I just stare at him, breathing as long and slow as I can.

Victor glances down, away from my glare, and hesitates a bit. He walks over to me.

I tense up. Both my hands close slowly into fists.

He says, Here.

And I see that there's something in his hand. A piece of paper.

I look at it. Then back at his face.

I say, Fuck off, Victor,

and start to turn back to my locker.

He says, Please.

He holds the paper farther out toward me. His face looks pained.

He says, Just . . . take it.

Something about the way he's looking at me convinces me to.

So I do.

The second the paper is in my hand, he turns and walks away. Fast.

I watch him disappear around the corner into the next hallway. He doesn't look back.

After a while I look down at my hand. It's a small piece of lined notebook paper, folded three times. The edges are perfectly straight. I unfold it slowly.

In the very middle of the note, in thick black ink, Victor has written,

I'm sorry.

I stare at the words. I look up again, at where he was standing. Then I run after him, hurrying the way he went.

I see him at the far end of the next hallway, and I rush to catch up to him. A teacher yells out in a bored voice not to run, and I ignore her.

Victor turns when he hears my footsteps.

I slow down, stopping a few feet away from him.

Then I realize I don't actually know what I was going to say to him.

There are so many things I want to say. I want to tell him that I hope he gets held back and has to repeat freshman year. I want to ask him what it was like to have Ronald punch him in the face in front of everyone. I want to ask him when he first realized he was in huge trouble.

324

Was it when the school board called their emergency meeting, or before that, when the news started picking up on the YouTube video? Or was it when he first heard Sean was dead? Did he guess what had happened and that he was connected?

I want to blame him for Sean's death.

But.

There's a part of me, small but persistent, that gets that that's not really fair. I don't totally get why, and I don't really want to care about being fair anyway, but that stupid small part of me stops me from saying it out loud anyway, stops me from making everything Victor's fault.

So instead I just say, Why were you such a dick all year?

Victor doesn't say anything for a long time. He looks really uncomfortable. It makes me feel a little better.

Then he says, I don't know.

His answer makes me angrier.

I say, I never did anything to you.

He says, I know. It's not like I hated you or anything. You were just . . . an easy target.

I stare at him. He looks away.

He says, And then it became a habit.

He clears his throat. He looks miserable.

He says, And then it sorta got out of hand.

Slowly, I feel my hands opening, and realize I'd been clenching my fists again. My face relaxes a bit, my jaw unlocks. I stop pressing my lips together and breathe slowly.

I watch Victor for a while, and after a few seconds, I notice my anger's blocked by something. He's just standing there, tensed but not meeting my eyes. I get the weirdest urge to laugh, even though nothing's really funny, at all.

But mostly I just don't want to be around him anymore.

He looks up but I've already turned away. There's nothing more to say.

I left my locker open.

There are still lots of kids walking around when I get back, so no one's really noticed. I reach in to grab my backpack and realize there's something in my hand.

It's Victor's note. I look at it for a minute.

I'm sorry.

Then I fold the piece of paper back the way it was, three times, and put it in my backpack.

My eyes flick back to the locker door. Carefully, I take down the drawing of Mill Point Beach and put it in my backpack too. I take the backpack and shut the locker.

I walk slowly down the main hallway.

Kids pass me on either side, so eager to get out, but I walk slowly.

Through the double doors, into the sunshine of midafternoon, first bit of spring warmth.

Across the entranceway and lawn, around groups of kids huddled together making plans, through the pack of diesel engines and past Ronald's bus, beyond the track field and the early runners, across the street, and onto the middle school's side lawn.

I say, Hey, Toby.

That voice is strong and almost cheerful. I smile at her.

She smiles back and picks up her bag.

For a moment we look at each other. I think about all the times she's had my back, even at the worst times.

She says, Colin's been avoiding me.

My smile gets a little bigger, just barely. I have her back too. It makes me happy.

She says, Like he won't even make eye contact. Weird, right?

Her voice sounds kind of sarcastic and she's giving me this look.

I say, Maybe he's not into girls.

I put my hand on her head and ruffle her hair.

Toby giggles and moves her head out of the way.

She says, Let's go.

And we walk home.

ACKNOWLEDGMENTS

Damien. You first, of course. You're my husband, best friend, biggest cheerleader, and strongest advocate. When someone asks what I do, you force me to add that I'm an author. Thank you for that.

To Brianne Johnson, a Hermione-grade witch who amuses herself by putting all that power toward literary representation. Lucky for me.

To Liz Bicknell. Not everyone gets to work with a dream editor, someone who brings together graceful expertise with vigorous enthusiasm, who is equal parts talent and champion.

To Zack Clark, who saw something salvageable in an early draft and gently nudged me to smooth it down. Some of my favorite tiny moments in this book are due to him.

To Matt Roeser, whose cover design made me sort of flip out for three months. To Tracy, Phoebe, and Allison, for their endless help and patience with a first-time author. To the full Candlewick team, everyone who worked behind the scenes to put this thing out. It means more to me than you know.

To countless friends and family members who lent their support, their random bits of advice, their insights on how teens affectionately insult one another, or just their excitement. There are too many of you to name, but: Yono and Britta Mittlefehldt; the Butvicks, Mahers, and Blacketts; Sally Pell; Nate Manske; Nick Manske and Summer Dinh; Elisa Mason; Jacquie Osman; Chris Uhland; Rachel Younger; Aruna Jahoor; TJ Martin; Becky Amsel; Marquise Lee and Paul Blore; Jonah Detofsky; Donald Harrison; Melissa Nguyen; Brittany McCulloch; Clint Brody; Angelina Hemme; and three or four thousand others.

To I'm From Driftwood (http://imfromdriftwood.org), which I've worked with, and to The Trevor Project (www.thetrevorproject.org), which I've admired: two excellent nonprofits that work tirelessly on behalf of LGBTQ youth and adults.

And to my parents and Damien's: Nurit and Dave Mittlefehldt, and Kathryn and Bill Butvick. So many gay kids have to wonder what true support looks like, but we never did. It looks like this.